BANGKOK WHISPERS

STEPHEN SHAIKEN

(2020 EDITION)

Published by Stephen Shaiken
Cover design by Cal5086

Visit Stephen's website at www.stephenshaiken.com.
Follow Stephen on Twitter: https://twitter.com/StephenShaiken.

First Edition: August 2020
Print ISBN: 978-1-732147430
eBook ISBN: 978-1-732147423

TABLE OF CONTENTS

1

I STILL DON'T know how Sleepy Joe persuaded me to hear Phil Funston play. Neither of us could stand him. He is the most obnoxious of the regulars at the NJA Club, where I spend the lion's share of what passes for a social life. Phil never stops talking about his exploits in the naughtier parts of town, which does not interest me. What did catch my attention was the venue. Phil's gig was at the Blues Club on Samsen Road in Banglampoo, a place I knew well. Actually, the place was named Club Adhere the 13th, but no one ever called it that. Whatever its name, they have some of the best blues this side of America, in every style: Delta, Chicago, Memphis, Kansas City. Blues in Bangkok sounds crazy, but it's true. The first time I visited the Blues Club, I was skeptical, until this skinny Thai guy, an aging hippy with a graying ponytail, started playing his Strat. I later learned it wasn't even a real Fender, but a cheap Chinese knockoff. Phil himself once told me that more expensive guitars don't make better players, but better players can sound even better on a first-rate model. Phil sometimes taught guitar, and ridiculed his rich young students, the offspring of wealthy Thai Hi-So families or expats, who insisted on buying, as their first guitar, a really expensive model any pro would be proud to own. "They still stink," he said. "It's the guitarist, not the guitar."

When Thailand built the BTS to glide above congested Sukhumvit and Silom Boulevards, and the MRT to wind beneath Bangkok's teeming streets, they forgot to include Banglampoo. Unless I want to spend an inordinate amount of time stuck in traffic in a cab, listening to the driver-with-an-attitude gripe every centimeter of the way, the only option is the old-style, motorized riverboats operated by Chao Phraya Express, that ply their way along the busy river. They can carry scores of people and make frequent stops on both sides of the Chao Phraya. It's a bit confusing, as the stop announcements are made in Thai through a scratchy sound system, but Banglampoo's Phra Arthit Pier is the first stop when it recrosses. Easy to remember. Hundreds of thousands of people use the riverboats each day to commute within the city. They join the large volume of river traffic, with every vessel imaginable: crusty old tankers, sleek dinner-party boats, overloaded barges, an occasional pleasure boater. The riverbanks are an eclectic collection of top-flight hotels, expensive condos and shopping malls, decrepit old wooden houses, and a few historic churches, going back to the days when the Christians thought they had a shot at converting these devout Buddhists. They've gotten no further with them than with my people. I don't practice any religion, really, but the one I choose to not practice is my own.

Phil's gig was on a Thursday night. He was hired to fill in for the visiting band's lead guitarist, who was looking the wrong way when crossing the street and was hit by a car. (It takes some foreigners a while to get used to the "British side of the road" rules they use in the Kingdom.) He survived, but wouldn't be playing for a while. Phil's name has long been floating around town as the go-to guy when you need a quick fill-in who can play well in any style or genre. Problem is, Phil being Phil, there is never a second time with any band.

I have no great desire to see Phil Funston any more than necessary, which is at the NJA Club, but am always up for a visit to Banglampoo. Sleepy Joe knew that much. Banglampoo is the oldest part of Bangkok, sitting along the Chao Phraya River. After disembarking, it's pleasant to be greeted by the ruins of Phra Sumen, an ancient fort from the first days of Bangkok, near a nice green park, a low-rise look different from the international big city look that has taken over the rest of Bangkok. Banglampoo is the closest Bangkok has to San Francisco's North Beach, or New York's Greenwich Village. It's filled with hip, trendy and fusion restaurants, little bars and cafes, many with live music, all of which, not too long ago, were traditional Thai shophouses. The area is home to Thammasat University, one of Thailand's leading institutions of higher learning. The streets are narrow and crowded, and with no BTS or MRT to whisk people to Banglampoo above or below the streets, traffic is everything you imagine when you think of Bangkok.

I met Joe at the big Isan place on Ekamai, not all that far from my condo. It's actually two restaurants: a small, family-style restaurant, and a cavernous, barn-like structure next door, that can—and usually does—hold hundreds of diners, mostly people from Thailand's northeast Isan region, working in Bangkok, and the occasional smart *farangs* like us, who know where to get the best food in town. I prefer the barn. We shared a whole barbecued chicken, Joe pouring on even more hot sauce than I did, and a side of *som tum thai*, the spicy papaya salad to which we both have become addicted.

Sleepy Joe looked like a hippy who stuck around Haight-Ashbury a few years too long. His straggly gray hair, two-day stubble, and Salvation Army castoff clothing firmed up that image. Of course, the image was an illusion. Joe was a former member of the Australian Special Forces. After an honorable discharge, he moved to Thailand to deal and smoke weed, and enjoy movies, music, and good massages. He looked like a strong exhalation might blow him away, and bookies might offer even odds in a fight with a dead man. Witnessing Joe disable and kill armed thugs disabused any such notions for me. He sprang into action when I was coerced into carrying out a kidnapping for the CIA. The only reason I'm here today is because Sleepy Joe is the most loyal and faithful friend a person could ever have. He will never allow me to face danger alone. When danger calls, there's no one I'd rather have at my side than Sleepy Joe.

"Funston's a real asshole, granted," Joe said between mouthfuls, "but have to admit, he's a hell of a guitarist."

"You've seen him play?"

"A few times," Joe said. "Once at the Saxophone Club," he said, referring to the venerated music venue over by Victory Monument. Any musician of note, local or visiting, especially jazz or blues, expects to play there. They've probably got the best music in town, though definitely not the best food, and absolutely the worst bathroom. They are also conveniently near a BTS stop. If you want to hear the very best of different genres, that's where you go. Jazz, blues, rock, pop, all show up sooner or later. For strictly blues, head out to Samsen Road, Banglampoo, and the Blues Club.

We walked down Ekamai to the BTS stop and got off at the Sepan Taksin station near the river. The boat was just about to leave when we reached the boarding area, but we were able to buy tickets, board, and squeeze into two bench seats along the port side of the long, thin motorized vessel. We forced our way to the street through the narrow, enclosed pier, lined with hawkers selling chachkas to tourists on their way to get drunk or maybe catch a comedy show at nearby Khaosan Road. The main street bustled with people rushing to and from the busy sidewalk cafes and bistros. Thai street food, art galleries, even a chess club, were interspersed amidst this collage. Khaosan Road, for decades the redoubt of backpackers, is growing more upscale, with some nice restaurants and a good comedy club. It still has a way to go, but is moving in the right direction. Banglampoo was still a place for students, hip expats, locals, and anyone hungering for a taste of what Bangkok looked like before it became the cosmopolitan city of today. There aren't many nice condos in the area, and transportation is a pain. So, much as I like Banglampoo, I am not about to move there.

The Blues Club is too small to hold the crowds it draws nightly, and many would stand or sit outside among the smokers. Joe and I pushed our way through that crowd—gently, in a Thai manner—and grabbed the two empty seats at a small table near the stage, already occupied by two couples. From snatches of the guys' conversations, and their bad haircuts, I surmised they were Brits, on holiday, as they say. We all nodded at each other. The waitress came. It was beer for Joe, Coke Zero for me. I was still feeling the effects of the fat joint we had smoked on one of the side *sois* off Ekamai after dinner.

The band was setting up. They were all *farangs* in their mid-twenties, and this being one of Thailand's premier music venues, ambiance notwithstanding, meant they were good. Thai owners are not about to pay a foreigner more than they have to pay a Thai of equal talent. People expect very good music at the Blues Club. Even on open mic nights, the musicians are all top-flight.

Funston was bent over an amplifier, plugging in his guitar. I was close enough to see that it was the Gibson Les Paul he occasionally mentioned. Phil's was an early twenty-first-century reissue of the classic "Goldtop" guitars of the fifties, the original model, considered by many the Holy Grail of electric guitars. Phil once told me an actual vintage model was worth six figures, and I have no reason to doubt him. His reissue was worth at least five grand, he claimed, and he knew better than me. He was somewhat dodgy on how he acquired it, except to say that he brought it with him, so it must have been quite new at the time. He's had it the eight years I've known him, but this was the first time I heard him play. He would be playing rhythm and lead, and surely frequent blues riffs.

The rest of the band consisted of pale and scrawny British guys on drums and keyboards, a black man on bass, and a white guy with dreadlocks as lead singer.

"Should be interesting," I said to Joe.

The singer with the dreadlocks tapped his microphone, and hearing the electronic snap, looked pleased.

"We're the Dirty Dawgs," he said, in a Manchester accent thick enough to cut with a steak knife. "We're the best, most kick-ass blues band ever to hit Bangkok, maybe all of Asia. And with us tonight, as our special guest, is Mr. Phil Funston, guitar virtuoso, originally from America, but a fixture on the music scene here ever since the only place I was rockin' was in the cradle."

Funston scowled. He was sensitive about his age, never let on exactly how old he was. He had to have at least a few years on me, but with a shaved head, it's hard to tell for sure.

"We're gonna open with a blues classic, 'Smokestack Lightning,' the singer said. "Written and first recorded by the great Howlin' Wolf, covered by a whole bunch of masters, like John Lee Hooker and the Yardbirds. Now we'd like you to hear our interpretation."

I liked the way he said "interpretation." It's a level above "version" and a world apart from "cover."

Joe leaned over so I could hear him better above the chatter of the conversation and clinking of glass that filled the room just before the band started playing.

"The Wolf wrote that one himself," he said. "Covered a lot of Willie Dixon's stuff. 'Spoonful.' 'Wang Dang Doo.' 'Back Door Man.' But then again, hasn't everyone covered Willie?"

One of the young English guys at our table stared at Joe.

"Wow, you really know the blues," he said. Then the band struck up, and Joe patted the young man's arm.

"Later," he said.

The dreadlocked singer wasn't half-bad. He was no Howlin' Wolf, but then again, few are. He didn't howl or scream like the late blues icon, but he threw his entire self into it, bending forward, arching back, throwing his arms out, all the while sounding more like an authentic Chicago blues singer than a Brit trying to pass for a Rastafarian. If I ever got a chance, I'd ask why he sang blues and not reggae.

But it was Funston who stole the first half. If I thought that skinny Thai guy with the ponytail was hot, that was before I heard Funston. I've been listening to the blues for over thirty years, the past eight with Sleepy Joe to help improve my understanding, and I think I know a bit about the genre. Phil Funston was as good as they come. I grew up listening to Mike Bloomfield, Buddy Guy, Howlin' Wolf, Big Bill Broonzy, the Allman Brothers, Billie Holiday, John Hammond, the Kings (B.B. and Albert), Big Mama Thornton, Son House, and I loved the British Blues as well. Funston had that feeling, that mix of joy, sorrow, mystery, and universality that is the blues. He could bend and curl notes, and make the strings cry and wail, or hammer and scrape to evoke anger or hurry. His melodies were classic blues riffs, his chords filled with sevenths and sharps and inversions I didn't recognize. He played riffs I'd never heard before, because they were his own creations. He sure kept things interesting, and all eyes were on him when he soloed. Phil Funston's lead on "Smokestack Lightning" may have been the best version I'd ever heard from anyone, anywhere, aside from Howlin' Wolf. He was that good.

"Told you he was something," Joe said during a break between songs. Couldn't argue with him.

Joe is always right when it comes to music. I never wanted to see Funston play, mainly because I couldn't stand the sight of him, but on stage that night was a very talented guy. Let's just say it's a matter of attitude; Phil has no regard for anyone in the world save himself. No manners, no courtesy, no limits. He'll say and do whatever fancies him, insults included, and everyone else be damned. That explains why after all these years in Thailand, he has no real friends, and everyone who knows him dislikes him. One thing stood out: when I watch great guitarists at work, the look on their face is usually one of concentration, ecstasy, pain, love, joy, anger, determination, tranquility, of being lost in the clouds, sometimes even insanity. But with Phil Funston, it was attitude. His face didn't say that he was into the music, or that he cared about the crowd; he wore the look of a man whose mind is elsewhere, not connected to the here and now. He was probably thinking how he would take the money he earned that night, and after the show, blow it all on drinks and a bargirl at Soi Cowboy.

The Dirty Dawgs went through a total of eight numbers, mostly old blues standards, and one their singer wrote. It sounded an awful lot like Willie Dixon. I liked it.

Phil joined us between sets. The English boy's jaws dropped when this virtuoso bluesman came by to say hello. Joe introduced his new friend to Phil.

"Likes American blues," Joe said.

"What's there not to like?" Phil asked in an accusatory tone. "Even a Brit knows that," he added with an angry verbal flourish. The young man smiled, but I sensed it was forced.

"Well, we did give the world The Yardbirds, Eric Clapton, John

Mayall. And we acknowledged them."

Phil ignored him and started talking to the two young ladies, who looked to their boyfriends for guidance. I had the impression that whatever he said to them was inappropriate. Then again, just about every word out of Phil Funston's mouth is inappropriate. Joe's new friend stood up and faced Phil.

"I think it's best you go backstage and practice," he said.

"I don't need to practice," Funston bleated. "I know every blues song there is. I can play them all in my sleep!"

"No, I mean practice your manners," the English fellow said.

Funston moved toward the younger man, who was a head shorter. Before contact was made, Sleepy Joe stood in front of Phil, blocking his way. I faced the English kid and motioned for him to stand still. A beefy Thai guy moved toward us, an enforcer of some sort. Joe told the man to take Phil backstage until the next set, and he hustled Phil off, over his loud objections.

Turned out the English kid was an okay person, as was his friend, and their English girlfriends too. Joe and I knew they were right about the history of British blues. The British accepted African American blues at about the same time as we American whites, but they didn't have all these racial hang-ups and history that made it difficult for white American blues artists to acknowledge where their music came from. Not so with the Brits, and white British bluesmen like the Rolling Stones, Eric Clapton, and Jeff Beck, made no secret of who inspired them, and lavished praise upon their heroes like Muddy Waters, Howlin' Wolf, and B.B. King. Made them a lot of money with those London sessions along the way. Compare that to how Elvis took the music, softened it enough to play to white people and never acknowledged his debt to African American artists. Elvis was a simple guy, who probably would have done the right thing, but he was never in control of his career. A marked difference from Howlin' Wolf, who took no guff from anyone, played his music his way, and treated his band well. Funston was not pleasant like Elvis, and his rude and condescending dismissal of British blues didn't go over well. The Brits smiled when Phil was shuttled off to the back room.

Phil did not come out for the second set. Not to worry, the very same ponytailed Thai who played like Buddy Guy happened to be present, and it didn't take much persuading to get him on stage. It's a mystery how he happened to have a guitar, but maybe musicians always have their instrument with them. I could always ask Phil. Then again, I could also not.

The Thai guy gave his usual virtuoso performance, almost as good as Phil. The dreadlocked singer did really good jobs on covers of "Bell Bottom Blues" by Derek and the Dominos, and "Little Red Rooster," another Willie Dixon number first recorded by Howlin' Wolf, then by the Rolling Stones, and only after them, by Willie Dixon himself.

After the show, the band went backstage. The singer came out shortly and sat with us for a while. He had heard the chatter of our table mates and seemed pleased to be among his countrymen.

"That Yank was just too much, wasn't he?" the singer asked no one in particular, except the message was clear: as an American, I didn't even make the "no one in particular" cutoff. The singer looked through me when he spoke. "Had to let him go, mid-show, insouciant bastard. Didn't like it, but he left me no choice. Can't work with a maniac," he explained, without further elaboration. "Typical American," he added, cementing my intuition.

"Not this American," I said. "Sorry if my countryman offended you, but rest assured, he offended me too."

The singer looked at me and nodded. His dreadlocks danced around his face.

"Fair enough," he said. "America did give us the blues, after all. And they were kind enough to send Stanley Kubrick over to us," he said, naming my favorite director of all time. That can win anyone over to my side. He had the waitress take our drink orders. This time it was ginger ale for me. I doubt the band had to pay for drinks.

The singer's name was Frank, and Joe and I had a good time talking with him and the other four Brits. I have no idea where the remainder of the Dawgs went, but with four young foreign men here to play music, Funston-type hangouts showcasing booze and women were most likely. Whatever they earned that night, they'd put back into the Thai economy by daybreak. The remaining Brits were impressed with our musical knowledge, and even more that we had actually seen some of great blues singers close up. We liked that these English kids could embrace original American music as if it were their own. I guess after all those great British blues artists, it is partly theirs as well. Isn't music always changing? Does it really belong to anyone in particular?

After the show, the seven of us stopped off for a drink at a little bar and restaurant tucked away on a side *soi* near the University. We all sat together, chewing the fat about the blues, and charting the course of influences: Delta Blues for Clapton and the Stones, Chicago for Mayall. At Frank's suggestion, we played a few rounds of Blues Trivia. These Brits knew quite a bit. But when Frank asked who first recorded "You Gotta Move" before the Stones, and when one of the Brits said Mississippi Fred McDowell, Joe corrected him.

"Fred recorded it in 1970," he declared. "But Reverend Gary Johnson cut it first, back in 1965." One of the kids googled it on his phone and pronounced Joe correct.

"How the hell did you know that?" Frank asked.

"Aussie Special Forces," Joe replied.

"How the hell does that help with the blues?" one of the Brit tourists asked, a tall, thin fellow, starting to go bald in front. "I thought what those guys did was kill people."

"We kill them so quickly there's plenty of time to study the blues," Joe replied. Frank laughed and ordered a round for all of us. I switched again, this time to water. Bars love guys like me, as they can charge the same for water as for a real drink. Joe said Frank could pay for that one round only, and when the evening was over, Joe reached into his pocket and grabbed a few bills to cover the rest.

"Just to show there's no hard feelings about exiling my great, great, great grandfather to Australia," he said as he set the bills on the table. I threw down two red one-hundred baht notes as a tip.

"Because we're over King George III," I said.

JOE AND I were standing on Samsen Road, trying to hail a cab that would take us back to the Green Belt. A lot of Banglampoo cabbies didn't like the traffic over there, and often tried to extort outrageous fares out of what they perceived to be helpless tourists. The first cabbie to stop wanted three hundred baht, almost ten US dollars, about four times the normal meter. Joe waved him off. A few minutes later, another cab pulled up to us, rolled down his window, and asked for two hundred. I waved off this one. A third cab stopped, even though he had a passenger and the top light was out. The passenger rolled down their window.

"You guys really screwed me over!" Phil Funston yelled. The top of his shaved head was illuminated by the streetlight above us, and at first, I thought he was mooning us. "I won't forget this," he added. "I'll get you two, you can take that to the bank!" He rolled up the window and the cab sped off.

"What did we do to him?" I asked Joe.

"Acted like normal people with those English kids," he said.

"And look where it got us," I replied. "Like we said back in my criminal law days, 'no acquittal or good deed shall go unpunished.' Now we've got this maniac on our case."

"Don't worry about Funston," Joe said. "He steps out of line, I'll talk to him."

"You mean he's not out of line now?"

"Not out of line enough to require a sit-down with me," Joe said. "And by the way," he continued, "we've hardly been punished. Those two couples just got back from India. They somehow got a ball of hashish through Customs. They shaved off a little piece to show their appreciation of our blues knowledge. It's in my pocket. Frank suggested we smoke some and listen to the blues until we drift off. Told him it sounds good, and that's what we're going to do right now. Grab the next cab, pay him what he wants, and let's hang out, get high, listen to some blues. It's not even midnight."

The next cabbie let us in and threw the meter. I gave him a nice tip for being straight up.

Lek, my condo's doorman, concierge, security guy, and my friend, waved at us as we walked to the elevator, and handed me my *New Yorker* magazine when I passed him. In the elevator, Joe told me he suspected the white lines in the piece of hash might be opium. At least he hoped it was.

"I'm not really sure I want to smoke hash laced with opium," I said.

"You will if you have to," Joe answered.

He was right.

2

IT WAS JUST after eleven when I left my morning Muay Thai lesson for my condo. The plan was to shower, smoke a joint, and meander over to the NJA Club for my afternoon martini with my friend, the General. I discovered the Club shortly after arriving in Bangkok eight years ago, and it quickly became my tavern, salon, and daily group therapy session. I spend hours a day there and cherish every minute. I'm not much of a drinker; it is the company, not the alcohol, that draws me. In my previous life in America, there were never friendships like the ones formed at the NJA Club. The Club is a rare Bangkok venue where the regulars include Thais and foreigners, and all my closest friends are NJA Club devotees. I can't imagine life without them: the General, a retired Thai military officer; Sleepy Joe, an aging hippie and former soldier with the Australian Special Forces; and Oliver, the finest purveyor of information in the Kingdom or anywhere else.

The early lunch crowd spilled from offices and construction sites along Sukhumvit Road and its side streets as I headed home. People scurried along as the Skytrain glided above. Common laborers and maids brushed against office staff and construction workers sporting hardhats, as they all lined up at food carts. Motorcycle drivers in orange vests stood by parked bikes, waiting for customers. Buses drove by, some with open windows and doors, in lieu of air conditioning. A sprinkling of tourists meandered about, and some snapped photos.

Near the Thong Lor BTS stop, a blind musician played his accordion as a young girl led him along the street. I dropped a twenty baht note in the cup she held out. A group of orange-clad monks hurried past, some glued to smartphones.

I approached my favorite grilled chicken cart, right after turning off Sukhumvit. The couple who own it speak little English, and with my useless Thai, we never converse. I ordered my usual piece of chicken with sticky rice. The man smiled as he handed me a drumstick in one plastic bag and the rice in another. I used the bag to hold the drumstick at its bottom. It was tender and juicy, tastier than any chicken in America.

I ate while walking home, drumstick in one hand, sticky rice in the other. Bites of chicken alternated with rice as I hand-shoveled them into my mouth, Thai-style. Chicken juice merged with the sweet coconut flavor of the sticky rice. My ex-wife would have strongly disapproved of eating with my hands. Maybe that's why she was an "ex". I concentrated on the food, which never disappoints. The bare hand added flavor.

THE INTENSE SMELL of fresh-ground Jamaican Blue Mountain beans filled my kitchen. I found them at the new upmarket Dean & DeLuca deli in the All Seasons Mall near the US Embassy. Greenwich Village has nothing on Bangkok. Beans are more expensive here than in America, but a coffee snob pays the premium. I poured the last stream of boiling water into the plastic cone that held the drip filter. There has never been a better way to prepare a single cup. The calming patter of drops was falling into the cup when my phone rang. The screen said it was my old friend Charlie.

Whenever Charlie seems out of my life, he blows back in like a hurricane, with me in its eye. The last time we spoke, he graciously volunteered me for a CIA kidnap plot. Charlie stayed safe in America and collected his ten percent of the fee, while my closest friends and I nearly lost our lives. Charlie's CIA connection, a thug named Billy

Sloane, was killed, and if it bothered Charlie, he kept it to himself. Perhaps he agreed with me that the death was no great loss. By the time we met, Billy was a rogue agent and homicidal maniac. We NJA Club guys survived and were well paid, but nothing changes the fact that when Charlie calls, it means trouble.

"Hey, good buddy," Charlie said. "How are things in Bangkok?"

"Great, because I'm twelve thousand miles away from you, and plan to keep it that way," I replied.

"Come on, Glenn," Charlie said. "You should break out the champagne every time we speak. Usually means you make a ton of money."

True, and I'd give Charlie half of it if he promised to leave me alone forever. I just couldn't be sure he would keep his word.

"It's never enough to make it worth dealing with you," I said.

Charlie let out a short laugh.

"Well, no worry today, Glenn. This time there's not a cent in it for you."

"That makes it even worse," I said. "Why deal with you for free?"

"Favor for an old friend. Actually, two old friends. And you get to show that you're still the guy we all knew and loved."

"One of the 'we' being you?" I asked.

"Only in the sense that I get great joy helping others," Charlie replied.

"Who is this friend? And how am I supposed to help?"

"Gordon Planter," Charlie said. "He needs to get out of town yesterday and I know you can keep him safe for a while."

My jaw dropped so far down I thought it would pierce my chest.

"Gordon Planter?" The words emerged as a croak. "He's coming to Bangkok?"

"Already there," Charlie said. "Just landed. Checked the airline. Should be at immigration in fifteen minutes. Meet him at the airport and keep him safe. He'll be at the arrivals meeting point."

In my mind, I saw the pistol my good friend Oliver kept in his condo. He would surely loan it to me. My aversion to firearms checked the idea; fifteen years as a criminal defense lawyer soured me on guns.

Seeing a client gunned down before my eyes cemented my feelings. Almost being shot by Billy Sloane didn't move the dial back any.

"Charlie, there's no way I'm going to the airport to greet Gordon Planter," I said. "Anyone else, maybe, but Planter, never." I recovered enough to pour a cup of hot black coffee and sipped it as Charlie spoke.

"Do it for me, buddy, and I'll owe you one. You know I'm a man of many talents."

"Charlie, if I ever have a problem, you're the last person I would call."

"Funny, you didn't feel that way eight years ago when you woke me from a hangover to help with a certain situation."

I had called Charlie eight years ago after snatching over six hundred thousand dollars in cash from a murdered drug-dealing client before the police could seize it. He helped me get the questionably obtained cash out of the US and into Thailand.

"Guy like you might need someone like me again. And besides," he added, "I'm asking you as a friend. We were friends long before you hired me. Always figured you for a stand-up guy."

True or not, I thought of myself as a stand-up guy. A *mensch*, as my late father would have said. One of the few Yiddish words I remember.

"You know what they said back in law school," Charlie said. "*You're never alone with Glenn Murray Cohen.*"

"And they were right," he continued. "Personal problems, school troubles, you were there to prop us up, Glenn. How many of our buddies got through Criminal Law because you helped them? No surprise you turned out to be one of the best defense lawyers I ever knew.

"Guess now that you got what you needed, you can turn your back on your old friends. Nothing I can do if you're going to be that way."

I really regretted taking Charlie's call instead of rolling that joint.

"Let's not confuse business with friendship," I said.

"I guess that was my mistake," Charlie replied. "Sorry to waste your precious time."

It was unfair of Charlie to bring up my law school moniker, which led me to think about my father and menschkeit. He had no right to draw me backward.

"Okay, Charlie," I said, "be straight. Why would we help Gordon Planter? You know I never liked the son of a bitch even when we were supposed to be friends. Neither did you. And you never do anything for free."

"He's in trouble and needs to lay low for a while," Charlie replied. "Needs help. We can give it and we should. He's far from perfect, but we don't want anything bad to happen to him. Lawyers are also people, you know."

"Lawyers like you make me forget that, Charlie."

"You're the one who hooked me up with Gordon," Charlie said. "When you left, he was mine alone. We fell out over some nonsense. Tell you about it some time. Hadn't heard from him in years, and then yesterday when I got to the office, he was waiting for me."

Charlie's historical account was accurate. I met Gordon in college and introduced him to Charlie when we two were in law school. Neither of us liked Gordon, but we somehow became a trio. Everyone else Gordon knew had cast him away, but he managed to hang on to us. It's still a mystery why. After my marriage, I saw Gordon far less often. Charlie and I ran into each other at the courthouse or Bar events, but contact with Gordon withered, and eventually ended. It didn't bother me, because I never really liked or trusted him, and still have no idea why I became his friend in the first place. As time passed, and Charlie and I became professionals, I came to see Gordon not as a friend, but as a conniving deadbeat and fraud. I still don't understand why it took me so long. Maybe that is a tribute to Gordon's skills as a con artist. The details, though, were a little foggy, as Gordon hadn't been on my mind for many years. Behind the fog lurked an unpleasantness at the thought of him being back in my life. I just couldn't remember exactly why.

I came to Bangkok to escape the past, and recalling it is something I try to avoid. Studying meditation with a Buddhist monk has helped me. Sometimes, when I'm very stoned, I wonder if I actually lived that past. Was it any different than the flashes of past lives experienced me-diators might experience? Hard to believe I was once a hard-charging lawyer in America. Harder to believe I was once married. Hardest to believe Gordon Planter was once my friend, though the mention of him makes me unhappy.

Charlie brought me back to the present.

"Do what's right, Glenn. Be the stand-up guy you know you are. If not for him, then for me."

Being the stand-up guy Charlie remembered was one thing from the past that I treasured. It's one thing that can never be taken away, because that's who I am. Charlie had been my closest friend in law school, and he learned to play me like Segovia plays classical guitar. He was a real bastard for springing the stand-up-guy line on me.

"I can be at the airport in forty-five minutes," I said.

I never asked Charlie what danger Gordon was in, or how I would keep him safe. I should have.

3

I THREW ON a pair of grey Dockers and a short-sleeved white shirt. Enough Asia had seeped into me to ban footwear at home. Lined up neatly at my door were designer sneakers, plain walking shoes, and my favorite Italian loafers. I chose the walking shoes. Gordon would see nothing that hinted at my finances. As the fog in my mind was burned off by sparks my brain cells were generating, I began to recall he was drawn to other people's money like a politician to a potential contributor.

The Airlink Train to Suvarnabhumi Airport is the most reliable way to get there. No need to worry about Bangkok's world-class traffic. As the train glided along, my thoughts gravitated to Charlie's reference to his breach with Gordon. What happened? Why was he still willing to help Gordon? How did he so easily get me to help someone I don't like? Maybe Charlie was an even better lawyer than I thought. Better than me. After all, Charlie reaps profit when I take risks. Was this another such instance?

During the half hour on the Airlink, I plumbed my memories of Gordon. He claimed to be a photographer, but never carried a camera. He evidenced no means of support, but drove a Porsche. He never paid for meals or drinks; there was always a wallet left home, or an expired credit card. Often there was no excuse, just a request to "cover me this time." Gordon never showed embarrassment, behaving as though support by others was his divine right. He coasted through life on other people's nickels, often claiming he was on the cusp of financial success.

We knew Gordon was playing us, but we never resisted. Gordon was neither intimidating nor threatening. He made us feel that if we protested his freeloading ways, we were the ones in the wrong. He had an impressive arsenal of tactics. It might be a hurt look, a few words of praise, or an apology. It always worked. We were young, and few young men want to be the bad guy. As a criminal lawyer, I learned to recognize Gordon's tactics as part of the toolbox of a good con man. With age, I learned that being perceived as the bad guy can sometimes help against men like Gordon Planter.

AN ESCALATOR ROSE from the Airlink stop to the Arrivals level. I moved left, walking quickly past stationary travelers. About two-thirds of the way up, I brushed against a man, and instinctively turned to apologize. He was tall, with a beard and long hair. It was the eyes that hit me. They were deep, and flashed with the intensity of lasers aimed at my chest. I wanted to say "sorry," but the blazing stare clamped my vocal cords like hands wrapped around my windpipe. *Probably having a bad day*, I thought, and hurried up the escalator stairs, not daring to look back.

My eyes scanned the crowd at the meeting point, hoping to recognize Gordon. Someone called my name. Gordon. I knew him at once. His face was lined and creased beyond what is expected at our age. His hair was mostly gray, with small patches of white and a few teases of original brown. He wore a suit and tie. It was May, when the heat and rain produce humidity that can steam-clean a suit while the man is wearing it. I felt itchy and sweaty just looking at him.

Gordon embraced me. I smelled alcohol on his breath while trying to wriggle free. Gordon always liked his scotch. He introduced me to single malt, a habit given up years ago. Of course, I bought for both of us, always, and often. I haven't drunk that much in years. At a certain point in life, a man has to choose between alcohol and drugs. For me, the choice was weed. Alcohol is a filler, a socially acceptable way of loosening up. Like my daily vodka martini with the General. The day they legalize weed in Thailand, and I can smoke it at the back alley of the NJA Club, will be the last day I drink.

I slipped from Gordon's embrace. His face was covered with a two-day stubble.

"It's good to see you again," he said.

"You need a shave," I replied.

"I'll shave when we get to your place."

Charlie had asked me to meet Gordon at the airport. Nothing was said about taking on a roommate.

"Sorry, Gordon, I don't have the paperwork to operate a hotel, and the authorities here are pretty strict about these things." This was true. The Thai government has been waging a war against Airbnb and other rental gig outfits. They don't like what they are doing to the city, taking reasonable rentals off the market in favor of high prices for short-term *farangs*. My condo's board prohibits owners from renting by the night.

Then it dawned on me that Gordon had no baggage.

"Airline lost your suitcase?"

"No time to pack," Gordon replied. "I'll fill you in on the ride home."

I didn't like the way he called my place "home."

I did not want to leave the meeting point until Gordon explained his presence in Bangkok and understood that after a few hours in my place we would find him a good hotel.

"Before we leave," I said, "we have to set a few things straight. You tell me why you came to Bangkok and I'll tell you where to find a nice, cheap hotel."

"I can explain it all in the cab," he said.

"Planning to treat me to a cab ride, Gordon? I usually take the train."

He flashed a smile, the same one he used all those years ago. His teeth were no longer gleaming white.

"Didn't have a chance to get cash or let my credit cards know I was leaving the country."

Here we go again.

"Let's take the train," I said. "Be faster than sitting in traffic. Just stay next to me."

I bought two tokens for the Airlink and we walked to the turnstile. The station was filled with travelers, and a crowd swarmed around us. I looked about carefully. Gordon was not at my side. He was only a few steps in back of me, and he caught up. Something clicked in my brain, and I focused on a tall *farang* man in the crowd, barely ten feet behind us. It was the eyes, piercing eyes that looked like they were on fire. The eyes I'd seen on the escalator. They were fixed on us. He saw me staring at him. A cold chill crept up my spine. The man disappeared as quickly as he had materialized. I grabbed Gordon and pulled him onto the train. The chill lingered in me the entire half hour on the Airlink.

4

THERE WAS NO chance to speak privately with Gordon on the Air-link. No wonder he didn't protest taking it. I should have figured that out and sprung for the cab. Gordon was supposed to be the deadbeat, not me.

"When we get to my place, you tell me everything," I said. "Otherwise, you are on your own."

"Don't I first get a stoning?" Gordon asked. "Figure by now you get the best Thai sticks."

Actually, no one in Thailand smokes such a thing, at least not since the end of the Vietnam War, and we were too young to have tried any that the GIs brought back from their jaunts to Thailand. If there were still any around, Gordon would surely bum some for free.

"We'll see," I said. I needed a smoke myself, and once again, Gordon Planter would get something without paying.

As we neared the entrance to my condo building, a tall *farang* cut between us and faced me on my right. Gordon stood behind me, inches from the building wall. I heard my own voice say "this isn't right," though I wasn't speaking. I shoved Gordon off to the side, pirouetted to face the stranger, and adopted the defensive posture my 23 Muay Thai teacher had drilled into me over eight years. The man's eyes bored into me, through my body and into my soul.

They were the piercing, burning eyes of the man at the airport, and they spoke as clearly as if they were lips.

"*I'm going to kill you,*" they said.

Those eyes did not see my right arm pull back and then release forward. I had thrown a right hook that would have made my teacher proud. My fist hit him right on his jaw. He went down, flat on his stomach, and didn't move for a moment. Then he rolled over on his back and started to raise himself. I kicked him in the face, and he fell onto his back again. Maybe that would not make my teacher proud, but at least I'd have the chance to tell him. My foot hurt when it collided with his face, but his face surely hurt him more. Blood flowed from his nose and mouth. Gordon's own mouth was wide open, but no sound came out. I grabbed him by the arm and pulled him the half block to my condo entrance, stopping after a few steps to take a photo of the fallen man's face on my iPhone. Things happened so quickly that the eyes had not caused a chill as before, but inside the lobby, my spine became an icicle. My friend Lek—the doorman, concierge, and security guy rolled into one—greeted me.

"That was fucking awesome," Gordon said when his jaw had slackened enough to speak.

I ignored him and turned to Lek.

"Two things, Lek. One, there's an unconscious *farang* up the block to the left. Could be a heart attack or a drug overdose. Never know these days. Call the cops and get them over here right away." Lek's cousin was a patrolman in the local precinct, another of the many reasons why the condo board loved having him. We had some of the best police response times in Asia. Of course, we regularly showed the police our appreciation.

"Second, this is my friend. I don't want anyone to know he's here. Anybody asks, you never saw me with anyone." I didn't say Gordon's name.

"*Mai khongwon*," Lek said, telling me not to worry.

I wouldn't. Lek was born in Isan, the northeast region of Thailand, and as a teenager, came to work in Bangkok. He was already a fixture when I moved into the building. We became friends over the past eight years. Lek helped me through episodes with girlfriends gone violent, hailed taxis when I couldn't get them to look at me, and taught me most of my scant Thai. His friendship has given me insight into Thai people and their ways. He explains anything I ask. He is discrete and trustworthy. My favorable view of Isan people was shaped by knowing Lek.

Many *farangs* complain that while it is easy to make friends with Thai women, it is difficult with Thai men. That may be cultural, or perhaps because Thai men find many *farang* men in Thailand not worth knowing. This is changing as younger digital nomads replace the older expats, a change I wholeheartedly embrace. Too many of the old guys came only for easy sex and cheap living. There's much more than that to embrace in Thailand, starting with the people.

Some cynics might argue that Thai women are friendly to *farang* men for less than honorable reasons. I am the last guy anyone would want to consult on the psychology of Thai women, or any women, for that matter. But I do have some tried-and-true Thai men as friends, Lek being one. Maybe I'm more likable than I believe, or Lek is just a good actor.

Or maybe the many thousands of baht I give him every Songkran, the ancient traditional Thai New Year and Water Festival, plays a role in his thinking. I'm sure he'd like me anyway, but it doesn't hurt. And he deserves every baht.

It wasn't safe for Gordon and me to stay at my place. We had been tracked from the airport to the condo building, and with the stalker incapacitated, it seemed like the best time to get out of sight of whoever was in pursuit.

I needed a place where we would be safe and protected, where our privacy could be assured, and which we could get to easily.

The NJA Club. It was within walking distance, and I know shortcuts through side *sois* and alleys known only to motorcycle taxi drivers. The General would be there with his two bodyguards, Sleepy Joe would head to the Club the minute I called him, and woe be to anyone who misjudged him as a harmless old hippie. Oliver would be there with his information. It was after three and Ray the bartender would be working. If I told him we needed privacy, no one would bother us. The waitresses, Mai and Joy, would also chase away any busybodies. Wang the cook might seem preoccupied with his work, but I have seen him scare off armed Russian thugs with nothing more than a stare and saw him kill a Thai gangster and Charlie's rogue CIA agent friend within the space of one hour. We would be safe at the Club.

AS SOON AS my condo was out of sight, I pulled Gordon against a building wall on a quiet side *soi*, and called Oliver.

"I just sent you a photo," I said when he answered his phone. "Need you to find out everything you can about this guy." Oliver's line of work is getting information, and there are none better. My team relied on him when we snatched the Russian, and his information was better than the CIA's. I told him everything that had happened, starting with Charlie's call. He was most interested in how and why I disabled my attacker.

"What was he trying to do, steal your weed?" Oliver asked in his booming Australian baritone.

"Nothing that bad. Just tried to kill me. But I knocked him out cold with a right hook and a kick to the head."

"Trying to put Sleepy Joe out of a job?" Oliver asked, referring to Sleepy Joe's past service with the Australian Special Forces. Joe's skills were not diminished after decades of never-ending cannabis consumption. I saw Joe in action when we captured the Russian, and it takes more than one lucky kick to make a Sleepy Joe.

"What exactly did this fellow with the eyes do that makes you think he wants to kill you?" Oliver asked. "Might you have misread the situation?"

I paused, cleared my throat, and answered. "He turned up at the airport and followed us onto the Airlink. Pushed his way in between us near my place. No need to ask what he was up to. One look at those burning eyes told me why he was there."

"Because of that, you gave him a concussion? Because you think he wanted to kill you?"

"Not think, know," I said. "I spent too much time representing killers to miss one when they cross my path. It's not by coincidence that he shows up at the airport and then tries to take me out in front of my condo.

"Oliver, this guy Gordon is in big trouble. Charlie sent him here, but he never explained why. This guy with the sci-fi eyeballs is mixed up in whatever Gordon is running from. Nothing else explains him. I need you to find out everything you can. Then maybe we can figure out what Gordon has gotten himself into, and with who. And how to stop them from killing me.

"Or Gordon," I added.

"Facial recognition software is amazing these days," Oliver said. "Just got the best program in the world. Israeli, of course."

"Don't pander me," I said. "If my name weren't Cohen, you wouldn't say that."

"Never intended to pander, my friend. Fact is, Israelis are the best in this stuff. Pleased to say they share with yours truly. I've been known to give them a hand at times as well. Scratch each other's backs, you might say. Just so you don't feel bad about being pandered, you have as much in common with these tough Israelis as a pussy cat to a tiger."

I tried to think of something appropriate to say, but before I could utter a word, Oliver spoke.

"We'll find out who this guy is and if he was sent to kill anyone.

"See you at the Club in an hour," he added.

"TELL ME WHAT the hell is going on!" I said to Gordon as we walked on a narrow side *soi*. "Don't even think about lying."

"I'm in trouble, Glenn. Real serious trouble. Not the Mickey Mouse shit I used to get into."

"I hadn't spoken with Charlie in years," Gordon continued. "But when I had this problem, he was the only person I could think of calling. I didn't know how to reach you."

"What was your beef with Charlie?" I asked. "You two were good friends last I recall."

Gordon frowned.

"Let's start at the beginning, Gordon, The truth, no bullshit. I could have been killed out there. You owe me some answers."

Gordon looked down and moistened his lips with his tongue.

"Need some water?" I asked.

"Later," he said and began his tale.

5

EVERY CRIMINAL DEFENSE lawyer must learn how to extract the desired facts from clients. Many times, it is best not to have all the facts, as some might compromise ethical representation. Gordon wasn't my client, but facts had to be gleaned, even on a walk through Bangkok's hidden side *sois*. There wasn't a soul on the streets beside us, and no one cared what two *farangs* had to say to each other.

"It all began when I married the Prune," Gordon said.

"A prune?"

"That's what I said. Married the Prune," he repeated.

"You mean you married a desiccated plum? Is that what they're doing in California these days?"

"It's no joke, Glenn. Met and married her in a matter of weeks. It was a few months after you disappeared. Big mistake."

"Why did you do it?" I asked.

"I needed money. I always need money, Glenn, you know that. We met at the dry cleaners. They were steam cleaning my only good suit. The Prune was dropping off some fancy-looking gowns.

"She wasn't my type. Couldn't be more different. Too old, too skinny, nothing to look at. Eleven years older and an inch taller than me. Somehow, we got to talking while the owner was taking a call. Don't ask me about what. Anyway, we kept chatting as we walked out the door. I took her number.

"She was a recent widow. Never worked a day in her life, born to money, married into more. Husband did real well, big house in

Marin, Mercedes and Land Rover in the driveway. No kids. She was lonely and needed someone. I needed money. We got married six weeks later."

I stared at Gordon. When we were young, he was rarely without an attractive woman at his side. He was a handsome charmer, for which my friends and I envied him. Gordon knew how to talk to women, and how to make them want to be with him. That was never my skill set. He wined and dined them on our money, which only increased our envy.

Today those good looks had deteriorated into a worn, lined face decorated with moles and the red splotches of a drinker. His stomach showed the beginning of a paunch. A close look at his suit told me it was well-worn. Could it have been his one good suit of seven years ago?

"What happened between you and Charlie? He says you guys are out of touch for years before you called him for help."

Gordon shook his head and clasped his hands.

"Yeah, we fell out back in 2008, about a year after you left. Right before the election, when Obama won. It wasn't me; it was the Prune."

"What could the Prune do to break up a friendship of close to twenty years? What could Charlie have done that made the Prune force you to cut him off?" I had never met Mrs. Planter yet was already calling her the Prune.

"Badmouthed Hillary Clinton," Gordon said. The look on his face reminded me of a puppy caught taking a dump on the living room carpet.

I wasn't sure whether to be angry or just laugh. Gordon released his clasped hands and continued.

"The Prune was a big Hillary fan. Loved her. Don't ask me why. Charlie was all the way in with Obama, and you know Charlie. He's not quiet about his opinions. He came by one night during the thick of the primary war between the two. Called Hillary a crook and a liar. That was when the Prune pulled up the drawbridge. No more Charlie for me."

Part of me wanted Gordon to experience the same treatment I used on the man with the burning eyes, and not just because I too was for Obama. But doing that would mean never getting the story. My foot remained planted on the floor.

"You didn't tell her 'no way'? Tell her Charlie was your good friend and a solid guy who never let you down?" How did my needle get stuck in a groove that kept replaying a defense of Charlie, like an old turntable playing a scratched record?

"Remember when someone stole your identity and ran up thirty-five grand on a credit card? The bank called you night and day and was about to sue. Charlie was in a trial but he found the time to prepare a lawsuit of his own that he sent to the bank's lawyer, and that was the end of your problem. Remember?"

"Yeah," Gordon replied. "Charlie did good."

"Doesn't sound like you do." Gordon Planter was the only person on the planet who could turn Charlie into a saint. I soldiered on.

"And when your brother got arrested for sexual assault and you called Charlie in the middle of the night, he was again in a trial, but found the time to work his magic and have your brother home before dawn. Later got all the charges dropped. Do I remember it correctly?"

Gordon looked up as if summoning divine guidance.

"More or less," he said.

"Never charged you a dime, did he?"

Gordon paused at the next corner and pulled his tie knot a little lower down his chest.

"Don't let it reach your belly button," I said. "Tell me the real reason you threw Charlie under the bus over some stray remark about a political hack." The Prune wouldn't like me any more than she liked Charlie.

"Take me from the wedding to your showing up in Bangkok," I said. "Tell me why a blazing-eyed maniac followed us and tried to kill me."

"Never saw that guy before. And never want to see him again," Gordon said. "I just couldn't make it work with the Prune. Too old, too many miles on her. When we had sex, it was only because I thought about life without her money. Fantasized about other women during the act. Money. That's all she was to me. Then I made another mistake. An error in judgment. Got involved with a pretty young thing who worked in the supermarket near us. Hot little Chiquita."

"You mean Latina?" I asked.

Gordon smiled for the first time.

"Come on, Glenn, no need to play the liberal. We're far away from California."

"People don't change just because they change location," I said.

"Okay, Latina. Whatever. Anyway, she got pregnant. She didn't want me to marry her, not that it was on the table, but she wanted me to support that kid for the next eighteen years. Wouldn't think about an abortion. You know, the Catholic thing."

"Wasn't your mother half-Catholic? Doesn't that make you one of them?"

"I'm a universalist," he replied. "You remember that, don't you?"

"Of course," I said. "Tell me more."

"When the baby was born, she went to the prosecutors and filed a suit against me for child support. Served me right on my doorstep. Good thing the Prune was at her book club when the Sheriff came by. Fortunately, no one saw me hit with the papers. Maybe they didn't even notice the Sheriff's car.

"They were asking for ten grand up front and two thousand a month. No way I had that kind of dough. And I couldn't ask the Prune to help me out with this one. She would have tossed my ass out in the street in two-seconds flat."

Exactly what you deserved, I thought.

"So I did something stupid, but what choice did I have? I borrowed money against the Prune's house. Forged her signature on all the forms, brought in all her tax and bank records. Even made a fake notarization or two. Everyone at the branch knew I was her husband, and never doubted that it was all on the up and up. Gave me the money. Two hundred fifty grand. I was able to cut a deal with the DA, pay them a lump sum of a hundred fifty grand, and I was off the hook forever. Kid would not have my name, I'm not listed on the birth certificate, mission accomplished. Had a hundred grand left to service the loan until I could figure out some way to pay it off in full. Billing was paperless, sent to a special email I created. Seemed foolproof."

"But your being here tells me it was not."

"Yeah, my bad luck. The Prune got one of these free credit reports and when she opened hers, she saw that quarter-million second mortgage and freaked out. Told her it was used in a stock deal gone bad and I was only trying to make some money and prove myself to her. Don't know if she believed it, but it didn't matter. She was crazy, over the top. I tried to reason with her. She totally overreacted. A quarter mill on that house wasn't even ten percent of what it was worth.

"She told me to leave right away, taking only what I brought with me, which to be honest, was the clothes on my back. Everything else was from her money. She found out about the account I set up for the loan proceeds and got the bank to freeze it. Seven years of marriage and nothing at all. I was out on the street without a dime.

"I spent a few days at a motel, using what was left on my credit card. Then these weird-looking guys started coming around asking for me. Seems like the Prune had filed a claim with her homeowners' insurance and they paid her off but wanted to get it back from me. Maybe they thought I still had some of the money. I felt like the Jean Valjean in *Les Misérables*."

I was impressed that he knew Victor Hugo. Maybe he got free tickets to the Broadway musical.

"And Charlie?" I asked. "How did he get dragged in?"

"Who else could I turn to? You know Charlie has a good heart, and he can do things other lawyers can't. When I showed up at his office one morning, he greeted me like a long-lost brother, staked me to some cash, and set up this trip here. Even paid for the ticket."

"He didn't ask where you'd been the past seven years?" I asked. "Charlie is a lot more forgiving than I would have been. Especially if you threw me under the bus for Hillary Clinton."

"Never mentioned my absence for all those years, so neither did I," Gordon replied. "Just like you haven't mentioned yours.

"Charlie's no dummy. He knew it was really about the Prune, not Clinton, and he said so. She wanted total control over me, and an old friend from my single days was a threat. Especially a single guy like Charlie, with all his womanizing. Charlie gave her the opening she needed to justify cutting him off. He was right. I apologized, admitted that I'd been a real shit as a friend, but I had no one else to turn to for help. It was his idea to send me over here. He said you could keep me safe."

"Yeah, Gordon, but the question is whether I can keep myself safe."

IT IS ALWAYS a pleasure to enter the NJA Club, one that has not dimmed in eight years. Even when stress and fear grip me, entering the Club makes me feel less worried. This time was no different; seeing the General seated at his usual table relaxed me as much as any joint or martini.

The bar at the Club starts about twenty feet in from the door and runs almost the entire length of the wall. It's the first thing anyone sees when they enter. It is hardwood and brass, with a wall mirror and barstools running its full length. The Club offers an excellent selection of alcohol, including my favorite vodka, Tito's, made in Austin, Texas and distilled six times. Imbibing Tito's is like drinking water, perfect for people like me, who do not like the taste of alcohol.

As soon as we walked in, Ray, the daytime bartender, signaled that my martini was about to be made. I walked up to the bar and told him that I would be speaking with my friends and didn't want any uninvited guests. Ray nodded and went back to preparing my one drink of the day. Ray, a gregarious Irishman, was not only a first-rate bartender; he was also the best raconteur I've ever come across. He often held the entire bar in his thrall as he entertained them with one of his stories. No one knew a thing about Ray's past, but that's not unusual at the Club. Some of his stories were funny, like the ones about the Chinese tour bus driver going the wrong way on Rama IV. Others were a bit gruesome, like the one about the Russians who thought they could scare off Thai gangsters in Pattaya, only to wind up as heads on pikes outside a Russian social club. There was no story being told when we entered.

The tables at the Club are scattered about, wherever they fit. The General was seated in the far-left corner, facing the entrance. One of his bodyguards sat in front of him. Another waited in the General's armored Hummer, parked illegally in front of the Club.

The General motioned for me to sit. I asked if he would mind if Oliver and Sleepy Joe joined us shortly.

"It's obviously important, or you would not ask," he said.

I deduced from their past interactions that the General and Oliver had done business and were comfortable with each other. As for Sleepy Joe, he had gotten on the General's bad side when he tried to make an end-run around him and find a cheaper weed supply, which caused the General to have him arrested, since he somehow had a piece of the local weed business. The General then helped me buy his way out, and took a healthy cut of the bribe. We *farangs* tell each other that Thais love to carry grudges, but that is not the case with the General. After he learned of Joe's past with the Australian Special Forces, and Wang reported his observations of Joe in action during the Russian episode, Sleepy Joe found himself in the General's good graces.

The General was unpredictable, often unresponsive, always mysterious, occasionally intimidating. I long ago determined that this blend is his way of keeping others off-guard and controlling situations. I experienced this odd approach a few weeks after the kidnapping mission. We were sitting at this same table, toasting the fact that I was alive, when he reminded me I was indebted to him.

"Had to keep an eye out for you," the General said when I returned from the kidnapping mission alive. "And I'm sure I can count on you when the day comes."

Fear wrapped around my body like a winter cloak. The General had used his not-inconsiderable influence to help me free Sleepy Joe, my friend and weed supplier, from the clutches of the Thai criminal justice system, and when it was done, he told me he would someday collect an unspecified favor. Very much like a warning. Shortly afterward, the General sent Wang, his most trusted ally, to protect me against the Russians. Wang killed that maniac Sloane before Sloane could kill me. Without Wang, and thus the General, I wouldn't be around to hear reminders. Still, when a man who rides around in an armored Hummer with two gun-toting bodyguards tells me I am going to be called upon to return a favor, I worry.

The thought of that favor caused the cloak of fear to tighten around my gut like a vest on a suit that fit twenty pounds ago. Fortunately, the reminder was only the General's way of making certain my debt is not forgotten, and he didn't bring it up again. He did continue to badger me about accepting his standing offer to meet friends of whoever happened to be his current *mia noi*, or minor wife. *Mia noi* is a distinctly Thai version of the Western mistress, usually a young, attractive woman comfortable with what we in the West would call a sugar daddy. Unpleasant as the General's hectoring on this subject may have been, it was a return to normalcy. The thought of taking up his offer, if it would satisfy the debt, crossed my mind, but I determined that the General would see it as insufficient compensation. As time passed, my fear about the favor quieted and eventually disappeared into that secret place where fear hides until it sees the all-clear sign.

That was the past, and this problem was in the present.

I introduced Gordon to the General and related all that had happened since Charlie's call. The General did not respond, and changed topics. He spoke directly to me, as if Gordon were not present.

The new topic was the same old one: my ongoing refusal to agree to an assignation with a woman the General had personally selected.

"It would be perfect, Glenn," he said. "My *mia noi*'s best friend since childhood. The four of us go down to Hua Hin for a long weekend, and none will be the wiser. I could ask my son to bring down his *mia noi* and join us. You'd like him. He likes the same music as you.

I won't tell a soul."

Hua Hin was an upscale resort on the ocean, a few hours outside of Bangkok. There is a Royal Palace there. It would be nice to leave the city for a few days, but not on those terms.

"We'll just wait until I find the right woman, and then we can all go down there," I said.

"Glenn," the General replied, "I'm in my sixties. May not have enough time for that to happen. Let me make it easy for you. *Farangs* are supposed to come to Thailand so that life can be easy. I bet every other *farang* would give their eye teeth to have the opportunity you pass on." The General's years as a military attaché in the US provided him a command of American vernacular, which he sharpened by watching American television and reading our newspapers.

"Would you rather have their eye teeth or my company?" I asked. Oliver entered the Club before he could answer.

Oliver's round face, shaved head, and muscled arms were tinged red, a consequence of spending time on the island of Koh Phangan in the Gulf of Thailand. Oliver could conduct business anywhere, and had long threatened to pull up stakes in Bangkok and live on the island full time. He tried to persuade me to move there as well.

"Not a chance," was my stock reply. "Bangkok is the home I was looking for my whole life, and the NJA Club is my family." All true. I couldn't imagine living anywhere else.

Oliver came to our table before the General could answer. He sat across from Gordon and introduced himself by first name only.

The sight of the big Australian with the shaved head and baritone voice of an announcer at a heavyweight boxing match had its effect on Gordon. He gripped the armrests of his chair and sat erect.

"I know a bit about the man who my friend Glenn put to sleep," Oliver said to Gordon. "What I would like to know is who might be interested in you, and why. The truth, of course." He sounded friendly, the way a used-car salesman sounds friendly.

Gordon turned to me, with a silent, wide-eyed look that was a plea for help. None would be coming. Gordon threw his hands up to chest level, palms forward, and spoke to Oliver.

"You got it all wrong, guy. Had a little trouble with my wife, and that's it."

"Oliver doesn't get it wrong," I said. "Crazy thugs don't assault me because of the Prune."

Oliver patted my arm and resumed speaking.

"We're going to get to Burning Eyes. But right now, we need to hear everything Gordon knows. He has two choices. He can tell us everything, or I can tie him up, take him to my boat on Koh Phangan, and throw him overboard."

Gordon dropped his hands, and pursed his lips as if moistening them. He looked at me again with that pleading puppy face. I wasn't falling for it.

"What the hell have you gotten me into?" I asked Gordon. "Oliver knows something and you are holding back the rest!"

"Can you tell me who Burning Eyes really is?" I asked Oliver.

"Of course," Oliver replied. "Congratulations, Glenn, you knocked out Peter Clincher, a journeyman plumber from Santa Rosa, California. And he's only ten years older than you."

"A FIFTY-EIGHT-YEAR-OLD PLUMBER? That's who the mob sends out to kill me?" I asked Oliver.

"First of all," he replied. "Who said the mob sent him? Don't you think that a Latin American cartel or the Mafia would send out someone who knows how to get the job done? Not some bumbling idiot with red eyes who gets made twice at the airport, and then on the street? Surely your own gangster clients were more professional."

How could I not have seen that? I thought. Oliver was right; as a former criminal defense lawyer who had represented every kind of thug imaginable, it should have dawned on me that a professional does not get made, and if they do, the job is over. They don't keep following the target; that's a sure way to get caught.

Am I losing my skills? I worried.

Oliver must have extra-sensory perception, because it was as if he were reading my mind. "Don't worry, mate," he said. "You just need to get pushed back into that criminal lawyer mindset, just like you did with the Russian caper. Worked out well for us. You saw things coming."

He was right once again. I needed to get rid of the anger, the fear and the frustration, and start thinking the way I did when being paid to get people out of some very difficult situations. Usually, the people had gotten themselves in the mess, and deserved punishment, but my job was to do everything possible to avoid that fate. I was pretty good, but the constant stress drove me out before it drove me crazy. At least I hope it was before.

"Any chance of a mistake?" I asked.

"This facial recognition program is never wrong," Oliver said. We had your phone camera shot, and the booking photo Lek's brother got me. Matches up to the photo taken by Immigration at the airport, as well as those on his passport and California driver's license. Not to mention the photo on his web page and his Facebook account. Touched up those last two so the eyes look normal. Has the same red eyes in the others. Must be some medical condition."

"Why the hell would a plumber from Santa Rosa travel ten thousand miles to accost me on the street?" I asked.

"Apparently he wasn't there to harm you," Oliver replied. "He was visiting his brother, who happens to live across the street from you. Got that from his immigration card. Not very neighborly of you to assault his sibling."

"Maybe he lied to immigration?" I asked.

Oliver shook his head. "Turns out Lek's cousin knows your neighbor. Good thing for you, because he managed to calm the brother down, and the whole thing will be forgotten. He's working here without a visa and Lek's cousin reminded him that it might be averse to his interests to bring in the authorities, if you get my drift."

Gordon sat still. His eyes grew bigger and his right hand trembled.

"What's your problem?" Oliver asked him. Gordon remained mute as his tremble increased.

"Speak up, boy," Oliver said. "We haven't got all day."

"You think someone is still after me?" Gordon asked.

"No doubt someone is looking for you," Oliver said. "You wouldn't be here otherwise. It wasn't Burning Eyes. A drug cartel would send a killer, not a plumber. And they will."

My own hand twitched.

"How can you be so sure a real killer is on the way?"

"I'm an information expert, remember?" Oliver said.

"What's the information that says a killer is on the way?" I asked.

Oliver pulled his chair closer to the table. "Charlie said you had to keep Gordon safe, and Gordon is obviously terrified of something. I doubt he's telling us the truth, which certainly frustrates our helping him. Or you. The story he gave doesn't make sense. Tell me, Mr. Criminal Lawyer, if things happened like Gordon here says, what are the chances a prosecutor would file charges? Sounds more like a civil lawsuit."

Oliver knew his American law. Too much reasonable doubt for a criminal case. Which spouse has the right to sign a mortgage may not always be easy to determine, and on any jury, at least one of twelve would think stealing from one's spouse is not against the law. That's a hung jury right there. The local district attorney would have shuffled the Prune off to civil court, and good luck trying to collect a judgment against Gordon. That's something Charlie would surely know. So why did he send Gordon to me?

"No doubt at all that he is being tracked by someone," Oliver said. We need to find out who and why, and he's no use for that," Oliver said, tossing a thumb toward Gordon. "He's making fools of us, though you did a good enough job of your own, beating up that poor old plumber. At least I've solved that mystery."

"I need an information expert to tell me I made a fool of myself?" I said.

"Well, mate," Oliver said, "you did ask my opinion."

6

"HOW ABOUT A shot for me?" Gordon blurted. "I could sure use one. We are in a bar."

"Go buy your own bottle," I said.

Oliver stared into Gordon's eyes. The Australian's shaved head glowed under the ceiling light above him.

"You tell me everything I want to know," Oliver said, "and you'll get a drink.

"Your other option is Koh Phangan and the boat. Hope you can swim."

Gordon's breathing reminded me of a caught fish gasping on the dock. But he started talking.

"I FORGED the loan papers and took the quarter million, that part is true," Gordon said.

"I never doubted you are a thief" was my reply. "It's the bullshit about the girlfriend and the insurance collection that's the lie."

Oliver patted my arm. I shut up.

"What did you do with the money?" he asked Gordon.

"Bought cocaine."

"From whom?"

"From a Colombian guy I knew from the gym. Antonio. We had gone out drinking a few times. He hinted one night that he had some connections with drug dealers, and if I ever wanted to make some money, he could work with me. The stuff would be the purest available. He made clear it had to be big, minimum a quarter million. The stuff could be cut with baking soda to double the profit. Got the wheels spinning. It would free me from the Prune.

"I figured I could get the loan, work a deal, pay it back, and have a half-million profit, tax-free. As soon as the loan funded, I called Antonio."

"So far, so good," Oliver said. "What went wrong?"

Gordon took a deep breath and continued.

"We met at a motel I rented. I gave him the cash in a duffel bag, and he handed me a small suitcase with the coke. We tried it. Uncut. Great stuff.

"I didn't know squat about dealing cocaine. Only snorting it. So I called up Henry Blatt. Remember him?"

MY LAST MEMORY of Henry was a decade old. He was always clean-shaven and well dressed, styled hair, in great shape. Didn't look like anyone's idea of a neighborhood drug dealer, which I guess was the idea. He was in fact a drug dealer, and not an especially smart one. I'd represented him twice when he sold to undercover cops. Probation the first time, a year in County the second. Henry Blatt could get any drug on the shortest of notice. There was a lot of grumbling about his prices and plenty of claims that he shorted the amount, but what were we supposed to do, sue him? I bought from him no more than once or twice. Weed was not his big-ticket item; he was more of a powder and pill pusher. Gordon was a coke customer whenever he found someone to loan him money.

"Didn't Henry have a reputation as a sleaze?" I asked. Henry still owed me for my representation.

"Yeah," Gordon said. "But so does Charlie, and we both trust him."

Did I really trust Charlie? Did I even like him? Or did Gordon made him look good? Why did Charlie drag me into this nightmare? Why did I agree?

Those questions would be sorted out later.

Gordon continued.

"Henry came to the motel and picked up the stuff. He said he had a buyer for the whole kit and caboodle and would return the next morning with my money. I spent the night at the motel and woke up bright and early, waiting to become rich."

"Well, obviously that didn't happen," Oliver said. "What did?"

"When he didn't show up by noon, I was worried," Gordon said. "Maybe he had ripped me off. Could never rule that out with Henry.

"I went to his house." Gordon's face froze for a moment, covered by a mask of fear. His eyes glistened slightly. He opened his mouth and exhaled as he shook his head.

"The door was open. I walked in. I'll never forget it."

"Tell us what you saw," Oliver said, gently, like a grade school principal questioning a student who reported a stranger in the yard.

"Can I have a shot now?" Gordon asked.

"Tell us and it's a shot plus a few tokes later," Oliver said, looking at me. I nodded.

Gordon sat in silence, sweat beading on his forehead despite the Club's Thai-style arctic-level air conditioning.

"There was blood everywhere. On the floors, the walls, the furniture. Body parts all over the place. Legs, arms, chunks of flesh, stuff that looked like it came from his insides. Henry's head sat in the middle of the dining room table. I'll never forget the look on its face. Mouth wide open, like he was trying to scream. Eyes the size of Oreo cookies. Looked like he'd seen the Angel of Death. I guess he had."

"And the coke?" Oliver asked.

"Gone. No drugs or money. I looked everywhere. It wasn't easy, not with Henry's head watching as I went through the closets and cabinets. I had to at least try."

"Because Jack the Ripper or not, you needed the money or the coke," I said.

"Was the place tossed when you got there?" Oliver asked.

Gordon said no. Oliver looked at me.

"Would you concur, Mr. Criminal Lawyer, that if the drugs were missing and the place had not been turned upside down, then whoever took it was given it by Antonio?"

"Or they knew where it was. Or they just got lucky and found it right away," I said.

"Good points," Oliver said. "You might surprise us and come in useful."

"Here's something better," I said. "You walked in on Henry after he'd been robbed and butchered. Why they chopped him up is something we might explore down the road, but right now we need to know why anyone would be looking for you."

"I don't know," Gordon said, his voice rising. "I was already out the money and the dope. What more could they want?" He looked at the floor as he spoke.

"There's something you're not telling us, Gordon," I said. "My life might depend on the truth, not to mention yours. So you better tell us everything right now."

Oliver moved a half foot from Gordon, towering over him.

"If we dragged him down to the island, weighted him with some iron, and tossed him into the Gulf of Thailand, what are the chances he would float ashore?" he asked.

"With the right weights and far enough out, zero," I said. "Let's go somewhere and smoke a joint before we tie him up."

Oliver shook his head.

"No, let's tie him up first. We'll be too stoned to do it after we smoke. And getting the gag in his mouth so he doesn't choke is going to be real hard."

Gordon clasped his hands on top of his head.

"Wait a minute, guys!" he yelled. "Give me a chance to me finish!"

Oliver swept his hand toward Gordon, palm facing him. Gordon spoke.

"While leaving, I spotted a cell phone on the floor. I picked it up.

Figured maybe it was some kind of evidence.

"Soon as I got out the door, a guy came out of the elevator. Dead ringer for Vinny Vega."

Oliver looked at me. I explained.

"Vinny Vega. The hitman played by Travolta in *Pulp Fiction*." Sleepy Joe and I had seen the film often enough to act it out ourselves.

Gordon continued.

"He yelled, told me to stop, give back his phone. I ran down three flights, into the street.

"Caught the first Muni bus that came along. I was lucky. It stopped down the block from the building where Charlie has his office. You ought to see it, Glenn. Beautiful space way up in this skyscraper. View of the Bay Bridge. He's doing well."

When I was still practicing law in San Francisco, Charlie's office was no better than mine: a small room in a shabby suite in the low rent district at the end of Mission Street, near the border with Daly City. We didn't need downtown offices. My office was along Bryant Street, not too far from the Hall of Justice, maybe ten minutes from Charlie's. It worked well for my clients. Charlie never had any problem finding people to pay him, and they couldn't care less about a fancy office. From what Gordon said, Charlie had gone up in the world. Maybe I got him started on the road to success. He made over sixty grand off me for a few hours of his time, and then seven years later, a hundred grand for telling his CIA friend about me. Not bad work when you can find it.

I caught myself drifting back in time, and refocused on what Gordon was saying.

"I told Charlie everything. He thought about it while I sat there sweating. Said the guy was most likely the killer and came back when he realized he dropped his cell phone while chopping up Henry. Then he said he was sending me to Thailand to see you. Said he would explain everything when he called you. He had told me before that you were semi-retired and doing some legal work over here. I figured good for you. Had no idea you and Charlie kept in touch. Charlie peeled a bunch of hundreds off this roll and handed them to me. I still have them all. Except I spent a little on drinks at the airport and on the flight." At the airport, Gordon said he had no money for a cab.

"Still have the phone," he added. "Charlie said I had to give it to you sometime. Now is fine."

"Hand it to Oliver," I barked, and Gordon obeyed.

"That's good," I said. "We promised you a shot if you came clean. We keep our word. This time it's on the house." The General, who was listening without speaking, signaled to Mai, who took the order for shots of bourbon for all, except one Diet Coke for me. She brought the drinks to us in record time. Gordon reached for a shot glass like a drowning man grabbing a lifeline.

7

IN 1957, SONNY Rollins and Sonny Stitt, two of the greatest tenor sax players of all time, recorded *Sonny Side Up*, with the great Dizzy Gillespie on trumpet. My favorite cut on the album is "The Eternal Triangle," perhaps the best sax duet ever. Its sound oozed through the Club's speakers and took me to a world where only hardcore jazz lovers are admitted, where time and space become meaningless, where only rhythm, harmony, and melody matter, all confoundingly improvised. Ray played the album as a courtesy to Oliver and me. Gordon had fallen asleep in his chair, not surprising after a twentyfour- hour flight and several shots of Jim Beam.

"What do you think?" I asked Oliver.

"I think he's telling some of the truth, but holding back most," Oliver said. "He hasn't said a word about who might have killed Henry or why it had to be so gruesome. I suspect he knows, and that's who he thinks is after him. Probably right. Also, not a word about what the Prune is doing, now that she knows he ripped her off for a quarter million. That should be in the mix."

"What do you think he's hiding?" I asked. "Why is anyone after him? How did they know I exist? What is true and what is not?"

Oliver leaned back and tilted his shiny shaved head over the back of his chair. He remained in that position for a few seconds, and then raised his head just enough to level his eyes with mine.

"That's a lot of questions to throw at me all at once," he said.

"Can you find out the answers?" I asked.

"Of course," Oliver said. "Can your friend here afford me?"

I looked at Gordon, who sat with his chin on his chest, snoring loudly.

"I'll cover his bill. How soon can we have this?"

Oliver looked at his watch.

"It's late night in California. The right people won't be easy to reach at this hour, but I'll get through to them. I'll be back here after I speak to them. By six p.m. the latest. In the meantime, don't leave, and don't let Mr. Prune out of your sight. And get Sleepy Joe over here."

I called Joe, and he was on his way at once.

Oliver rose from his seat. I raised an arm, flapped my hand down, and he sat again. I rephrased my questions.

"Do the bad guys know Gordon is here? Do they know who I am?"

"Can't say for sure about you. All we know is Burning Eyes had nothing to do with this," Oliver said. "But I do know that the bad guys are tracking your friend, and I know how."

The look on my face told Oliver an explanation was required.

"You think when a phone is turned off like this one is, GPS does not work." He held the phone Gordon gave him and waved it in front of me.

"That's what I've always believed," I replied.

"That's true about the GPS that comes with the phone. That kind of GPS needs an internet connection, and when there is none, the connection is lost. There are after-market products that solve that problem." Oliver pressed two spots on the back of the cell phone, and the rear cover popped off.

"Take a look," he said. "See that little thing that looks like a small Valium?"

I nodded as I squinted at the small white disc inside the phone.

"It's a stand-alone GPS tracker. I'll wager whoever sent out Henry's killer likes to know where their guys are at every minute. Make sure they're not cutting deals with competitors or getting caught and turning. Whoever chopped up this Henry fellow surely understood this, and had to retrieve his phone. His bosses would never approve of leaving it at the scene."

"No more than they would approve of leaving an eyewitness alive," I said.

"Exactly," Oliver replied. He patted me on the back.

"And this little white disc told them where your friend Gordon was at every moment once he had this phone."

It started to make sense. It didn't matter where Gordon went; as long as he had that phone, his pursuers knew where he was. They knew he had gone to the airport, and that he flew to Thailand. They could put out a contract on him, and undoubtedly did. I just clocked the wrong guy. According to Oliver, the real ones were coming.

Oliver pulled the tiny chip from the phone. He walked into the nearby bathroom. I heard the toilet flush. Oliver returned and said he was leaving.

"We've got to get out of here as soon as possible, now that they can't track us," he said. "This evening the latest."

The General said something, speaking so quietly that we had to lean forward to hear him. Oliver remained long enough to hear what he had to say.

"Everything Oliver says makes sense," the General said. "I don't think we can say the same about Gordon. He is lying, but I can't figure out why.

"Thanks to Oliver, we know that the one you call Burning Eyes was not a killer, and he was not sent here by the people you should worry about. That is it for now. It is all we know for certain. We will know more at the right time."

"When will that be?" I asked.

"As soon as you return from Chiang Mai," the General said. "You're leaving as soon as Oliver returns. He has some research to undertake." He turned to the big Australian.

"You know the place I have in mind?"

"I certainly do," Oliver said. "What's the plan?"

The General motioned to Wang, who came over to our table. They spoke briefly in Thai, and then the General spoke to us.

"Wang will call Lek's cousin, who will have a car sent over to pick you up in the back alley. You'll be dropped off at Hua Lamphong," he said, referring to Bangkok's main train station.

"You will buy tickets to Chiang Mai, in cash. This is the safest way. It's possible that people at the airport can be bribed to tip off the bad guys if you show up at the airport. But I highly doubt they have staked out the train station, and no one will know you were there."

"Why Chiang Mai?" I asked.

Oliver smiled and explained.

"The General has a house tucked away in the hills up there. Over the years, we've used it for everything: love nest, private meetings, hideout when the heat was on. It's almost impossible to find, and if anyone did, they'd have to get past some fairly tough armed guards."

I debated asking Oliver what he meant by "when the heat was on," but the General interrupted my train of thought.

"You, Oliver, and Sleepy Joe will spend a night or two there," the General explained. That will allow Oliver time to learn more, and give me time to arrange for your safety here when you return.

"Your friend will stay up there after you leave, until we get this all sorted out," the General added, staring at Gordon, who flinched in his sleep.

"I'm going home to make those calls," Oliver said. "See you at six."

THE INSTANT OLIVER was out the door, Sleepy Joe arrived. I brought him up to speed. Our conversation woke Gordon, who wriggled in his chair, shaking off his stiffness.

"Meet your new protection, Gordon," I said, throwing a thumb in Sleepy Joe's direction.

Gordon stared at Sleepy Joe, who wore a wrinkled button-up shirt, bought on the street for two hundred baht—less than five dollars— and jeans with frayed cuffs and the beginnings of holes at the knees. His long, stringy, and mostly gray hair was tied in a ponytail. Joe was not more than five foot eight and weighed no more than a hundred forty pounds. He hadn't shaved in days, and dark bags hung beneath his eyes. He reeked of marijuana.

"You've got to be kidding, right?" Gordon asked. "He's just here to bring us weed, right?"

"That too," Joe said. Gordon leaned forward to catch Joe's slurred Aussie accent. "But first I may have to beat some information out of you. I understand you have been holding back on my friends."

Gordon smiled for the second time since his arrival.

"No offense, but today I watched Glenn put down someone he thought was trying to hurt us. Honestly, you don't look like you're in the same league."

"Quite right," Joe said, stepping within arm's reach of Gordon, and sitting in a chair to face him. "I'm better."

I didn't see Joe move a muscle, but as the words left his mouth, Gordon let out a howl and bent over, hands cupped over his crotch.

"Don't worry, mate," Joe said. "A few minutes and you'll be okay. But next time will be a lot harder on you. So think about being straight with us right now. When Oliver gets back, we're going to question you again, and this time you'll tell us everything. And it better all be true." Joe flashed a toothy smile at Gordon, who slowly straightened his torso.

SLEEPY JOE SHOOK me awake. I had fallen asleep in my chair shortly after Joe magically inflicted pain on Gordon's crotch, escaping into some of my favorite jazz as the events of the day caught up with me. When I focused my eyes, I saw Oliver standing next to Joe. My watch read a few minutes after six.

"Where's Gordon?" I asked. Maybe I got lucky and he ran away.

"Already in the car," Joe said.

"What car?" I asked.

"The car that's taking us to Hua Lamphong," Joe replied.

I followed Joe and Oliver through the Club's kitchen and into the alley. Wang was chopping vegetables when I passed him. He looked up at me and then went back to his chopping.

A van was parked in the alley. A side door opened. Oliver pulled himself in and called to me. I climbed in and sat next to him. Sleepy Joe sat next to Gordon in the row in front of us. The driver and another Thai man were in the front seats. The door closed and the van drove off.

I asked Oliver what he had learned.

"Verified most of what Gordon told us," he replied. "There is a Prune, rich like he says, and there was a Henry Blatt, and he was butchered like a prize hog. Cops found a bloody machete in one of the building's garbage can. No prints, of course."

"I'm waiting on a report about the calls made and received on the phone," Oliver added. "Should hear when we get to Chiang Mai."

"What about the bank fraud?" I asked.

"The loan was made, and the Prune cried foul," he said. "Raised hell with the bank, but no reports to law enforcement."

Sleepy Joe handed me a lit joint. I took a few hits and it helped shake off my fear. I passed the joint to Gordon, who nearly ripped off my fingers as he grabbed it.

"The General wants Gordon hidden away safely in Chiang Mai until we figure all of this out," Oliver said. "We'll deliver him to the safe house and take the train back to Bangkok in a day or two."

Gordon passed the joint back to me, and I handed it to Oliver. He took a hit and exhaled a cloud of smoke before continuing.

"We can assume that the trail to us ended at the Club when I pulled out the tracking chip," Oliver said. "There's no way anyone finds out we went to Chiang Mai and back."

When Oliver mentioned the Club, my stomach tightened.

"Could we have brought danger to the Club?" I asked.

"No worry," Oliver said. "With the General and his two body-guards, plus Wang, and whoever else they bring in, I'd be more worried for the bad guys who come looking."

Oliver was probably right. But we still didn't know who the bad guys were.

8

HUA LAMPHONG WAS bursting with people. I craned my neck trying to read the overhead signs. Our train departed at 7:30 p.m. Twelve hours later, it would pull into Chiang Mai Station.

The train station was almost a hundred years old, built during the reign of King Rama VI, known for modernizing his Kingdom. The old Bangkok Airport, Don Mueang, was also built during his reign. My Thai friends tell me he introduced both democracy and nationalism. The democracy part is still a work in progress. Most impressive, he somehow found time to translate the works of William Shakespeare and Agatha Christie into Thai.

"Is there a plane we could take?" Gordon asked on the cab ride to the station.

"Anyone with money can buy all the airport information they want," Oliver had said. "That includes passengers coming and going at airports. Very little record-keeping on trains."

To be safe, I showed my John Rawlings Canadian passport to buy the tickets. The agent didn't ask for the others' names. In the unlikely event the Rawlings name was recorded and discovered, it would do no good. John Rawlings was Charlie's creation and allowed me to keep my money in a Thai bank without alerting Uncle Sam. Canada doesn't know Rawlings exists. Charlie is good.

This was a popular departure hour for the night trains, with their sleeper cars and berths, and the station was abuzz with movement. There were a few foreigners sprinkled about, but almost everyone in the station was Thai. Many were traveling to their home provinces; several carried large bags filled with clothing to give or sell back home. There were businessmen in suits and ties, and Muslims from the South, the women identifiable by their hijabs, the men by their skullcaps. Travelers, with time to kill before their trains left, lined up at stands selling *phad thai*, grilled chicken, spring rolls, and soups. A Dunkin' Donuts kiosk sat amidst the Thai stands. It had a long line. Police in brown and soldiers in green camouflage were scattered around the huge waiting room, chatting with each other or with pretty women.

All seats on the long rows of wooden benches were filled. We stood together near the bathroom and showers. I caught a whiff of Gordon, and considered sending him in to freshen up, but fear that he would run away or be killed in the shower shuttered that idea. Sleepy Joe leaned against a wall, slurping a bowl of *tom yum goong*, the classic Thai soup made with spicy chili, lemon, and shrimp. A passerby would have thought him to be another burnt-out *farang* who drifted to the Kingdom, seeking a new shot at life, but only grew crisper the longer they remained.

Those passers-by would have been wrong. Witnessing Joe disable and kill armed thugs on our CIA mission disabused any such notions for me.

Oliver told us the train was boarding. We headed to the track.

"Do you think Charlie is in any danger?" I asked Oliver as we approached our car.

"I doubt it," he replied. "All they know is that Gordon went into a huge office building filled with lawyers, accountants, and consultants. That little disc wouldn't tell them more than that.

"Besides, gangsters almost always leave lawyers alone. Never know when they'll need one."

"Does that apply to me?" I asked as I clambered up the metal steps into the railway car.

"Not at all," Oliver said.

WE SAT IN pairs opposite each other, two seats facing forward and two facing the other way. Oliver sat next to me and studied his phone, Sleepy Joe dozed, and Gordon looked out the window to his left. Eventually, he joined Sleepy Joe in slumberland.

"When they make up the berths, Gordon and Sleepy Joe take the lower and we take the uppers," Oliver said after he put away his phone. Sleepy Joe held the one Gordon had stolen from Henry; we knew it was as safe with him as any place on earth. "If we have any trouble, Joe will be in action, and Gordon will have a chance to get away."

"What about us?" I asked.

Oliver smiled.

"You'll clamber down that ladder and deliver your patented right hook to the head of anyone Joe hasn't killed. I can sleep through it all. Wake me up when it's over, mate."

"Aren't we really taking the train because it's safe?" I asked.

"*Safer*," Oliver said. "I'm pretty sure Lek's cousin shook any tails, but one never knows." The driver had taken a circuitous route to Hua Lamphong station, doubling back a few times, going too far in one direction and then correcting, pulling into parking lots, making U-turns.

"I hope you're right," I said. "You don't sound like you're ready to fight."

"I get information and let others risk their lives," he said. "At least I try to keep it that way."

The attendants came by after an hour and a half and turned the seats into bunk beds. I took the berth above Sleepy Joe. Oliver climbed into the berth above Gordon. It was surprising how easily he fit his six-foot-plus frame into the space. The other two seemed none-too-pleased about being awakened; Gordon scowled and Sleepy Joe mumbled to himself. Within minutes, their snores leaked through drawn curtains. Oliver and I lay on our beds chatting for a while, mostly about Koh Phangan. Oliver bid me good night and drew his curtain. I followed suit. Thais love arctic-level air conditioning, and the upper berths are notorious for their frigid temperatures. I regretted not bringing a sweatshirt, but the motion of the train and the boredom lulled me to sleep. A dream took over after I lost consciousness.

In the dream, my phone rang and the screen showed it was Charlie, but it was not Charlie who answered. A deep voice spoke in Spanish, a language I learned from representing Latino drug dealers, who didn't like court interpreters in the holding cells with their lawyer. It became my second language. Perhaps if there were a financial motivation, Thai would become my third.

"*Olvídate de tu amigo y vives. Intenta salvarlo y morirás. Usted ha sido advertido,*" the voice said. "*Forget about your friend and you live. Try to help him and you die. You have been warned.*"

Oliver's big hands on my shoulders pulled me from my dream.

"MUST HAVE BEEN quite a world you dreamt yourself into," Oliver said. "You were screaming like someone just kicked you in the nuts. I could hardly hear your phone ringing a few minutes ago." Charlie had called. I tried reaching him but there was no reception.

"Coincidence," Oliver said.

I knew a prosecutor or two who liked to say that there are no coincidences.

AFTER ASSURING MYSELF we were safe on a train to Chiang Mai, I closed my curtain again. I had almost succeeded in falling back asleep when the soft patter of footsteps stopped outside my berth and triggered my trial lawyer radar. Through the space at the end of the curtain, I saw the bottom half of a man. I was sweating despite the freezing air conditioning. Sleepy Joe was only a foot below me. One signal to him and the man would be dead. Then the man bent down to tie his shoelace and moved on. He was an older Thai, thin and slow-moving. I stuck my face a half inch outside the curtain and watched as he went into the bathroom at the end of the car. I sat still until he was done, and watched silently as he made his way to the other end of the car, where he climbed up to his bed.

Probably not our assassin, I told myself.

I remained awake for the rest of the train ride.

A WOMAN CAME through the car, taking orders for coffee. Oliver ordered four cups and woke up Sleepy Joe and Gordon. Before the coffee arrived, an attendant turned our beds back into seats. We were soon sitting and sipping.

"How does this stack up against those fancy beans you brew?" Oliver asked.

"It doesn't," I replied. Actually, it wasn't bad coffee. It's just that when it comes to the bean, I am an admitted snob. After sleeping no more than an hour or two, my system required caffeine to get a jump start on the day. It was six thirty in the morning. I would have drunk instant coffee if necessary.

When the train pulled into Chiang Mai Station, Oliver led us out of the small depot, down a narrow *soi* that we would have otherwise missed. A red pickup truck used as transportation, *songthaew* in Thai, was parked at the end of the little street. We climbed into the bed and sat on hard wooden slabs set along the sides. Without a word to the driver, the *songthaew* made a left turn and wound its way through a series of narrow side *sois* lined with small wooden buildings. I recognized one as a brothel for Thai men by the red, yellow, and green Christmas lights draping the front, turned on even when closed. Did I mention that Christmas is not a Buddhist holiday? Nearby stands were selling food, but those for clothing and household supplies were not yet open.

"You wouldn't believe the ladies in that place," Oliver said as we passed by the flashing lights of the brothel. "When all of this blows over, we have to stop by."

"Not me," I said.

"Oh, I forgot we have a Puritan with us. Okay, Glenn, we won't force you to have a good time. You can stay home and brew coffee while the rest of us work off our tension."

"I'm no Puritan!" I said louder than I intended.

"Of course not," Oliver replied. "You're just against sex, cursing, and degeneracy."

Oliver was not going to sucker me into a debate. He knows I enjoy sex as much as the next guy, but only when there's no bill presented. A man who earned a living as a mouthpiece can't fathom substituting intelligent speech with vulgarity. As for degeneracy, it's case-by-case with me.

A familiar scent filled the bed of the truck. I turned to Sleepy Joe.

"Why you smoking a joint at seven in the morning?"

"Because I couldn't light up on the train," he replied. He passed the burning joint to me. I looked at Oliver.

"This is our private limo," he said. "Do as you like."

I took two long drags and offered it to Oliver, who declined. I passed it back to Sleepy Joe, who instantly had it between his lips.

"What about me?" Gordon asked. "Don't I get some smoke?"

"Sure," said Sleepy Joe, and he blew a mouthful in Gordon's face.

"They're going to be looking for Gordon," Oliver told me on the *songthaew* ride. "Gordon saw the killer and took his cell. Or at least we know he has a phone. In the wrong hands, that's big trouble for whoever wanted Henry dead.

"Gordon is always trouble," I said. "Why would I make the list?

"The fact that you are with him would convince the criminals that you know enough to sink them," he added, staring at me. "They may or may not know of you. Don't know if they were at the airport. The good news is that it's doubtful they have any idea about Sleepy Joe and me."

Gordon squinted and shook his head.

"Does that mean you two live and Glenn and I die?" he asked.

"I'd normally lay odds on that," Oliver replied. "But no one should bet against you when Sleepy Joe is around." Joe was slumped on the bench, against a corner of the truck bed, snoring softly.

"You're sure about that?

"Positive."

A HALF HOUR later, our "limo" deposited us at the bottom of a long stairway carved into the side of a steep, forested hill. We followed Oliver up the stairs to the large wooden door of a substantial house hidden from view amidst a grove of trees. On the way up, we passed two Thai men with blank looks on their faces and semiautomatic rifles in their hands. They ignored us.

At that early hour, the sun was a soft, buttery yellow, and the sky a fuzzy baby blue. The air in the hills was clean, and smelled of earth and leaves. We were months away from the burning season, when farmers clear their fields by fire, and the smoke smothers the North for weeks. It was good to get out of Bangkok every now and then, I thought, before remembering why we were in Chiang Mai.

A Thai woman opened the door and let us in. She looked somewhere around thirty, a few inches above five feet, with the light skin of the North, her black hair pulled into a bun.

"This is Nahmwan," Oliver said.

"She works for the General," he explained. "If you need anything, let her know. Whatever she can't handle, she'll pass on to me."

"Works for the General?" I asked.

"Her sister is his girlfriend," Oliver explained.

"Wait a minute, Oliver," I said. "I thought the General has a *mia noi* in Bangkok."

"What, a man can't have two these days? Makes up for the one you don't want."

Oliver left us and went off to one of the many rooms in the big house. Nahmwan showed us the rooms we could use during our stay. Her English was excellent. She smiled at Sleepy Joe and me, but not at Gordon.

"You stay in your room," I told Gordon. "If he leaves, let us know," I said to Nahmwan as I steered Joe into my room.

As soon as the door was closed, he pulled out a joint and walked to the window. Oliver hadn't said anything about smoking in the house, but veteran potheads like Joe and I are always aware that it might be frowned upon. We stood by the open window, passing the joint back and forth. It was not yet eight in the morning, and we were on our second joint. I promised myself not to smoke any more until I felt out of danger. Of course, the way things are going, that might never happen.

"What do you think?" I asked.

"Thinking is your game," Joe replied. "But I'm having a very difficult time believing most of what your boy says. He's lying about something important."

I felt uneasy, in the way one feels when they are about to throw up. I breathed in and out a few times and the feeling slipped away.

"What makes you say that?"

Sleepy Joe looked at the joint and stubbed it out on the windowsill. He put it into a shirt pocket.

"Finish it later," he said to himself, and answered me.

"Oliver showed us how someone was tracking Gordon, and that the one you call Burning Eyes was not mixed up with them. Professionals would never send a fool like him on such a mission."

"You ought to speak to the CIA," I said. "They sent me out to kidnap a Russian gangster."

"Which you did," Joe said, "Because you had me."

"Any ideas on what the hell is really going on? What did Gordon do, and who did he do it to?" I asked. "Any thoughts at all will be appreciated."

Sleepy Joe pushed a lock of hair away from his eyes.

"Like I said, Glenn, thinking is your game. Now go and do some, mate."

9

THERE WAS A small desk in my room, stocked with paper and pens. Pencils would have been preferable, as I like to erase and replace. No doubt word processing is faster and more efficient, but some ideas need to flow through the hands. Criminal lawyers do this all the time.

The first entries on paper were the names of all the characters in this drama. Criminal lawyers differ on where to start, but this always works for me. The names started to flow.

Charlie
Gordon
Henry Blatt
Henry Blatt's Killer
Burning Eyes

You've forgotten someone, the criminal lawyer lurking in my subconscious called out.

It was true. I added a name.

The Prune

Still missing someone, the voice imparted to me without sound.

Right again. I added the missing character.

Myself

I DREW ARROWS between people who were connected. Me to Charlie and Gordon. Same connections for them, but they were both connected to the Prune, Gordon, and Charlie.

Henry Blatt was connected to me, Gordon, and Charlie. He was also connected to his killer, as was Gordon.

My list looked like a post-urban modernist pen-and-ink drawing. There wasn't quite enough room for clean lines between the actors.

Next came the chronology of events, as best as I could discern. In this case, the chronology was a blend of what Gordon said and what I personally observed. Sometimes the order of events just can't be known for certain, and we do the best we can.

I started writing, and kept going until I had a complete timeline:

Gordon takes fraudulent loan on Prune's house
Gordon buys cocaine from Antonio
Gordon advances cocaine to Henry Blatt
Blatt is murdered
Gordon sees murderer and grabs his cell phone
Charlie calls me
Met Gordon at airport
Spot Burning Eyes following me by condo
Knock out Burning Eyes
Lek's brother takes Burning Eyes to police station
Burning Eyes released
Gordon gives different stories
Oliver finds GPS device in phone
We come to Chiang Mai.

I went over the notes several times. For each event, I added the actors. Gordon was in every scene, except for Henry's murder, my first encounter with Burning Eyes, and Burning Eyes taken to the police station. Since Gordon landed in Thailand, we were together every second.

Gordon was at the center of everything, that was clear. Willing and knowing or not, Gordon set everything in motion, and directed it all along the way. When he gave us bad information or held something back, it was to protect himself. Neither Oliver, Sleepy Joe, or I had cracked his veneer of secrecy and lies. Gordon acted, we reacted, and we still had no idea what we had gotten ourselves into.

It was almost one in the afternoon. A little more than a day had passed since Charlie called. I felt like a man trapped in a cave, trying to find his way out with a penlight. Putting everything down on paper helped magnify the light, but not nearly enough. I had to do a better job of getting the facts.

As I pondered the meaning of my cast of characters and timeline, someone knocked on the door. It was Nahmwan, who handed me a manila envelope. "From *Khun* Oliver," she said. When she was gone, I removed the document inside the envelope. It was the San Francisco Homicide Inspector's report of the murder of Henry Blatt.

Will help with the timeline, I thought, and sat down to see if that was true.

When I was finished reading, I stood up and entered Gordon's room without knocking.

10

GORDON FELL ASLEEP in his suit, which was rumpled and smelled like the socks at the bottom of my gym bag. I held my breath to avoid the scent. Gordon woke up when I yelled at him.

"When we're done talking, you take a shower and we'll get you clothing. But first I've got me questions."

"What's the problem?" he asked. "I need some sleep." For the first time, I was confident Gordon was being honest. He hadn't slept more than a few hours over days and he looked it.

"I need some answers," I said. "And I'm going to get them now."

Gordon sat up in bed and leaned against the headboard. He was fully awake, and his eyes were wide open. I aimed my words at them.

"What does the Prune know? No more bullshit, Gordon."

Gordon's eyes remained as wide as half dollars.

"She found out. Someone at the bank said something to her. They all thought she was on board as a cosigner. That was right before I left to pick up the money I expected from Henry."

"I thought you said she found out through a free credit report," I said.

"I lied," Gordon replied.

"Have you spoken to her since?" I asked.

"Not a word," he said. "What I said about her kicking me out with nothing was true. She told me to get out and never come back. Didn't bother me at all, because I was on my way to pick up money so I could pay back the loan and live like you."

I felt as if someone had punched me in the stomach. I wondered how much Gordon knew about me.

"What do you mean, 'live like you?'" I took a step toward Gordon. He curled up into a seated fetal position.

"Whenever I asked Charlie how you were doing, he always told me you lucked out and got a law gig over here in Thailand. I know Thailand is cheap to live in, so I figured a lawyer like you must be doing really well over here."

It made sense to me. Charlie couldn't expect that no one would ever ask about me, and it was an easy-to-believe story he gave Gordon.

"Did the Prune know this?"

"Yeah, I'm sure I mentioned you to her a few times. Your name came up a few times. She knew Charlie, and you know, a wife can be curious about her husband's life before marriage."

"Obviously not in this case," I said. "Or the Prune would never have married you."

I sat on the edge of the bed and stared at Gordon.

"You're not being honest with me, Gordon. I just know it." The inner sense that trial lawyers possess was sounding four alarms whenever Gordon opened his mouth.

"I don't know what the truth is here, or what your plan might be, but you're not being straight with me or Oliver, and that can be dangerous for all of us."

Gordon got up from the bed. His white shirt, like his suit, was wrinkled, and he sorely needed a shave. He didn't look very dangerous, but the warnings were ringing in my head.

"Maybe I can get a cup of coffee," he said.

That was the first good idea Gordon had since his arrival.

"This is the General's home," I said. "No doubt the coffee is the best."

I LEFT GORDON to ask Nahmwan about coffee. She was in the

living room, just a few meters from Gordon's room. She smiled when she heard my request and asked what kind I wanted. There were a least a half dozen choices, as the General rivaled me in love of the bean. Nahmwan recommended the imported Ethiopian Highland, and I agreed. Afternoon light poured through the kitchen window, and I saw how pretty Nahmwan was, with light brown skin offset by perfect white teeth and dark eyes that shined with a soft glow. Nothing at all like the coal-glowing eyes of the man I kicked in the head, who turned out to be an innocent plumber with pink eye.

"Brewed with one cup filters," I added.

"The General always asks for French Press," she said. "Oliver too."

"I don't want to share anything with that guy," I said, jerking my thumb in the direction of Gordon's room. She opened up cabinet doors and gathered together what she needed. I sat at the table.

Watching Nahmwan prepare the coffee was akin to watching ballet or modern dance, perhaps the Alvin Ailey or Bill T. Smith companies. When I was in college, a young lady introduced me to modern dance, and it must have pulled some strings deep within my soul because I have been drawn to it ever since. My favorite performances were those set to jazz; the movements and sounds take me places I never imagined existed. Whenever there is a top-flight modern dance performance in Bangkok, I attend.

Nahmwan's hands and arms flowed in coordination as her body gently swayed in the opposite direction. A soft smile was fixed on her face as her eyes moved subtly from the grinder to the filters as she worked. Her long black hair and smooth skin made me recall at least two former loves. I vowed not to hold that against her.

NAHMWAN BROUGHT THE coffee to Gordon's room. I sat by the little desk, and Gordon sat on the edge of the bed, balancing a cup and saucer on his knees. I turned my chair to face him.

"I've got some more questions for you," I said, "and the answers better be true."

Gordon rubbed his eyes.

"Can't it wait?" he asked. "Be better after some caffeine."

I told him he was smart enough to drink coffee and talk at the same time.

"You sip while I ask, then you stop and answer," I explained. "I sip while you talk."

The first question out of the box was about Antonio, the gym buddy Gordon claimed as his coke contact.

"How long have you known him?" I asked.

"Oh, a few years, maybe three, four maybe," Gordon said. I noticed him clenching and unclenching his fist, and not because he was getting ready to slug me.

"You're lying," I said.

Gordon gripped his cup and saucer as if he were on a ship rolling about on the ocean.

"Why would I lie about something like that?" he asked.

I took a long sip of my Ethiopian Highland. Nahmwan was right; it was exquisite, though I might have brewed a stronger cup.

"There is no Antonio," I said. "You made him up to divert attention from the real supplier."

Gordon shook his head rapidly several times. I held out my hand and thrust it forward with such force that were it one millimeter closer, it would have flattened his nose.

"No one would trust a casual gym acquaintance with a quarter million dollars, let alone in an illegal cocaine deal," I said. "So if you ever had any coke, you got it somewhere else.

"I'm betting Charlie had something to do with it," I said. "That's why you ran to him when things went south."

Gordon stood up and placed the cup and saucer on a small desk. He moved backward, away from me, his arms up in surrender.

"Charlie?" he said. "Charlie's a lawyer."

If there was any lawyer who knew where to buy kilos of cocaine, and any lawyer who would get involved in such a deal, it was Charlie.

But with Charlie, things always turned out well, and that didn't seem to be happening here. Maybe I was wrong to suspect him of involvement.

"Give me the name and location of your gym and a description of this Antonio," I said. "A last name if you have one. Anything else you can tell me about him. His workout routine. Where he lives. Car he drives. Oliver will get the manager of the gym on the line and we'll see if there's such a guy at your club."

Gordon tried to speak, but no words came out. He looked like a fish on land, gulping for water. Finally, his words tumbled out.

"Why do you think all these things?" he asked. "Why the hell would you think I lied to you or that Charlie was in this?" I thought he might start crying.

"You want to give me the information?" I asked. "Or would you prefer Sleepy Joe squeeze it out of you?"

Gordon instinctively looked at his crotch.

"There's no Antonio," I repeated, "and your story about finding poor Henry is also a crock.

"I've seen the police reports, Gordon," I said. "We've got ways of finding out everything.

"According to your story, you went over to see Charlie right after finding Henry, and right after you told Charlie everything, he sent you over here. I know what time Charlie called me to say you were landing, and I know when you arrived."

Gordon focused his eyes on the wall, as if he were deep in concentration.

"What difference does that all make?" he asked.

"Makes all the difference in the world," I replied. "By taking the correct times we already had and matching them with the police report, I was able to construct a fairly accurate timeline.

"According to your story, the total time from discovering the butchering until the time you landed in Bangkok was between twenty-nine and thirty-four hours. That was easy to figure out, based on Charlie's call and your arrival."

Gordon sat on the edge of the bed, head in hands.

"You guys really don't believe me," he said, sounding more like a foregone conclusion than a shocking realization.

"We can't," I said. "Not when the police report says Henry Blatt's body parts were discovered in his apartment at two a.m. the day you say you came upon him. Problem is, they were on the scene at least ten hours ahead before you claim to have arrived. I doubt the cops left the door open and Henry in pieces laying around for you to find."

Gordon released his hands from his chin and made a downward pushing motion while shaking his head "no," as if he were trying to calm an aggressive Rottweiler.

"I'm through screwing around with you, Gordon. I never liked you and I remember why. You're a liar and a deadbeat. We're going to find out what really happened. And how you really got that phone."

"You're going to hurt me?" Gordon cried out.

"Of course not," I said. "That's Sleepy Joe's job."

11

NAHMWAN STOOD A few feet away from Gordon's room. I asked where I would find Oliver, as I wanted him present for the questioning. She told me Oliver had left the house while I was working, and he told her he'd be back in a few hours. I couldn't wait for him.

"Watch that door," I said, and walked to get Sleepy Joe. "If Gordon tries to leave, scream."

Sleepy Joe was lying on his bed, watching a Batman movie.

"The General has satellite, and the reception is great," he said. "Val Kilmer as the Batman. Tommy Lee Jones, Jim Carrey, Nicole Kidman. Bob Kane said it was the best he'd seen," he added, referring to the Batman's creator. "Of course, Kane died before he could see Christian Bale, in my opinion, the best of them all."

"We'll go back to the comics later," I said. I filled him in on my work and discoveries.

"That was pretty good," Sleepy Joe said when I told him how I had caught Gordon in the lie about finding poor Henry. "If I ever get in trouble again, you're getting another call."

"Next time, I'll charge you up the wazoo," I said. "Now that you can afford it." Our Russian gangster escapade may have been dangerous, but it paid Sleepy Joe a hundred fifty thousand US dollars.

Joe had untied his ponytail, and his hair hung down over his shoulders. He looked like an anorexic Viking.

"What's my assignment, Sarge?" he asked.

"Get the truth," I said. "About who he's running from and why."

"We've got to know who gave Gordon that phone, what the hell he's really doing here, and Charlie's role," Joe said. "In any order."

I was haunted by one mystery.

"Was Charlie duped into helping Gordon, or is he somehow mixed up in whatever caused him to flee?"

"He's your mate," Joe replied. "I never met the man. What's your gut tell you?"

It didn't take long to answer.

"My gut, and every other body part, tell me that Charlie doesn't get duped by bozos like Gordon. We saw through him right away. Just couldn't get the whole truth. Whether Charlie must be mixed up in one way or another, I just can't figure out how. And I'm wondering why he tried to call me when we were on the train."

"Probably Charlie just wanted to make sure Gordon arrived safely. How else would he know? Let's take a small break. You'll go back to work after I have a little chat with Gordon," Joe said.

A fresh joint appeared from nowhere and rested between Joe's lips. He was a magician, a sleight-of-hand master. I'd seen him take out men when it looked like he hadn't moved a finger. He saved my life from Russian gangsters and Thai thugs without a weapon. Gordon had no idea what was coming his way.

"Hard or soft?" Joe asked.

I saw the faces of the men Joe had laid to rest defending me, and the murdered client whose money brought me to Bangkok.

"Medium to hard," I replied.

I noticed the joint was lit, though I hadn't seen a match or lighter.

"That's surprising," Joe said. "Thought a refined gentleman like you would say to go soft. Queasy about the rough stuff."

"Not anymore," I said. "But not yet all the way to hard."

"Hang on to this," Joe said, handing me the lit joint. We were sitting near the open window. "But don't smoke it all. I'll finish it when I get back. He left the room. I heard him call to Nahmwan to unlock Gordon's door.

I didn't put the joint to my lips. It remained between my fingers until it went out.

IT COULDN'T HAVE been more than five minutes before Joe returned.

"Come with me," he said. "Our friend is happy to tell all." He looked at the dead joint in my hand and shook his head.

"Never as good when you have to relight it," he said.

GORDON SAT ON the edge of his bed, eyes wide open, his mouth an open oval. No words came forth. I stood in front of him and detected no sign of recognition.

I called his name and shook his shoulders, with no response.

"What did you do to him?" I asked Sleepy Joe.

"Gave him an idea of what it will be like if he doesn't tell us what we want to know. I think he will."

"Will he ever speak again?" I asked.

Gordon ended his silence with a gurgling sound that segued into a sentence.

"He made me hurt. And he didn't even touch me," Gordon said. "Hurt me here again," he added, pointing to his crotch.

I put a hand on Gordon's shoulder. I felt a slight movement.

"Gordon, he touched you. You just didn't see it coming. Joe's a master at this. It's a form of sleight-of-hand with more of a punch to it. Think of him as a magician. A magician who can make you laugh or make you hurt. Now get yourself together and talk so that the magic show doesn't resume."

Gordon sat there and stared at us without moving or speaking.

"Hurry up and start spilling your guts," Sleepy Joe said as he waggled his fingers in Gordon's direction. "Act Two coming up."

Gordon stood and threw up his arms in surrender.

"Wait a minute, I'm telling you everything I know. Just give me a chance."

"You've got ten-seconds," Sleepy Joe said.

JOE SUGGESTED WE head to the living room and sit at the big table, where we would be more comfortable. We were just out of Gordon's room when my phone rang. It was Oliver. I told him what he had missed.

"Quite impressed, mate," Oliver said. I'll be back soon. "Don't let up on Gordon. Keep our prisoner mixed up and worried."

"Like he's done to us," I said. "By the way, where are you?"

"At that delightful little establishment we passed on the way," he replied. "The one with the pretty lights. Care to join me? Sleepy Joe can watch our prisoner for a little while."

"No thanks," I said. "Hurry back soon as you finish with your pleasures."

After the phone went quiet, I realized he had referred to Gordon as our prisoner.

WE WERE SEATED at a square wooden table in the General's large dining room. Gordon sat at the head, and Joe and I were in the seats to his immediate left and right.

"You're right," he said, looking at me. "I never set foot in Henry's place after he was murdered. I heard about it from Charlie."

"How did Charlie find out?" I asked.

"He was Henry's lawyer," Gordon replied. "The cops may have called him to let him know his client was dead and to see if he could give them any leads on who might have wanted Henry dead."

"And of course, Charlie lied to the cops," I said.

Gordon cocked his head to one side as if he had never considered such a possibility.

"But Charlie is a lawyer," Gordon replied.

I heard Sleepy Joe laugh. "Well, that solves that," he said.

"Hold on," I cried out. "Let's not forget I'm a lawyer too."

"Do I ever give you the weed before you give me the money?" Sleepy Joe asked.

Our banter relaxed Gordon enough to start him talking.

"And it was Charlie who cooked up the story about coming upon Henry. I didn't think you'd believe it, so I made up my own story about knocking up that Chiquita."

"I told you not to talk like that in my presence," I said.

Sleepy Joe held up a finger. I shut up.

"Why would Charlie want you to tell such a lie to our good friend Glenn?" Joe asked Gordon.

Gordon grasped the edge of the table and leaned as far back in his chair as he could without tipping over.

"Because he figured that if Glenn knew the truth, he wouldn't agree to help me."

I wanted to do to Gordon what I did to that poor plumber, the difference being that Gordon deserved every blow. Instead, I yelled at him.

"You told me yesterday that Charlie believed your story about finding Henry's body all cut up. He sent you here because he thought whoever killed Henry wanted to get rid of a witness who could identify the killer."

"There's more to it," Gordon said.

"So now you're going to give us your latest version of the truth? More lies?" I asked.

Sleepy Joe held up two fingers this time.

"No, Glenn, Gordon is going to tell us the truth, as you Americans like to say, the whole truth and nothing but the truth. Aren't I right, mate?" he said, staring at Gordon with a grin that exposed his yellowing teeth.

"Of course," Gordon said, in a voice like a croaking frog.

"That's good," Joe said, "because otherwise I'll rip off your testicles and feed them to the General's koi. Probably wouldn't be missed," Joe added. "Watching you snivel, they're about as useless as a pair of balls on a brass monkey."

Gordon grabbed my arm.

"Glenn, this guy's crazy," he rasped.

"Exactly," I replied.

"The truth," Joe said in a soft voice, his grin reduced by half.

"I killed the Prune," Gordon said.

12

"YOU KILLED YOUR wife?" I screamed. "You committed a murder and expect me to help you hide from the law?"

"It was an accident," Gordon said. He slumped so far down in his chair I feared he would slide onto the floor.

"It was an accident," Gordon repeated. "It was nothing I would ever do or even think of doing. Charlie told me it was not a crime, at most negligence. He said that it might look bad if I ran, but it wasn't proof that I did anything illegal besides leave the scene, and that's not a felony unless they can prove I knew she was hurt. I was the only one who could say that, and Charlie told me not to say anything to anybody except lawyers like you and him."

The suppressed lawyer within me burrowed through the barriers my mind constructed years ago when I left the law. In the state of California, fleeing immediately after the commission of a crime can be introduced at trial as evidence of guilt. Doubtful a judge would give a jury that instruction if the crime itself consisted of leaving the scene. A sharp lawyer would argue that the jury would be misled into thinking that if the defendant ran away from the jurisdiction, that's the end of the case, that he must automatically be guilty. The jury would never be able to draw the distinction between flight from charges being mere evidence bearing on guilty conscience, and the actual crime of leaving the scene. None of this really mattered here, since Gordon fled America before any charges were lodged, and didn't flee immediately; he departed only after a lawyer's assurances that he probably had not committed a crime, or at least one that could be proven. We didn't even know if the body had been found.

In my day, the retainer would have been ten grand up front. When the client learned there were no charges or the only charge was a misdemeanor leaving the scene, with a fine and a stern warning, that client would think the money was well spent.

A check-in with Charlie was needed as soon as possible. No attempt at reaching him had been made since the train. That was not even twelve hours ago, though it seems like weeks.

"Now start again and tell us what really happened," Sleepy Joe said to Gordon as he produced yet another joint from between his fingers and set it on his lower lip while he reached across the table for a lighter.

"Tell me the truth and you get two tokes," he told Gordon. "Tell me a lie and I shove the burning joint up your nostrils." He inhaled a cloud of smoke.

Gordon sat up in his chair. His face was bright red, and looked like it might shoot off from his body like a Roman candle erupting from its holder.

"It was the night she found out about my loan scam," he said. "The night she threw me out.

"There was no arguing with her. I grabbed a bag with some clothes and a toothbrush and razor, and the keys to the Mercedes. That was the car I'd been using for five years. Problem was, it was bought with her money in her name. She told me to drop the keys on the floor and use my feet. Instead, I rushed out the door, jumped in the car, and started down the driveway.

"I didn't see her running out. It was dark, and the driveway lights were not on. Never saw her run in front of me. She came out of nowhere. But I'll never forget that sound. A thump followed by a scream. Flew right over and across the hood. Then a heap suddenly appeared off to the side of the car. I knew what it was."

Sleepy Joe blew out a long draft of smoke and stubbed out the joint.

"And you immediately called the police and told them there was an injured woman at your home, didn't you?"

Gordon stammered and mumbled something unintelligible before answering.

"I thought that if I did that, the cops would arrest me."

"That doesn't make any sense," I said. "It was clearly an accident. Forensics would prove that. The car was in the driveway, accident reconstruction would have shown you were pulling out when she ran in front of the car. They would have checked the position of the body, figured out where it came from. No one would have doubted it was an accident."

"Easy for you to say," Gordon replied. "You're a lawyer, just like Charlie, you know the laws and what to say and do. The rest of us don't.

"It would have taken the cops no time flat to learn about the loan. How would that look?"

"It would look like what it was," I said. "A wife finds out her husband is a deadbeat and a cheat, throws him out, they argue over whether he can take a car, she runs out in the dark, right in front of him while he's driving away, and he hits her by accident. Up to that point, you hadn't committed any crime. Certainly not an intentional, violent crime. The minute you drove off, you were potentially guilty of a felony hit and run, leaving the scene of an accident after a serious injury. If you were trying to avoid arrest, you went about it in the worst way possible. If you had Charlie make the report and you kept your mouth shut, it wouldn't have been too bad at all. I'm sure Charlie told you that, after the fact."

The redness drained from Gordon's face. He didn't look as worried or scared as he had up until this point.

"Glenn, you've been out of the criminal law game for a long time. Maybe you don't remember. It doesn't always work that way. The loan, and the Prune's discovery of it, made this more than an accident. They'd find out for sure I cheated on her all the time. Cops and DAs are going to be looking for some way to pin the rap on the bad-guy husband."

Before I could answer Gordon, Sleepy Joe chimed in.

"He's got a point, mate," Joe said, looking at me. "It's like a friggin' soap opera. Lowlife seduces and weds a rich widow, can't keep it in his pants, and is an embezzler to boot."

"It's not embezzlement," I said, cutting Joe off. "Embezzlement requires that the thief take legal possession and then feloniously steals it. In this case, it's actually grand larceny and forgery. Maybe identity theft as well, since he had to use the Prune's personal information without her consent." I had to let the others know who was in charge when we talk law.

Joe waved a hand as if to shoo me away.

"Thanks, Professor, and I think you've made Gordon's point. The long arm of the law might find some crime to pin on him and drag him off to prison," he said. "Looks like the only real crime he committed was leaving the scene without reporting, which is what Charlie told him. Maybe he thought Charlie was his lawyer and would handle the report, like you suggest. Not entirely unreasonable. Maybe a good defense. I get why you aren't buying that was the reason he ran, and it's something else that he's hiding from us."

How the hell does Sleepy Joe know all this US law? I thought.

"You have the makings of a good criminal lawyer," I said.

"But you really are a criminal lawyer," Joe said. "Why don't you resume questioning the witness?"

I looked down for my notes, and realized we weren't in court and I had no notes.

"Did you tell Charlie the whole truth?" I asked.

"Of course," Gordon replied. "How else could he help me?"

I wanted to ask Gordon why he didn't apply that same logic to me, Oliver, and Joe, but decided finding out what happened was more important.

"And what did he tell you?" I asked.

"Exactly what your hippie friend said. It was a total accident, probably her fault for running in front of a car in the dark. But I needed to make a report."

"Which you didn't do," I said.

"Not entirely true," Gordon replied. "I told Charlie. When he said I had to leave America, I figured he would take care of it for me. Like your friend said."

"You were wrong," I said. "It's always up to the driver to make the report. They're the ones with the actual knowledge of what happened."

Oliver walked into the room before I could ask Gordon if he had any contact with Charlie since he left his office.

"Mate, you wouldn't believe what I learned about that phone," he said to me.

"Not a phone as we know them," he continued. "Can only make or receive calls to or from very limited numbers. Like a closed-circuit phone system.

"And all of those numbers are North Korean," he said.

DARKNESS FELL UPON me for a moment, as if someone had crept from behind and thrown a blanket over me. For an instant, it felt as if the blanket was smothering me. Then the darkness lifted, and I was back in the room in the General's safe house in Chiang Mai, frightened of the figure from my past I thought I knew, but clearly did not.

"North Korea?" I shouted at Gordon. "What are you doing with a North Korean phone? And why did you bring it to me?"

"It gets worse," Oliver interjected. "My contacts in your FBI and CIA tell me the numbers are all North Korean intelligence agencies. We're dealing with spies. Maybe our friend Gordon is one of them." Oliver smiled in a way that showed his bright white teeth.

"You're a North Korean spy?" I asked, grabbing on to the back of a chair to keep myself from keeling over.

Gordon scanned the room, giving Joe, Oliver, and me quick glances.

"It's complicated," he said.

13

"THE PART ABOUT getting the loan by fraud is all true," Gordon began. "So is the part about me wanting to double my money with a cocaine deal."

"But there was no Antonio?" I asked.

"You busted me on that one," Gordon said. "I was trying to hide the truth, that everything was to be done through Henry. I would give him the money; he would both buy the coke and sell it for me. It was perfect for both of us. Henry said he could get the stuff at a great price, but the seller wanted cash on delivery, which I would have. No doubt Henry would make money off me on both ends, but as long as I doubled my money, I couldn't care less.

Sleepy Joe stood up and stretched, arching his back with hands at hips. He stood across the table from Gordon and placed those hands on the edge, leaning toward Gordon, who blinked his eyes in fear as Joe spoke.

"And now poor Henry's dead and headless, and we're here with a North Korean phone. And you didn't want us to know that Henry was the guy who got the coke. Connect the few missing dots, please."

Gordon looked at me. I thought I saw the tip of a tear in the corner of his eye.

"You won't let him hurt me again, will you, Glenn?"

"Depends on your answer," I said.

Gordon lowered his head, and his mouth settled into that hard-to-find place between a smile and a frown. It was a look I had seen on clients or witnesses caught in a lie and compelled to tell the truth.

"Henry was getting top-quality cocaine at really low rates from North Koreans. I wasn't supposed to know about this but I found out."

Oliver had been quiet, listening carefully to the rest of us. Now he spoke.

"Tell me exactly what you learned and how you learned it," he said to Glenn. "Don't even think of lying, withholding, or shading. If you do any of those, one thing is certain: You will die. Either by the North Koreans or by me."

Sleepy Joe rose from his chair again.

"Now, mates, there's no reason to be so rough with poor Gordon here. He was just about to tell us everything Oliver wants to know, right, Gordon?"

The room remained silent for a few seconds before we heard from Gordon.

"It was a one-in-a-million thing," he said. "Before applying for the loan, I stopped by to see Henry, just to be sure he really could handle that big a dope deal. Just talk with him, reassure myself one last time before forking over a quarter mil. Make sure he had it all lined up. Wouldn't give him the money otherwise. He convinced me he could, and agreed he wouldn't get the money until he showed me the coke. What I learned about his sources, that was unbelievable.

"After we talked business and smoked a joint, Henry told me he had a few calls to make, which I took as my sign to go. I headed toward the front door, and Henry went into the bedroom. As I was about to close the door behind me, I realized my phone was still on the table where we'd been hanging out. I walked back to pick it up. It was right next to Henry's iPhone."

Six eyes were glued to Henry's face, six ears fine-tuned to his every word.

"I guess Henry thought I was gone, because the bedroom door was half-open. He was talking kind of loud, and I could hear every word.

"And those words were?" Oliver asked. He spoke softer and slower than usual. I wasn't sure if he was trying to make Gordon trust or fear him. Maybe both.

"I'll never forget what I heard," Gordon replied. "No doubt I heard right.

"Henry asked whoever was on the other end of the line 'You are sure there will be no problem getting cash from California to Pyongyang?' Then later he said, 'Of course, I'll only use this phone with you. Think I want to get shot as a spy?' Then he laughed and hung up. Since his iPhone was on the table, it didn't take a genius to figure he was talking on a special phone. I scooted out the front door as soon as I heard him say goodbye."

"Based on that snippet of a conversation, you assumed he was working with North Korea?" Oliver asked.

"Yes," Gordon said. "Back home, you can't go two days without hearing something about North Korea. Everyone knows Pyongyang is their capital. And everyone knows they're up to their neck in smuggling and dealing drugs. I saw a special on Fox News."

"And the phone?" Oliver asked. "How did you get your hands on that?"

"Easy," Gordon said. "A few days later, after having time to think up a plan, I went over to see him, supposedly just to update him on the progress of the loan, assure him the money was coming."

"But really, you were there to find that special phone," Sleepy Joe said.

Gordon nodded.

"Why did you want it?" I asked.

"I knew it was worth a lot to our government," Gordon said. "Maybe wouldn't have to do any coke deal, never even keep the loan money, just sell the phone to the CIA. Must be worth millions."

"You're not as dumb as I thought," Joe said. "And a lot braver, too. So how did you do it?"

Gordon sat up straight and a smile worked its way across his tired face.

"I told Henry that I needed to use his bathroom. Upset stomach.

Probably something I ate off a food truck. The bathroom was in his bedroom."

"Good work!" Sleepy Joe called out. "You figured out that was where he kept it."

"Right," Gordon said. "I closed the bedroom door and locked it while I started rummaging around. If he tried to get in, I'd have a minute to open it, tell him I must have locked it by mistake and needed a minute to get off the throne. But he never tried to enter, couldn't possibly think I knew about his ties to North Koreans. Took me maybe two minutes, and there it was, buried amidst a pile of underwear in a drawer."

"Total amateur," Joe said, and Oliver agreed.

"Slipped it in my pocket, said goodbye, and that was the last time I saw Henry," Gordon said.

"So the deal never happened?" I asked.

Gordon shook his head.

"No," he said. "After I took the phone, there was no need to take that kind of risk. I knew that I could help myself much more with that phone than with the money. With something like that phone, I could make all my problems go away. Or Charlie could. Besides, Henry was killed before I could get my hands on the money."

"Has it dawned on you that taking the phone may have caused the Koreans to kill him?" Sleepy Joe asked. We all looked at Gordon.

"Of course," he said. "But he was a traitor. Working with the North Koreans, giving them dollars they needed to kill us. Maybe he got what he deserved."

"Let's just hope you don't," Joe said.

"What happened to the quarter million you were stealing from The Prune?" I asked.

Gordon let out a long sigh.

"Like I said before, she found out by sheer luck, when someone at the bank mentioned the loan. I had just taken the phone from Henry, and was planning to see Charlie the next day. He'd know what to do. He would figure out how to make us rich. I wouldn't need the Prune or her money. That was the night she threw me out." He paused, "The night I ran her over by accident. Ironic, isn't it? Got rid of me when I really didn't need her anymore. I drove the car in reverse back up the driveway, which was curved, and shielded from the street by trees and shrubs. Put it right back where it started out. I walked down a footpath hidden by the trees and made my way to the nearest bus stop. Caught the last one into the City. Paid cash for a room at a dive near the San Francisco bus terminal, and made my way to Charlie at first light."

"You mean you just left your wife lying there?" I screamed.

"Calm down, Glenn," Joe said. "No doubt she was already dead."

"She was," Gordon said. "Her head was off at a crazy angle, and there was blood coming from the back of her head. She wasn't breathing.

"Funny thing, there wasn't a mark on the car. Mercedes are built like tanks."

14

I KEPT GORDON talking. Giving him a break would allow him to think up more lies. We knew by then that Gordon was smarter and quicker than he appeared. He was up against the wrong three people: an experienced criminal lawyer, a man who earned his living getting information, and a former soldier who knew how to force the reticent to speak.

"You thought Charlie could help you, maybe make you rich?" I asked.

"Charlie is real smart, and he thinks in ways nobody else does. He's not one of these lawyers that gets too hung up on the law, you know."

"And what did he tell you?" Oliver asked. "Not the bullshit you've been feeding us. We want the real deal. Don't we, Joe?" Sleepy Joe grinned at Gordon, who kept talking.

"He told me that I was sitting on a fortune. He said that the phone was worth a fortune to US intelligence agencies, and those were the only people who would ever see it. I remember him saying that he might be greedy, but he was also patriotic.

"He did tell me that I probably wasn't going to be charged with any crimes, especially with the fraud victim dead. Besides, the government wouldn't care less about the fraud, or even a dead wife, if they could get their hands on a North Korean spy phone with all those contact numbers. The government could prove that North Korea was selling drugs in America."

"Why did he palm you off on me?" I asked.

"Charlie thought that sooner or later, the North Koreans would find me. Maybe they had surveillance on Henry, or they could monitor his phone calls, or maybe he had to give them the names and contact info of anyone he dealt with. He said that you and your friends here could protect me until he worked everything out and it was safe for me to return."

"And he let you take the phone with you?" I asked.

Gordon nodded his head.

"Charlie's real smart, like I said. He figured if he took the phone, the North Koreans could find it sooner or later, and there would be no reason for them to keep him alive. Or me. But as long as I had it, and he was the only one who knew where I was, he could probably talk them into letting him live. That's how Charlie thinks. Too bad he never thought they might be tracking me through the phone. But your friend here figured it out," he said, gesturing toward Oliver with his thumb.

"When did he expect you to tell us about the phone?" Oliver asked.

"He said to keep it secret as long as I could, but when it became necessary to tell you the whole truth, that's what I had to do. He said Glenn could always be trusted."

"In other words, he was hoping to put my life at risk without letting me know there was money involved?" I asked.

The look on Gordon's face told me that was not how he saw it.

"No, Glenn, that's not what was going on. Charlie didn't want any communication of any sort between us about North Korea until it was necessary. For everyone's safety. And he told me that when this is all over, you and your friends were going to get money."

"I think this son of a bitch is finally telling the truth," Joe said. "Now all we have to do is figure out how to make that money."

"But first, time for a smoke," he said. Next thing I knew, he was passing a lit joint to Gordon, who had it between his lips in less than a second.

15

IF THE THOUGHT of being pursued by a cocaine cartel sent shivers up my spine, the realization that North Koreans were after Gordon turned me into an icicle. North Korea as the enemy meant that whoever they sent would be trained, skilled, and backed with the resources of a government. Not just any government, but a nuclear power run by a murderer. I passed on the joint when Sleepy Joe tried to hand it to me.

"What do we do now?" I asked Oliver. "You're the guy who knows it all."

"Thanks for the compliment," Oliver said. "But my experience with North Koreans is somewhat limited."

"I'm waiting for my contacts in the American and Australian intelligence services to get back to me with a bit more information about who exactly might be on Gordon's tail and where they might show up," he added. Gordon looked none too happy upon hearing with such authority that the North Koreans were seeking him. Like the rest of us, he must have wondered when and where they might swoop down upon him.

"Right now, our number one goal is protecting ourselves," Sleepy Joe said. "If we do it right, we will come out of this alive. And with some money, if that phone is worth what Charlie thinks."

"It is," Oliver said. "That's why we're the only ones who touch it right now."

I told the others to wait a minute while I made a call in my room.

Oliver and Joe nodded, aware of who I was calling.

THE GENERAL LISTENED to my account and did not say a word until I was done.

"I'll have a few of my best men guard the house," he said. "Secure your friend, and the rest of you get out right away. My driver will bring you to a safe place. You can eat and relax until it's time to return to Bangkok. Take the girl with you."

"And be really careful," he added before ending the call. "I know you're smart, you proved that with the Russian. But, Glenn, even the Russians are scared of North Koreans."

SLEEPY JOE TIED Gordon to a chair and wrapped a gag around his mouth. Gordon's prior experiences with Joe must have impressed him, as while his face showed his displeasure, he offered no resistance. One of the guards we passed on our way up the stairs stood over Gordon, rifle slung over the shoulder, pistol holstered on his belt.

"I'd like to keep you alive long enough for you to collect your share," Joe told Gordon. "After that, we'll see," he added. He waved goodbye.

Nahmwan called us to the front door. She wore old jeans and a T-shirt, her hair still tied in a bun. She looked like a maid. Probably the idea, I thought. She led us into the same *songthaew* that brought us to the house. We climbed into the bed. I sat next to Oliver.

Oliver let out a loud laugh as we rode down the hill.

"What could possibly be funny right now?" I asked.

"Just think of it," he said, shaking his big, shaved head. "Every major intelligence agency in the world has been trying for years to prove North Korean drug dealing in the US and Europe. Some smoke, but no fire. Now this amateur, this nitwit, this grifter, pulls off one of the intelligence coups of the millennium. A direct link of Pyongyang to American drug dealing. The phone's got all the calls to North Korean intelligence agents. From all we can determine, it's been handled only by Gordon and me since it was taken from Henry. Henry's DNA should still be on it. Its provenance will be established."

"Wouldn't there be all sorts of contamination issues?" I asked. "It's not like we handled the phone according to proper procedure."

"Maybe in a court of law, a smart defense lawyer like you could raise reasonable doubt, just like Johnny Cochrane and Barry Scheck did for O.J.," Oliver said. "But in the real world, if Henry's DNA is on that phone, every government in the world is going to accept Gordon as credible on this one. The chain is established. How the hell do the prints of an American drug dealer wind up on a phone linked to North Korean intelligence? If you think North Korea sets off alarms in your country now, wait until this story breaks."

I WAS AMAZED at how the driver maneuvered between endless small motorcycles, autos, and trucks that crowded every street. The *songthaew* made several right turns, then a few lefts, and a U-turn. A few blocks later, it pulled into an alley and stopped in front of a corrugated steel door which immediately slid open. A man's voice called out in Thai, and Oliver and Nahmwan replied. It was one of those times I wished I had studied the language a little better. Over eight years in this country and I still couldn't understand most of the population. Yet somehow, I felt I belonged here. Life is odd.

Nahmwan explained that we would have a meal of fine Northern cuisine while the General and his people arranged for safe passage to a very private airport, and then on to Bangkok.

We were soon inside a small but well-appointed restaurant. Several tables were covered with fine linen, and gleaming silver utensils peered out from the top of white napkins. A young Thai man wearing a dark suit and tie approached us when we were all inside. I heard the door shut with a metallic ringing sound.

"Sit where you like," the man said. "Friends of the General are always welcome here."

"And you as well, Miss Nahmwan," he added. I saw her smile at him. *Wonder if they've got something going*, I thought. Then I wondered why I cared.

THE RESTAURANT PREPARED whatever we wanted. Oliver's steak was top-flight Australian beef, and my fish was fresh enough to have been swimming in the ocean not long before. Sleepy Joe and Nahmwan were enjoying Thai dishes I did not recognize.

"Would you like to try some of my *khao soi*?" Nahmwan asked, and I looked at the noodles swimming in green broth in her bowl. "Special egg noodles. Chiang Mai is famous for it," she said. "Never as good anywhere else."

I nodded, and she set a small mound of noodles on my plate, spooning the green broth over it.

"This is green curry *khao soi*," she explained. "Maybe spicy for a *farang*. You can add some of these if you like," she said, pointing to a collection of silver bowls filled with sliced shallots, pickled mustard greens, lime wedges, and chili oil, all familiar to me. I told her I would first try it unadorned.

I picked the noodles up with my fork and let them sit in my mouth for a few seconds. Then the burning began, and didn't subside until after I had downed my glass of water and Oliver's as well. He didn't mind, as he was nursing a pint of Singha.

Everyone laughed as I struggled to regain my composure.

"*Arroi maak*," I managed to say, one of my stock Thai phrases, meaning very delicious. It probably was, once you adjusted to fire-eating.

"Not even one of our more spicy dishes," Nahmwan said as the young Thai fellow refilled my water glass.

"Maybe next time, we'll have you try *khao soi gai*," he said. "Made with chicken and coconut cream. Like your friend is enjoying." He looked at Sleepy Joe, who was wolfing down the last remnants of his dish.

"I like spicy food," I said, feeling the need to rehabilitate myself. A foreigner living many years in Thailand is expected to be capable of handling spicy food.

"I think you also like sweet," he said. "I see you looking at Nahm-wan."

Nahmwan tapped me on the arm.

"Don't mind my brother," she said. "Ever since our sister got involved with your friend the General, he's been pushing me to find a *farang*." She was looking right at me.

"Would I be right if I said the General owns this place?" I asked, turning from her gaze.

"You are right," she said. "Only for him and his guests."

"Well guarded," she added.

I tried to make small talk with Nahmwan, but that was not my strong suit. Nahmwan sensed my awkwardness at this basic social skill and took charge.

"For a lawyer, you don't ask good questions," she said. I caught a slight smile, which made me feel better.

"That's because we're not in court," I said.

"Can't you make believe we are?" she asked.

I sat still for a moment, picturing my days standing before podiums in courtrooms, questioning witnesses out to bury my client.

"Okay, Madam Witness. Don't you find it at all concerning that your entire family depends on the General?"

"Not at all," she replied. The General is a powerful man. Also very generous. We live well and are safe from any possible harm."

"But what happens if the General gets tired of your sister? Surely you don't think a *mia noi* is forever." As soon as the words left my mouth, I realized how offensive and embarrassing they might be to Nahmwan. That's never a good thing for a *farang* to do to a Thai.

"The General is a man of honor," she said. "No doubt, when he and my sister are no longer involved, he will treat us well. He paid for me to go to college and study English with a private tutor. And my brother has a small ownership in this place. We have no complaints."

Her words made me feel a bit better about my friend. His treatment of women clashed with my values. Seemed like there was more to him than met the eye, at least more than met my eye.

"I'm glad to hear that. I too know him to be a man of honor." That wasn't a hundred percent true. Not that it could ever be one hundred percent true about any human being.

"What is the General like when he is down in Bangkok?" Nahmwan asked. "I only see him here in Chiang Mai. He's always very relaxed and carefree up here. Just meets with his friends, drinks, stays at the house with my sister."

"He's not all that different in Bangkok, except not quite so carefree and relaxed. He has a lot of businesses, and interests in all kinds of things."

"Like making sure your friend Joe gets his monthly supply of *ganga* to sell?"

I sat frozen in place for several seconds. It seemed so out of character for the General to tell this to anyone. Who knew what else he might have told her, especially about me?

"Don't be surprised at the things I know," Nahmwan said before I could speak. "If the General cannot trust me with such small matters, I have no business keeping his safe house."

"Distributing weed is a small matter?"

Nahmwan threw back her head slightly and laughed.

"Oh, you *farangs* are all the same. You think everything about you is so important. *Ganga* is for *farangs*. Hardly any Thais like it. It helps make a lot of cops rich, and happy police are good for the General. But really, the rest of us Thais couldn't care less about *farangs* and their habits. If you don't bother us, we don't care what you do."

"Does that include me?" I asked. Nahmwan studied my face for a moment.

"I haven't figured that out yet."

She's a better lawyer than me, I thought. She got out everything she wanted to know, and I was still in the dark about her.

"TIME TO LEAVE," Oliver announced. We headed out the door to our *songthaew*. Nahmwan sat next to me, and a few times as we bumped along the streets, her leg pressed against mine. I tried to ignore it. Oliver explained that we were heading to a small military airport outside the city. The General had arranged for us to be flown to Bangkok, where his security people would meet us and bring us to my condo, with around-the-clock guards, until this was settled. If we were going to be found, and maybe have to fight, it would be more convenient to be at home with my music, my coffee, and my weed.

"Does it look like the North Koreans have found out about us?" I asked.

Oliver spoke loud enough for Joe and Nahmwan to hear.

"We know that they were able to track Gordon right up to the Club. That means they know he was with Glenn in his building. If they are as good as I think they are, it wouldn't take them long to speak to some people, maybe bribe or hack their way into some data, and figure out who is missing and where they might have gone. If they pick Chiang Mai, we could have some problems."

"Do they have any help in Bangkok?"

Sleepy Joe answered.

"There are two North Korean restaurants in town. One is pretty fancy, with music and dancing. They say it's to raise hard currency, but here's one old Special Forces guy saying they also use it for spying and making trouble."

"Amen," Oliver said.

"So once they knew Gordon was in Bangkok, they could have sent one of their people on him as a tail, and followed us to the train?" I asked.

"Now you're putting on your criminal lawyer cap," Oliver said. "That's good, because we may well need it."

"Can my legal skills stop bullets?"

Sleepy Joe reached across the bed of the truck and tapped my arm.

"Mate, intelligence and spying are all about the brain. When guns get used, it means the spymasters failed. Even the North Koreans would prefer to avoid messy violence.

"But I must say they are more willing to use it than just about anyone else."

I heard another "Amen" from Oliver. It was not a joyous "Amen" like I used to hear at services, back when I attended.

"WE HAVE TO assume that the North Koreans know that Gordon is in Thailand, and they have a pretty good idea of who he's with," I said to Oliver and Joe as our *songthaew* bumped its way along a dusty dirt road to the airport, the kind of road used by farmers and drug smugglers.

"If it were me," Oliver replied," I'd chat up everyone I could at the Club. Don't look too nosy, just the kind of small talk that comes from alcohol in bars."

"Wouldn't take a sharp fellow too long to figure out which regulars are missing," Sleepy Joe added.

"Don't you think the General and his men would take notice of a few North Koreans walking into the place?" I asked.

Oliver and Sleepy Joe first looked at each other and then at me. Oliver spoke.

"Mate, has it ever dawned on you that they wouldn't have to? As if they can't find Thais, or even *farangs* like us, to do this for them."

I felt I had to defend myself against the unspoken allegations of stupidity.

"Wouldn't they be afraid that the North Koreans might decide to get rid of them when they were done?"

Oliver shook his head.

"Sometimes you can be so smart, and other times so damn thick," he said. "I'm quite certain our friends from the North would claim to be from some South Korean corporation and were investigating some foreigners in Bangkok for whatever reason they come up with."

"They pay in dollars, you know," Sleepy Joe added.

I felt the heat in my face, and it must have been red, because Nahmwan briefly lay her hand across my arm.

"Don't feel bad," she said. "These two have experiences you don't. But you're smarter and quicker than them in many other ways. Important ways."

"How would you know?"

She touched my arm again.

"The General tells me everything," she said.

I WAS THINKING about the two arm-touches, and debating whether to communicate with Nahmwan in a reciprocal manner. My pre-erotic thoughts were interrupted by the sound of our tires crunching on the cracked dirt road as we slowed to a stop.

Oliver slid open the window between the bed and the cab and spoke to the driver in Thai.

"Police roadblock," Oliver said. "Looking for drugs. Pretty much all drugs come through here on their way to Bangkok and the islands."

Sleepy Joe walked to the gate of the truck and peered out.

"Dressed all in black, topped with berets," he reported.

"What does that mean?" I asked.

"Means they can't be bribed," Joe said.

The driver shouted something through the window.

"What did he say?" I asked Oliver.

"Don't know," he said. "Speaking Lanna." Lanna is the language of the Chiang Mai region. "Too different for me to really understand."

"Because he doesn't want that fellow behind us to understand," Joe said.

I turned to the rear and saw a man in black pointing an assault rifle at us, while motioning with his head for us to get out. He looked like a soldier. Nahmwan pulled next to me, her body pressed against mine.

"The driver said this man's not Thai, and he's right," she whispered.

Joe, moving in a crouch, passed me and sprung like a frog over the gate of the truck. As he flew through the air, he extended his left arm, his right pressed against his chest. His left hand grabbed the soldier's rifle in the middle of its barrel. It dropped to the ground as the soldier fell backward, Joe on top of him. Nahmwan leaped from the truck and grabbed the rifle. She raised it to her shoulder and started firing. I heard a cry from the front of the truck. I saw the driver firing a pistol through his side window, while shots ran from somewhere in front of the truck.

Oliver had pulled himself up to the gate and grabbed a pistol from his rear waistband. He twisted his large frame around the corner of the bed and fired several times. The attackers were firing at us, but less and less as each second passed.

The firing stopped. Sleepy Joe rose from the ground, the soldier in black lying at his feet, head off at an impossible angle, like Gordon had described the dead Prune.

Everyone immediately got back into the truck. We suffered no casualties. As we drove off, I saw four bodies lying along the road.

"Sleepy Joe, I know," I mumbled. "But, Nahmwan, you jumped right in and knew how to use that rifle. I would never have guessed." She draped an arm around my shoulder.

"Why do you think the General insisted you bring me with you?"

"He trained me well," she added. The arm remained across my shoulder for the five minutes it took to reach the airport.

16

"I THOUGHT YOU didn't do violence," I said to Oliver as we boarded a small green army propjet.

"I arm myself whenever I'm up against North Koreans," he said.

"Which is, of course, never?" I asked.

"Wouldn't say that, but never before in a shootout."

I sat next to Nahmwan during the flight to Bangkok.

"How could you be so sure the driver was right about that guy not being Thai?" I asked her just before we took off.

"Don't you think we know our own people?" she asked. "And he's not a driver."

"Then who is he?"

"He's Thai, but he worked for you. I mean, your country."

Nahmwan was not the person I thought. I confused her orders to protect me with her personal feelings. Maybe she liked me, but not in that way. All too often, that's how it turns out for me.

Oliver was more familiar with armed conflict than I ever suspected. Gordon was running rings around me, tossing out one lie after another, and me falling for them. Sleepy Joe no longer surprised me. Something inside me cried out that I was out of my league.

"I don't suppose I'm much use in those situations," I said to Nahmwan.

"Glenn, that's not what anyone expects from you. Your talents are different."

"What are those talents?" I asked. "They're not so obvious to me."

"You are very smart, and when you focus on something and really concentrate, you can solve any problem. That's why you were such a great lawyer in America. The General told me all about you." It was tempting to draw conclusions from the tone of her voice, but I've been wrong too many times to rely on my own observations. No reason to believe this was any different.

"We're counting on you to figure out a way to end this problem," Nahmwan said.

"Soon as I come up with one, I'll let you know," I replied. I recognized the driver of the SUV that picked us up at the small airport just outside Bangkok. He worked for the General's security company. Nahmwan sat up front with him, and the two chatted away in rapid-fire Thai. The rest of us were squeezed into the back seat.

It was good to be back in Bangkok, especially without Gordon. It was a little past ten at night, and when we turned the corner onto Sukhumvit Boulevard, we were greeted with the usual nocturnal activities: vendors clogging the sidewalks, their stalls filled with fake Rolexes, counterfeit Viagra, pirated CDs and DVDs, clothing hanging on racks, food grilling; hookers calling for customers on the sidewalks or from small, dark bars; overweight, aging *farangs* shamelessly parading women a third their age and a quarter their bulk; motorcycle taxi drivers weaving between buses and trucks belching black smoke; *farang* tourists in large numbers waiting to be overcharged by sidewalk vendors before they folded their tables and went home.

The traffic jam lessened after we made it through the Asoke intersection. Asoke was formed by the confluence of both the BTS Skytrain and MRT subway stops, the upscale Terminal 21 Mall, and Soi Cowboy, a side *soi* dedicated to the proposition that there's a hooker for every *farang*, or at least for those willing to pay more than at Nana Plaza, a few blocks down on the other side of Sukhumvit. Include me out, as the legendary Hollywood producer Sam Goldwyn said.

The van stopped in front of my condo. The side door slid open, and Lek's policeman cousin motioned us to follow him. Inside the lobby, Lek gave me a *wai*. I told him to stop that years ago, even though my being older justified his actions. Who likes to be reminded they are old?

I was about to remind Lek that the *wai* was ordered dropped years ago when the elevator arrived. Oliver, Joe, and Nahmwan followed me in. Half a minute later, we were at my front door. Before I could reach into my pocket for the key, the door opened. The General beckoned me in.

"Make yourself at home," he said.

Wang and one of the General's bodyguards stood by the sliding glass door leading to the balcony. They were armed with assault rifles. Wang pointed a finger at Sleepy Joe, then Oliver, and then me. We followed him into the kitchen.

The General was not dressed in his usual finely tailored suits or designer casual clothes. He wore an olive green, lightweight tropical uniform. Several stars were sewn on the epaulets of the short-sleeved shirt.

"If we're ever at war, you'll be dressed for the part," I said.

"Glenn, we are at war," he replied. My eye caught the forty-five in his holster. I had seen enough guns in fifteen years as a defense lawyer to recognize that caliber.

"You're not a soldier anymore," I said. "You retired years ago."

"Good thing for you I really haven't," he said. "Glenn, there are some professions from which one never retires. General is one. Lawyer is another."

"We're going to get through this because neither of us has lost our skills," he added.

I looked at Wang and the security guard, their eyes periodically scanning the street and the buildings facing us, their fingers resting on the triggers of their assault rifles.

"Is this really a situation where a criminal defense lawyer is needed?"

"It's your brains we need," he said. "Hard as it may be to believe."

The General had set up the French siphon I used to brew Black Ivory Coffee, the world's best and most expensive bean.

"Figured you'd want to celebrate still being alive," he said.

My French siphon looked like the scales of the Libra zodiac sign, one side holding an opaque vessel, the other a clear one, joined by narrow piping. The clear one is for ground coffee. The opaque vessel sits atop a tiny tank for methyl alcohol. No doubt the General ground the beans by hand in my small wooden grinder, and carefully measured the powder into the clear vessel. When the water boiled, the heat caused it to be siphoned over to the ground coffee in the clear vessel. Once the brew had cooled ever so slightly, it was magically siphoned back into the opaque vessel. The General set four small cups before us and poured coffee into them. We drank it black, always the case with great coffee. I savored my first sip, full-bodied without any bitterness.

"Tell me everything that happened since we left the Club," I said after the coffee had snaked its way down my throat.

"Okay if I light up a joint?" Sleepy Joe asked. The General said nothing, and Joe lit up. I passed.

"Not too long after you left, three *farangs* showed up. No one knew them. Claimed to be British, but who knows, could have been Russians. They seemed to have some training, but not enough. We spotted them right away."

"What tipped you off?" I asked.

"One of them sat down at Edward's table. That told me they could at least figure out the weakest link right away. I heard the whole conversation. Spending all those years fighting the Reds in the forests, one develops sharp hearing. Or else one dies.

"Guy said he heard about the Club from some American at the gym. Couldn't recall the man's name, but remembered the fellow mentioning a friend from the US Said the American told him to stop by for some good company and drinks, not to mention Wang's cooking. Asked Edward if he knew either of these Americans." The General lifted his cup and took a small sip of Black Ivory Coffee.

Sleepy Joe exhaled a cloud of smoke, and then coughed. His eyes were red.

"No doubt your men invited these customers into the back alley for a chat and learned they were sent by the North Koreans."

"Quite right," the General said. "The Koreans were able to track Gordon to the Club, but when Oliver figured out the GPS tracker, they lost the trail afterward. They still had enough time to round up three agents, if we can call them that, and send them to the Club to snoop around. Not really bad, when we consider that they had to find *farangs* with some basic skills. Not every one of you is a Sleepy Joe or an Oliver."

"Most likely they were down on their luck, and probably didn't even know they were working for North Korea," Oliver chimed in. "They're famous for sucking in the totally unaware. Avoids other intelligence agencies walking back the cat to Pyongyang."

Sleepy Joe stood, helped himself to the last small cup of coffee, and returned to his seat. After stirring in sugar—barbaric by my Black Ivory standards—he looked at Oliver and then the General.

"You can tell the difference between their guys and the hired help. That guy I killed by the truck, he was North Korean. Were I a millisecond late on my delivery, it would have been me left dead on the road. The other guys, the Thais, our pretty lady killed," Joe said, glancing at me. "Really didn't have to shoot all of the Thais," he said. "We could have gotten away after we shot the first one. He smiled at Nahmwan.

"Yes, she did have to shoot them," the General interjected. "Have to send a message. Anyone working for communists on our soil gets killed. Thais included."

"The General does not like communists," Nahmwan said.

"So I've noticed," I replied.

The General eyed his empty cup and then at the empty siphon pot.

"I didn't spend all those years fighting Reds up North just so that these North Korean commie bastards could run around my country like they own the place," he said.

It was now clear why the General was risking his own life. It wasn't to save Gordon Planter, maybe not even to save me, though I wanted to believe that was at least one of his motives. The General was still fighting his war against the communists. It looked like he was helping

Gordon and his own NJA friends, but in truth, he conscripted us into his army.

"Did Edward tell them what they needed to know to find us up in Chiang Mai?" I asked.

"We'll never know for sure," the General said, as Oliver nodded in agreement. The fluorescent light from the fixture above us bounced off his shaved head. That told me those three men were dead. Like Nahmwan said, the General doesn't like communists. Or their flunkies.

And the General didn't believe them or Edward. Edward was not devious, just weak. He knew how to launder money, so the General tolerated him.

The General's tolerance would not likely extend to the three North Korean agents, dupes or not. Three *farangs* trying to work the NJA Club to help kill its most loyal members were a problem. I would never ask the General how he solved it. Criminal lawyers rarely wanted to know if their clients were actually guilty. Maybe the General and his men gave the three a good scare and told them to advise their bosses to leave Thailand. Maybe they beat them up and warned them not to come around asking too many questions. Asking too many questions about expats was often considered over the line, since no many of us don't want to talk about the past and many want to create some mystery about themselves, often because the truth just isn't something they want to live with. Then again, if the poor fools were killed before they could pass on what they learned, then why were there North Koreans around my condo building? It's possible they texted their info before meeting an untimely end, or maybe the General decided it was a better strategy to allow them to live and talk. Doubtful he would ever say, which was fine by me.

If those North Korean agents asked Edward about American Club regulars, he surely gave them my name. Dumb as they might be, they couldn't miss the fact that I was not present. Once they had my name, the North Koreans would find me. They could glean a hoist of information just by knowing who I am. My cell phone, for starters.

Unlike my main bank accounts, my cell phone account was in my real name, Glenn Murray Cohen. If they could get the number, they could find me. Getting such information is not hard if you are Oliver, and no doubt the North Koreans had their own Oliver. I shared these thoughts with the others.

"Now you're acting like the brilliant lawyer we know you to be," Oliver said. "Keep thinking and you'll figure out their next move."

Sleepy Joe pushed a lock of hair from his face.

"You're starting to think like them, which is the key," he said.

"You're quite right," the General interjected. "If you want to catch a snake, you have to think like a snake. Learned that from fighting the Reds forty years ago. I'm just as ready to kill them now as back then."

"They couldn't find your house up in Chiang Mai, but on the road, they could follow us," I explained.

"No doubt," said Oliver.

I wasn't done.

"Which means they know where I live and they know we are here right now. They could attack any time."

The General stood and held his rifle over his head.

"Except they know I'm here, along with Wang and my guards. And they probably know Sleepy Joe is here with us. Not to mention Nahmwan."

"Did you see her take out those commies?" Sleepy Joe asked. "She's tougher than me and Wang put together."

"Toughness saved you so far, but from now on, it's brains that will rule," the General said. "The commies know they can't expect to survive a fight with us, not here in my city. They will want to get out without losing everything. From here on, it's Glenn's brains that will get us out of this and let those Reds know they can never again do this in my country. He's our lawyer. He will figure out some way to end this without anyone else being killed. Not even Gordon, though he surely deserves it."

"Works for me," Sleepy Joe said. "And who else gets to smoke *ganga* with their lawyer?"

I was starting to feel so good about myself that I didn't notice Nah-mwan move over and sit next to Joe.

"We'll make sure nothing happens to our friend, won't we, Joe?" she asked, leaning against his shoulder. If that was supposed to make me feel better, it didn't."

It was decided to shut me up in the second bedroom I called an office, though there was never any office work to be done. It was really a combination storage and guest room, though I never had any guests. There was a small desk stuck in a corner, and when I needed to focus on something, I sat there. I had started focusing on Chiang Mai, and Nahmwan thoughtfully brought the notes I'd made. She would have made a great legal assistant, not to mention other relationships, but it was clear her interest in me was assignment-related only. I grabbed a yellow legal pad and a pen from one of the drawers and started writing. This practice began with my first legal case: write down everything known about the case—people, places, actions, things—and then tie them together, as I tried to solve a mystery. Usually, the mystery was how to come up with a viable defense. The system must have had some merit, because I always came up with one, and it worked more often than not.

My eyes scanned the lists I had prepared only a day before, though seemed longer. I added Nahmwan, our drivers and guards in Chiang Mai, the restaurant owner and staff, and the crew of the plane. That was everyone we had been in contact with. If anyone were with the North Koreans, it would almost surely be one of them. Then I remembered to add the North Koreans and Thais who had ambushed us. They had to come from somewhere. I needed a straight line from some unknown party to them. The best I could come up with was that, somehow, the North Korean agents who visited the NJA club managed to get their information to their handlers, and the North Koreans tied me to the General, and somehow know that he had his tentacles in Chiang Mai. I went over the list of events I had prepared in Chiang Mai and added nearly being killed on the road up North, the meal, the flight, and arrival at my place. There were still missing links. Maybe they'd always be missing.

Of course, Gordon was the thread that tied the loose ends together. There would have been no need to flee, no shootout in Chiang Mai, no need to have armed men standing guard at my window.

I drew circles and wrote names inside them. I drew concentric circles, linking the actors in every configuration possible. I rearranged the sequence of events in my head. I tried to think of any possible connection between every name written down. When done, all I knew was that the North Koreans wanted Gordon because he had taken one of the phones they used to control their drug dealers, and they wanted it bad enough to risk a serious rupture of diplomatic relations with Thailand.

That was where the secret was hidden. What was so special about this phone? What was so special about Henry Blatt, a sleazy and inept drug dealer, who in the end was so unimportant to the North Koreans that they sliced him too thin to fry and left the pieces for the police?

American law enforcement knew all there was to be known, aside from the North Korean involvement.

Now, there was solid proof of the North Korean network of drug dealers in America, directed by Pyongyang. The stolen phone would establish this beyond all doubt and provide the US government with information to root out and prosecute the drug ring. While America was unlikely to apprehend the masterminds, who were surely safe in the Hermit Kingdom, North Korea would suffer a humiliating intelligence failure, not to mention the loss of a key source of hard currency.

Even a jackass like Gordon would realize the value of what he had, and that sooner or later he would be able to sell it to one of the world's intelligence agencies, probably America's. His days of money worries would end for good and any legal problems would disappear. He might even inherit everything from the Prune, with a good lawyer like Charlie. Gordon, however, was greedy and planned to keep every penny paid for the phone for himself. That's why he didn't tell us about the phone until it was forced out of him. He wanted us to protect him while he had the phone, and nothing more. Gordon was still the same: using other people, while giving them nothing but trouble. If any of us were killed along the way, that would not be his problem. He planned to stiff Charlie as well. But Gordon was not nearly as clever as he thought, and now we were on the run from North Korean assassins.

Perilous as our situation was, at least we knew Gordon's real intentions. We knew what the North Koreans wanted. We did have the phone, the trump card, though Gordon came along with it. We would decide if he came out of this with anything more than his life, and at that point, I wasn't even inclined to assure him that much.

The riddle was solved. It was clear why we were in such danger.

What was missing was a way out.

I had an idea that just might work. All it needed was some help from the General.

17

THE GENERAL SAT on my couch, watching automobile racing on television. In Thailand, there is a channel that broadcasts these races twenty-four hours a day, seven days a week. I never understood the attraction, but the General was clearly absorbed in the spectacle of a dozen speeding race cars zooming around in a huge circle. A pot of coffee sat on a tray on the table before him, a steaming mug in his hand. He called out something in Thai, and before I could seat myself next to him, Nahmwan appeared with a cup for me and filled it.

"Sumatran," I said after a quick sniff.

"You have quite a nose," the General said.

"I've been told that's what my people are known for."

The General put down his cup and face me.

"So, *Khun* Lawyer, what have you decided?"

I LAID IT all out to the General, everything I had determined from the evidence. How Gordon was working a drug deal with Henry, but when he learned about the phone, he figured it was worth far more than any drug deal. Charlie sent him to Bangkok to protect the valuable phone, and he wasn't too concerned about the loan scam or the Prune's death. The worst Gordon was looking at was a misdemeanor for leaving the scene of the accident, a no-jail misdemeanor for a first-time offender, and even that was assuming that the prosecution could even prove he had any connection to the death. With the Prune dead, there would be no case for the mortgage fraud, or any way of proving that Gordon knew she was seriously injured when he left, making felony prosecution impossible. Gordon would have a story, and with no one alive to refute him, he'd walk. The DA would know that, so there would be no charges. But of course, with the phone, Gordon would have none of those worries, because the US government would want that phone and wouldn't care less about the Prune being dead or the victim of a mortgage scam. Charlie knew all of this.

So why did Charlie tell Gordon to run away, and why to me?

The one piece of the puzzle that was missing was the one needed most.

Isn't it always like that?

THE GENERAL RAN his fingers up and down the barrel of his rifle.

"Did Gordon expect that we would protect him until he could sell the phone?" he asked.

"I don't think he was expecting violence," I said. "Most likely Charlie sent him to Bangkok, where anything can be bought and sold, and where he knew we could protect him. Or thought we could."

The General looked down at the floor and shook his head.

"I don't like this, Glenn. Something is not right. That old soldier's instinct. Three years fighting Reds up North. Training with Green Berets in your country. There's more to this."

My trial lawyer's sixth sense told me the same. Something was not right. No matter how the story changed, no matter how much we figured out, there was always something not right, something that we knew couldn't be fixed.

"We still don't have the full truth," I said.

The General set his rifle across his lap, holding it at the stock.

"Have you asked Charlie about this phone?" he asked. "Do we have any proof he really knows about it? Until we know, we can't be sure why he sent Gordon here."

I explained that I had tried to call Charlie several times without success.

"Have you asked Oliver to find him?" the General asked when I explained.

"Oliver finds information, not missing people," I replied. It was a poor answer, caused by my embarrassment at missing this obvious solution.

"Interesting how you say *missing*. But isn't a person's whereabouts information?" the General replied. "Get the big man on this," he said, issuing me an order as my commanding officer. He gestured toward the kitchen, where Oliver sat reading an Australian newspaper.

"Should be able to get something quickly," Oliver assured me when I told him we needed to find Charlie. "Can find out if he's been using his phone, or his credit cards. If need be, someone can go looking for him. On your tab, of course."

I JOINED SLEEPY Joe out on my terrace. It was growing dark.

"Bangkok is always prettier when the light is softer," he said.

"I didn't know you had a romantic streak, Joe."

"I don't, but I think Bangkok is prettier in soft light."

Joe laughed when I told him about my analysis and the General's decision to find Charlie.

"I was wondering when you guys would figure that out," he said. "Seemed obvious to me right away that we still didn't have the truth about why Charlie sent Gordon to you. Your idea that he sent him here for protection and to market the phone has some merit, but also a lot of holes. I'd say it's still only a hunch. Maybe even an educated guess."

"We should know soon," I said. "Oliver has a lot of contacts in the San Francisco Bay Area."

What exactly do you want to know?" Joe asked.

I thought for a moment. There were a lot of things I wanted to know, but there was only time for the top two.

"Why Charlie sent him here, and whether he really knows about the phone."

Joe lit a joint and passed it to me as soon as the tip was burning.

"And what do you plan to do, assuming you find out?"

"I can't think of any reason why Charlie would send Gordon here, except for something connected to the phone. Charlie wouldn't send him away on only a moment's notice if there were nothing to worry about, and if he thought Gordon had committed crimes, would never tell him to run away. Even Charlie wouldn't do that. Just like he'd never send Gordon over here if he thought it might cause me harm."

Joe blew a cloud of smoke above him just as the last light of the sun disappeared below the horizon. The smoke faded into the darkness. Oliver opened the sliding door and joined us on the terrace.

"Well, mate, we're about to find out, aren't we?"

Oliver sat in a chair pressed against the wall looking out over the balcony. I didn't notice him come out to join us.

"Charlie is going to call you in a minute. You can take the call in your office."

"How did you find him?" I asked.

"Easy, he answered his phone. He's been out of sight for a few days. He'll tell you."

THE MOMENT THE phone rang, I accepted the call and spoke.

"Don't say a word except to answer my questions. The first is: where have you been the past few days?"

"I had a visit from some rough-looking Korean gents not long after we spoke," Charlie said. "They wanted to know where they could find Gordon. I told them that hypothetically speaking, even if I knew, I couldn't tell them. Client confidentiality."

I had known Charlie to bend the majority of the Rules of Professional Conduct, but never the one governing confidentiality.

"They weren't happy, but they left without making any trouble," Charlie said. "One guy did the talking. The other two stood there like robots. Really creepy."

I asked Charlie if that was connected to his temporary disappearance.

"I figured I was dealing with some Asian crime syndicate. Gordon must have gotten mixed up with them, over his head, and maybe that was the real reason he filed that loan application. Needed the money to get out of a jam. Figured I'd been working too hard, needed a break. Spent a few days hidden away in a cabin up north in the Trinity Alps. We once went river rafting up there, remember?" An image of me falling off a raft into churning white waters of the Trinity River came to mind. I smiled, thinking that was what passed for danger in those days.

"I called your number because I really wanted you to know all this, but there was no answer. Then I was out of cell tower range up in Trinity."

I laid out Gordon's string of lies about why he took the loan, and why he needed the money, but omitted any mention of Henry's murder or the North Korean phone.

"You never explained to me just why Gordon needed to hide with me in Thailand. If I can believe him, he might have been a suspect in a mortgage fraud and leaving the scene of an accident, but without the Prune, neither case sounds good for the DA. No doubt you told him so."

There was a pause that was just a little too long.

"That's exactly it, Glenn. The cops can have all the suspicions they like, but other than the Prune's apparent surprise at hearing of the loan, there's no evidence it was not made in the ordinary course of business, all legal and good. You think any bank officers are going to admit to being hoodwinked by a grifter like Gordon Planter?

"As for the poor Prune, no one saw what happened, and any forensic evidence of his presence is meaningless, because Gordon lived there. There were no cameras at the house, so there's no record of what happened. Even if Gordon was spotted running away, there's no way to prove he knew she was seriously injured, or even that she was struck. The Marin County District Attorney doesn't have a whole lot to do, so they might try to squeeze a misdemeanor with no jail, but I bet if you were still in practice, you'd laugh in their faces. Let them try that one. Never get past a motion to dismiss after the People's case. Without more, doubtful any DA even goes that far. But I don't have to explain this to you. Glenn Murray Cohen was the best."

"Doesn't California still have that ethical rule against counseling someone to become a fugitive?" I asked.

"It does," Charlie replied. "But where is the fugitive? What charges did he flee? My job as a lawyer was to make sure Gordon didn't wind up looking down the wrong end of a criminal complaint. You, of all people, know that, Glenn. They could never prove the mortgage fraud, and there's no evidence that Gordon was present when the Prune died. And as for running away, hey, those goons looking for him might be the reason. He is not required to speak with police, and if he did, he'd almost surely wind up getting charged with something. He'd plug up any holes in their case with his big mouth. My job was to prevent any of that from happening. I sent him to you to make sure of that, to protect Gordon from himself. He was, and as far as I know, still is, a free man. Free to not speak, free to leave."

"He's not free to leave the scene of an accident," I yelled. "Not free to leave a woman lying in a driveway instead of calling 911. And you're not allowed to use your services to help him commit a crime or a fraud!"

"Calm down," Charlie said. "How many times do we have to go over this? By the time Gordon came to see me, the acts you call crimes had been committed. He came for advice. The correct advice is that one is legally obligated to file a report. Failure to do so could be a felony when there's a death involved. But it is also sound advice to tell a client they don't have to say anything to law enforcement, and they are free to leave any time they wish unless legally ordered otherwise."

"You don't think advising a client to run away instead of making that report was an ethical violation? Maybe even obstruction of justice?" Something inside me wanted to make Charlie squirm.

I heard a laugh on the other end.

"Who said anything about running away to avoid a report? Nothing to stop him from making that report wherever he may be. By phone or mail. There was no damage to the car, and no sign it had been driven. It may well have looked like the Prune just fell and cracked her head. She was getting old, and I understand she liked a glass or three of wine every evening."

Charlie knew those ethical rules. If one is going to skirt them all the time, they better know them. He was also a damned good lawyer. He didn't have to be so shady. He just liked it that way.

"You're telling me the only reason you sent Gordon to Bangkok and me was so that he couldn't get himself in trouble trying to talk his way out of it with the law?"

"Exactly," Charlie said. "Right now, we got a loan that looks good on its face, a dead wife, and a missing husband. Sounds bad but what judge is going to issue an arrest warrant based on that? No known motive, no forensic evidence against our boy. No prior domestic violence, no past 911 calls by the lady. What DA would file a criminal case? What's the evidence? 'We think he did it'? Not good enough. The only person who could connect the dots is Gordon, and if he can't be found, he can't incriminate himself. With you still carrying a valid bar card, we've got confidentiality and attorney-client privileges for whatever he tells you."

Charlie didn't miss a beat. Then I asked about the phone.

"What phone?" he asked.

"The one you said was going to make you and Gordon rich. The one Gordon stole from Henry. The one Henry used to call the North Koreans. He would have kept it secret from us except he caved when we questioned him. We sort of pressured him to hand it over."

An extended quiet greeted my remark.

"Glenn, is everything okay over there? Do you know what you're saying? Gordon has a cell phone his dead cocaine dealer used to call North Korea?" Charlie's voice rose at the end of his sentence. Lawyers know when a witness really doesn't have the answer. We learn that from trials, not in law school. It was clear Charlie didn't know about the phone.

"Do you think I would send an idiot like Gordon over to you with a phone he stole from a North Korean drug ring without giving you the heads up?"

"I'm not sure, Charlie. It depends on what's in it for you."

Charlie acted as if he didn't hear this.

"This is quite a shock. Whatever Gordon's gotten himself into in the past, it was not training for dealing with the North Koreans. They can be a rough bunch."

"I know that, Charlie," I said. "My friends and I were ambushed by armed North Korean agents. We had to kill a bunch of them. The phone is safe with us, out of Gordon's hands. We're trying to figure out what the hell to do. We're looking for solutions. Feel free to weigh in. You sent him here."

I heard Charlie emit a sound that resembled "whew."

"Let me think," he said. Then he shared his thoughts.

I listened and, right after hanging up, told the others what Charlie recommended.

"CHARLIE SAYS JUST give the North Koreans Gordon and the phone?" Sleepy Joe shook his head as he spoke. We were seated around my dining room table.

"I don't care how big an asshole a guy is, they don't deserve what those guys will do to him," he added.

No one said a word as we pondered this option.

Nahmwan broke the silence.

"But if anyone does, it is Gordon."

"Are you suggesting we turn him over?" I asked. "You know what will happen. Think of poor Henry. We'd be accomplices to a murder. I'm with Joe."

Oliver joined us at the table. He had been listening from the living room.

"Charlie thinks it was not by mistake or by pressure that Gordon told us about the phone. Your colleague suspects it was all part of a plan to get us to protect him for free. We don't owe this guy anything. It's between him and North Korea, nothing to do with us."

Charlie did say that, and he was probably right. But I could not agree to turn a man over to certain death. I had to speak my mind.

Nahmwan reached across the table and grabbed my hand. I sat down as she spoke.

"Glenn, you are a lawyer. In your profession, sometimes you have to make a bad deal because it is the best choice you have. In my profession, same thing."

I wondered how anyone with such soft hands could sound so hard. Then I realized I didn't know what her profession was, and asked.

"I work for the General," she said.

"And that's all you need to know," the General interjected.

I pictured Nahmwan at the scene of the ambush, grabbing an assault rifle from a dead assailant, and killing several more. When we met, I thought she was only there to make coffee and phone calls. It didn't dawn on me she was there to protect us. Or at least me, as everyone else seemed capable on their own.

"We're not handing him over," I said.

"We will if we have to," the General said. "But I have a better idea."

"Any idea is better than Charlie's," I said.

THE GENERAL'S IDEA was simple: negotiate with the Koreans. This was Asia, where everything could be bargained.

"They are limited in what they can do in Thailand," the General said. "There can only be so many shootouts before we're the ones do-

123

ing all the shooting. They know this. North Koreans are evil but not so crazy as you Americans think. Their leader is no crazier than your new one."

The General had me there. I would never miss America as long as Donald Trump was president. And he was going to be sworn in in the very near future.

"Do we just walk into the local North Korean Embassy and ask for a sit-down?" I asked. "Assuming there is a consulate here."

"There is," Oliver said. "But I wouldn't recommend visiting. Rest assured, the intelligence agencies of all of our countries are watching that place day and night. Walking into the North Korean Embassy is only a good idea if you'd like a little more CIA in your life."

"I'd rather spend a night on Soi Cowboy with Phil Funston," I replied, referring to the NJA Club's resident sexpat, and the purportedly higher caliber stretch of go-go bars off of busy Asoke intersection, within sight of the upscale Terminal 21 Mall and the Exchange Tower skyscraper. The General, Joe, and Oliver laughed because they knew of my strong aversions to both Phil Funston and the sex industry.

"No, you wouldn't," Oliver countered. "Let me go in your place."

"I wasn't thinking of meeting them at their Embassy," the General said. "I'm quite certain the communists don't want to invite even more CIA scrutiny. Nor do we, for that matter. We can deal directly with the communists and keep your old friends from the CIA out of the picture."

Eight eyes turned to the General. I had no idea where one sneaks off to for a huddle with North Korean assassins. From the looks on their faces, neither did Sleepy Joe or Oliver. The difference was they wanted to know. As for Nahmwan, her face was as blank as a professional poker player. Eight years in the Kingdom taught me how well Thais conceal their emotions. Up to a point, that is. I caught her periodically glancing at Sleepy Joe. Once every so often, he gazed back at her.

The General tapped the table with the eraser end of a pencil as if gaveling court to order.

"The North Koreans operate restaurants all over the world. The workers are basically conscripts, and if they even think of defecting, their families get killed. Happened once in Japan, and our friends made sure it never happens again. Two of them are here in Bangkok. Easy way for them to raise hard currency. One of them is right off of Ekamai," he said, referring to the trendy and upscale street filled with high-end restaurants, clubs, and condos.

"But that's really too small and too public for us," Oliver interjected. "The other one should do just fine."

"Exactly," the General said. "The one on Soi 26, right near K Village mall. The building is set back from the street. We drop our team off in their courtyard right in front, and no one will see who we are even if they're watching."

I asked if the CIA would be watching the restaurant, if it really was a source of hard currency for one of our mortal enemies.

"It's not like they watch it twenty-four seven. You overestimate your agency's manpower and competence," Oliver said.

"Maybe manpower," I replied.

I LOOKED OUT toward the balcony. Wang and the bodyguards were still there, rifles in hands. A glance at the closed-circuit monitor on the wall told me that Lek and his cousin were keeping their eyes on the door.

"Why do I get the feeling that this isn't the safest place we could be?" I asked the General.

"Because it is a very dangerous place for us," he answered. "The communists have probably known your address for days now, and it wouldn't be hard for them to set up surveillance. They just say they are a South Korean company with offices here, hire a few *farangs* who need money, tell them they're watching for an employee suspected of stealing."

My stomach was catching fire as the General was speaking.

"Why did you bring us here?"

"Because this is how we fool them and stay safe," he said.

THE GENERAL ASKED Oliver to make sense of it to me. Everyone else already knew.

"It's like this, mate," Oliver said. "No doubt the North Koreans know exactly where we are and they're watching every possible way in and out of this building. It wouldn't have mattered where we went. They know enough about you to figure out where to look. Sooner or later, they'd find us. Me and the General figured the safest place for now was this tenth-floor apartment, with Lek and his cousin in the lobby."

"And we've got enough weed here to last us a while," Sleepy Joe said. He let out a cackle and rose from his chair. "In fact, I'm going to smoke another joint out on the terrace. Care to join me, barrister?"

I told him to meet me out there, and he walked to the sliding door. I turned my attention to Oliver and the General, still seated at the table.

"Are we supposed to stay here forever? Or until we turn over Gordon?"

Oliver rose from his chair and stood next to me, a heavy arm across my shoulder. Oliver was only an inch or so taller than me, but his thicker, wider body made me feel like a shrub beneath the shadow of an oak tree.

"Mate, since you haven't figured it out yet, let me be the first to tell you. To our Koreans and their watchers, it looks like we're hunkered down for the long haul, locked and loaded, as you Yanks like to say, waiting for that assault. Of course, that assault is never going to come, but the Koreans think that we believe it will. While they're thinking that you are holed up in this apartment, we're going to sneak you out for that meeting. In the meantime, enjoy your smoke with Joe." Oliver dropped his arm from my shoulder and returned to his seat.

"How come they don't shoot us when we're out on the terrace?" I asked.

"What good would that do them?" the General said in reply. "They're smart enough to know I've got men out on those streets, watching them just like they're watching us. They'd be dead in a minute. Besides, they'd rather have you alive to tell them where to find Gordon."

"Only then would they kill you," he added.

I joined Joe on the terrace. The sun was gone. From the tenth floor, I could see the hulking shadows of buildings, punctuated by soft amber lights from within. Joe leaned against a wall, staring out into the night. We passed the joint back and forth as we spoke.

"I'm not saying these two are as bad as Gordon," I said, looking back toward the General and Oliver. "But why do I have this feeling that they're not telling me the whole story either?"

"Because they're not," Joe said.

"And why is that?" I asked.

Joe stepped back from the wall and moved to the terrace rail, where he looked out upon the city.

"Probably because they aren't one hundred percent sure their plan will work, and they don't want to alarm you, so they keep their worries to themselves."

"What are they worried about?" I asked.

Joe turned to face me, and placed one hand on each of my shoulders.

"When you're in that restaurant, you're really in North Korea, and anything can happen to a foreigner in North Korea. Especially an American. But don't worry, I'll be there with you."

"I feel better already," I said, and it was true.

18

LEK'S COUSIN DROPPED us off in front of the restaurant on Soi 26. It was far enough off of Sukhumvit so that there weren't crowds of tourists or locals passing by. We looked like two foreigners hopping out of a cab for a fun evening.

Sleepy Joe and I walked toward the door. As we approached, three Korean women came out, dressed in what I took to be traditional Korean dress: long skirt, frilly, high-buttoned blouse, small bonnets in their hair. They were smiling and looked nothing like the fierce, humorless North Koreans we see on television. One of them addressed us in heavily accented English.

"Welcome," she said. "Is this your first time here?"

We nodded yes.

"Then we will make sure you leave feeling very good about us," she said. She turned to the entrance and we followed.

Inside, the lighting was soft but sufficient. There were about two dozen tables spread about a large room. Half were occupied, all by Asians.

"Mostly South Koreans," Joe whispered to me. "And probably all of them are spies."

The young lady led us to a table, and as soon as we were seated, she turned and walked away. We couldn't see her in the room, or figure out where she had gone. While we were pondering this, another woman came to our table. I recognized her as also one of the three who had greeted us outside, but she had changed into a western-style business dress and held a pad in one hand and a pen in the other. She introduced herself as our server.

"Since this is your first time here, allow me to make some suggestions," she said. Her English was nearly perfect, with only the slightest trace of an accent. We followed her advice and ordered North Korean kimchi, a noodle dish, and a spicy barbecued beef, all to share. Joe ordered a large North Korean beer.

"See how it stacks up to Foster's or Singha," he said as the server walked to the other end of the room and faded from sight.

"Must be some space along the wall where they can just slip in," he said. "Maybe a curtain."

"Looks like they leave this room unattended at times," I said. "Wouldn't expect that from a bunch of paranoid nuts."

Joe laughed.

"Whoever these ladies' bosses are, rest assured they are watching all the time. And you can bet they are heavily armed, just in case."

I scanned the room, spending a few moments watching each table. There were no women present, and the men seemed to be like businessmen everywhere, talking, eating, drinking, and laughing.

"You say they're South Koreans," I said to Joe. "What's the big attraction for them?"

"Not a hundred percent sure," he replied. "I get the idea that to a lot of Koreans, politics aside, it's still their people up North, and they're curious about them. This is about as close as most South Koreans are ever going to get to the North. Some may be hoping to make some business connections for the future. Wouldn't be shocked if one or two were South Korean agents. Nor would I be shocked if one or two were actually North Korean agents, looking to get info from the South."

"Sounds like this is really Oliver's turf, not mine."

The waitress arrived with the kimchi and Joe's beer. She poured water in my glass. This time, I watched her as she walked across the room. About ten feet from the wall on the other side, she disappeared.

"Must be something they do with the lighting," Joe explained before I could ask.

I kept my eye on the spot where she had disappeared, hoping to catch her when she returned with our entrees. My concentration was broken when she appeared directly in front of me and placed our meal plates on the table.

"How the hell…" I said half to myself.

"A parlor trick," Joe replied. "I'll explain it some time."

We ate in silence. My mind was on the instructions given by Oliver and the General: when the meal is over and they bring the bill, instead of cash or a card, drop a note that just says that if they want their phone, let's start talking. Then see what happens. If it became too much for Sleepy Joe alone, press the button on the key fob the General gave me; it would bring in enough of his men to wipe out a company of North Korean marines.

Just when we finished our meals, the lights dimmed and I saw people scurrying about in the front of the room. A spotlight came on, and it revealed a band made up of the three young women who had greeted us at the door, but now they wore miniskirts and tight, low-cut blouses. I wasn't sure in what decade the look thrived, only that it was before my time. The woman who led us to the table was holding a guitar, our server a bass, and the third woman was seated behind a set of drums.

"I never knew commies could be this hot," Sleepy Joe whispered.

LOUD, TECHNO-POP, BASIC rock sounds filled the room. I couldn't tell if the music was really them playing, or if it was piped in. The women moved and swayed like rock stars in the seventies, with a large dollop of a go-go dancer. They put down their instruments and headed toward the tables, and different music blared. They actually could play instruments, though hardly like Phil Funston. They went from table to table, pulling men into a conga line which soon snaked its way in a circle around the room. The woman who had asked me where I was from pulled me by the hand and ordered me to stand in line behind her. Unsure of the protocol, I placed my hands on her shoulders. She promptly pulled them off and placed them around her waist. Sleepy Joe's hands were on the shoulders of a pudgy Korean man.

During our second swing around the room, the North Korean woman turned her head to face me and asked if I was having fun. I said yes. She grabbed one of my hands, by now tightly gripping her waist, and led me back to my table. She continued to hold my hand after we were seated. Sleepy Joe was still shuffling along the conga line.

"So tell, me, Glenn," she asked. "Have you come to talk about the phone?"

I FELT LIKE I'd been smacked in the head with a two-by-four. The room was spinning, and I feared I might fall off my chair. My breathing grew labored. I was alert enough to place the thumb of my free hand over the button on the key fob in my pocket, then it dawned on me that Oliver and the General expected the North Koreans to know who I was and why I was there. My breathing returned to normal, and I released the key fob, which slid back into my pocket. I looked around the room for Sleepy Joe.

He wasn't there.

"Where's my friend?" I asked.

"He's being entertained in one of our private rooms. He's perfectly safe. As long as you cooperate." There was no longer a smile on her face.

"Just give us the phone and Gordon and you will never see or hear from us again.

"Unless you choose to visit us again for dinner," she added, still not smiling.

I appreciated why Sleepy Joe left the phone with Oliver. He would never risk it falling into North Korean hands on his account. Frightened as I was, my faith in Joe held true. If there was to be any killing, the dead would include North Koreans. I just didn't want it to also include Sleepy Joe.

"Let my friend go," I said. "He doesn't know anything. And let me talk to whoever is in charge around here."

"You are talking to the person in charge," she said. "And we are not so dumb as to fail to see that your friend is your bodyguard."

I forced a laugh.

"Him, a bodyguard? Did you take a look at him?"

She smiled for the first time.

"We don't place much on how a person looks," she said. "It is a great flaw of your people that they do."

Even in the subdued lighting, I saw how pretty she was. Hard to place her age, but she looked to be somewhere in her thirties, a little older than the other two women. I detected none of the lines, wrinkles, or folds that start to appear on people when they are in the vicinity of forty. Less so with Asians, especially women. But after a while, the *farang* eye grows sharp. I sensed her smiles were forced, and grimness was her default. I looked into her eyes. None of the pooled emotions I see in other people reflected back to me. Her eyes were dark marbles that showed nothing of what was inside.

"Whatever flaws we may have," I said, "they don't include turning a helpless person over to be murdered. You can have the phone, but not Gordon."

She was about to speak when we were distracted by a loud noise coming from our right, where the women had disappeared from my sight. I looked and saw a man in a dark suit lying on the floor. Not a second later, a second suited body sailed into sight and crashed to the floor. The conga line dancers, caught up in the loud music and their movements, paid no attention to the thuds sounding behind them.

Sleepy Joe suddenly appeared, moving toward us. He stepped over one of the still forms lying on the floor. He placed his hands on the edge of the table and glared at the North Korean woman.

"You people can't be trusted at all," he said. "We came here to talk peacefully, and you try to kill me? You think it was going to be that easy?"

I had to press my own hands on the table to stand up. I glanced at the two downed North Koreans and at the growing number of men dropping off the conga line to have a look.

"We better get out of here before they wake up," I said, looking at the two heaps.

"They're not waking up," Joe said, staring at the woman. "And your other friend will be joining them soon."

We looked toward the two bodies. A third man in a dark suit was crawling along the floor on his belly, a knife sticking out of his back. He slowly pulled himself forward, moving slower until he was dragging his bulky frame forward a few inches at a time. Then he stopped, and just lay there on the floor. I heard noises coming from the conga dancers.

"Grabbed it off a table while they were hustling me off," Joe explained. "Looked like the leader, so I stabbed him soon as I could. Then it was easy to snap those two necks."

"I was right about you," the North Korean said.

"Whatever that means," Joe replied.

He reached around the table, grabbed my arm, and pulled me forward. I pressed the key fob as we moved forward. Joe hurried us out the door into the courtyard. Halfway toward the gate, one of the General's Hummers pulled into the courtyard. A door opened and Lek's cousin called out to us. One of the General's bodyguards sat next to him, pointing a rifle at the nightclub. We ran toward them and tumbled into the empty back seat. Just as Joe was about to pull the door shut, the North Korean woman—the boss, if she were telling the truth—threw herself inside and forced herself between Joe and me.

"Surrendering?" Joe asked.

"Think of it more as defecting," she replied.

19

"I'M PROBABLY WORTH at least as much as that phone," the woman said as the Hummer pulled out of the courtyard and turned left onto Soi 26. The other two North Korean women ran on the sidewalk in the same direction, still wearing their dated rock-and-roll gear.

"Shouldn't we stop for them?" I asked.

"Not worth much to you or us," our uninvited guest replied. "They have nothing of value for your government, and mine won't deal for them. Just take it out on their families. They will be able to hide in Bangkok. Eventually, some South Korean Christian group will offer to help them, maybe to start a new life in South Korea. If they turn Christian, of course. I'd rather go to America.

"And please call me Cho," she said.

"Is that your name?" I asked.

"Call me Cho," she repeated.

Cho was probably right about her colleagues being able to hide out until they could make their way to Seoul. Anyone could hide in Bangkok. I'd been doing a pretty good job of it until Charlie found me.

"WERE WE BEING watched?" Sleepy Joe asked our intruder as we turned left onto busy Sukhumvit. Lek's cousin maneuvered the Hummer over to the right, into the U-turn lane.

"You killed the men who did the watching," she replied. There was no sorrow in her voice.

"You've got pretty nice legs for a commie," Joe told her. An embryonic smile crossed Cho's face and then disappeared.

We passed the streets where we could have turned to go to the NJA Club or my condo. I asked Lek's cousin where he was taking us. He didn't speak English, but Cho addressed him in Thai, and translated the reply.

"Safe place up in On Nut," she said, referring to a neighborhood not more than a kilometer and a few BTS stops from my place. On Nut was originally intended as an area where middle-class Thais could live in Bangkok and not spend hours commuting to work. It did fill that role in part but became a respite for *farangs* seeking relief from increasing rents in the ever-pricier expat-friendly areas around Asoke, Phrom Phong and Ekamai, all several BTS stops closer to the action than On Nut.

"Thai and English," Joe said. "I'm impressed."

"Our language schools are very good," she replied.

It was just past nine thirty p.m., and this part of Bangkok was gaining its third breath, after the business and dinner crowds were gone. Young and not-so-young foreigners mingled with twenty and thirty-something Thais seeking out the restaurants, bars, and clubs in the trendy Phrom Phong and Ekamai districts. A few blocks away, on side *sois*, lie the places known only to Thais, who don't tell *farangs* about them. I'm not sure I blame them. It's nice to live in an international and cosmopolitan city, but it's also nice to live where "Thainess" rules. Even after eight years of living here, I'm not really sure what constitutes "Thainess." It's like what US Supreme Court Justice Potter Stewart said about pornography: "I can't define it, but I know it when I see it." If we *farangs* find out about these places, they won't be Thai much longer.

"Do you ever make it over to this part of town?" I asked her.

"I'm not saying anything more," she answered, staring straight ahead. I waited for her to add she had already said too much, but maybe I've read one spy novel too many.

Lek's cousin made a U-turn to the right at the On Nut intersection, and turned left on to Soi 50, in the looming shadow of the Tesco Lotus Mall and On Nut BTS station. The mall's parking lot contained a few automobiles scattered about, and several taxicabs, motorcycle taxis, and tuk tuks waiting for last-minute diners and shoppers or BTS passengers. The busy complex befell behind us, as Soi 50 turned into an empty stretch, more like the outskirts as opposed to the center, of the huge metropolis that was Bangkok. Our driver hit the gas pedal, and we moved along at ninety kilometers an hour. Five minutes later, still not having seen a car on the *soi*, we turned right onto a narrow gravel road. Two hundred meters down this strip stood a large house surrounded by an eight-foot wall. A steel gate set in the wall slid open as we approached. When we were in the large courtyard, the gate clanged shut with a loud bang.

Several men in camouflage dotted the perimeter of the house.

"There are a few on the roof and at the windows," the General's voice called from behind me. I turned to him. The General wore a nicely tailored dark suit and a blue power tie.

"Just finishing a meeting with the Deputy Prime Minister when I got the call to get over here," he said.

My mother would be so impressed, I thought. *Her son having a friend who hangs out with Deputy Prime Ministers.* Amazing what comes through the mind in times of stress.

The North Korean woman was out of the car, walking between Sleepy Joe and Oliver. Upon seeing the General, she addressed him in Thai.

"Speak in English," the General said. "We're all impressed with your language skills, but my friends here don't speak Thai, no matter how long they've lived here.

"*Mai jing*," Oliver said, a note of pride in his voice. "*Phom pasa Thai put dai khrup.*"

"You're not a regular *farang*," the General snapped.

"And you're not a regular Thai," the woman replied. "And he's not a regular *farang* either," she said, turning her head to Sleepy Joe. "And I'm not a regular Korean." Oliver stamped his foot so hard I feared it might trigger an earthquake.

"You're a North Korean!" he yelled.

"Korean," she said softly. "Please don't tell us Asians who we are. You've been doing it for a long time, and look where it's gotten you. So perhaps we not-regular people can figure a way out of this mess."

"Does that include the only regular person here?" I asked.

"Of course," the General said. "There always has to be one normal person around. That's why I love you, Glenn." He clapped me on the back with a swat so strong it stung for half a minute. "But first, let's find out more about our charming visitor."

HER REAL GIVEN name was Cho, which means beautiful, and in her case, it was not just North Korean propaganda. As my fear of dying lost its grip on me, her fine features, her shiny black hair against light skin, obscured the reality that she was a North Korean agent, trained to hate and fear Westerners from her first breath. Especially Americans.

"I was born and raised in Pyongyang, our capital," she explained. We were seated around a table. Oliver, the General, Sleepy Joe, and Nahmwan sat facing Cho and me. Two of the General's men, both with assault rifles, stood behind the North Korean. "My father was a high-ranking official in the Foreign Ministry. His father had fought alongside Kim Il Sung, the founder of the country. I was sent to the best schools and universities. I even spent two years studying in Beijing, where I learned to speak perfect Mandarin, and to hate the Chinese."

"I thought you guys like China," the General said.

"We need them, but we know they don't like us any better than we like them," she said. "I saw how they treat Korean citizens in China. If I were not connected, they would have treated me the same."

Cho explained how she was trained in foreign languages and spy-craft. Her training was focused on America.

"For three years, all I did was watch American movies and tele-vision, read their periodicals, and speak their language twenty-four hours a day. I came out of it all with perfect American English and a love of rock and roll. You have to admit my guitar playing was quite good."

Actually, her guitar playing was not very good, no better than my own, but if I placated her, she would keep talking.

"Yes, I was admiring your musical talent," I replied. Oliver inter-rupted me before I could follow up with a better line.

"Why are you in Bangkok?" It was said as a demand more than a question.

"I think I have already said more than I should," Cho answered. "I will only speak with a US Consular Officer about this."

Nahmwan leaned forward and was about to say something, when the General raised his forearm from the table a few inches, bent his hand up and back, and lowered it at once. Nahmwan held back her words. The entire table was silent for a few more seconds. The General broke the silence.

"And I suppose you'll be needing a lawyer for all of this, am I right, Ms. Cho?" he said, looking at me.

OLIVER KNEW WHO to call and what to tell them. He always does. He handed Gordon's phone back to Sleepy Joe, and we all agreed that meant it was in the safest hands possible.

"Obviously, we can't have the two of you gallivanting about the streets of Bangkok right now," Oliver explained. "A North Korean defector and a pot-smoking American lawyer who can't properly fire a gun? Obviously, you will be protected. The other side knows this. They don't expect to snatch you two off the streets. The Americans know Cho would talk to them if they want. They will, of course. Someone from your State Department and, of course, from CIA will definitely want to have whatever information she can give them. Don't know if we'll be able to tell the difference these days."

"They're going to believe it, just like that?" I asked. "That we have a North Korean defector ready to talk?"

The General and Oliver looked at each other, and then at me. The General spoke.

"Glenn, when someone like Oliver tells your government that there is a North Korean defector at one of my safe houses, it's taken as a fact."

"That's how it works in my business," Oliver explained. "Relationships of trust are built up over years. Someone like me does not give bum information to your embassy. Not ever."

"Understood," I said, restraining myself from crawling under the table. "Is it safe for them to come here?" I asked, struggling to be relevant.

"I have men patrolling the streets for five blocks in each direction," the General said. "More surveillance cameras than the police. We're watching the North Korean Embassy, their restaurants, and businesses and safe houses they use as fronts. Keeping an eye on anyone we know to have worked for them, even if they didn't realize they were. Our visitors will be arriving in a van that says they clean pools."

"Who are these protectors you are talking about?" I asked.

"Some trusted Thai government agents I know personally," the General replied. "Other than that, it's my own people. Like you Americans say, 'If you want something done right, do it yourself.' Quite right. We'll handle things until your CIA takes over. They will be here first thing tomorrow morning at nine, because that's when we want them, and they'll be gracious. It's almost eleven p.m. now, time for us to get some sleep. Except for Glenn, who will be on a computer, researching American asylum law, so he doesn't make a fool of himself."

It was fine with me. I couldn't have fallen asleep anyway.

OLIVER WOKE ME by turning on the lights in the little room where I finally collapsed just after four a.m. He held a steamy cup of black coffee in his meaty hand. I grabbed it and took big sips while I sat on the edge of my bed.

"It's a little after eight," Oliver said. "Our guests will be here at nine. I suggest you take a shower and a shave in the guest bathroom. We took the liberty of having Lek gather up a suit, tie, shirt, and shoes from your place, so that you will actually look like a lawyer."

"Preferably navy blue for meeting with the government," I said, hoping to sound lighthearted.

"Actually, I told him charcoal pinstripe," Oliver replied.

While showering, I ran through the key points of asylum law I had gleaned from my self-taught online studies. The leading law books on the subject were not cheap, but they were good. I could put it on the bill, but I doubted Ms. Cho was expecting a bill.

I went to the kitchen dressed like a high-class lawyer on his way to a merger and acquisition. Nahmwan and the General were standing by the coffee maker. She looked at me as if she'd never seen me before.

"You look like such an American," she said. "Like an American lawyer in the movies."

The General reached over to a chair around the little kitchen table and picked up a black leather briefcase.

"Carry the briefcase when you meet them," he said. "A real lawyer must always carry a briefcase," he said.

"I'll try to remember that," I said. "Do I get to keep it when this is over?"

"No," he said. "I want it back."

20

I WAITED IN the small library-office, nursing my mug of black coffee. Lek and his cousin had done well in selecting my outfit. The dark pinstriped suit, stiff white shirt, and red-and-blue repp tie made me look every bit the kind of lawyer a North Korean defector on Cho's level would retain. The only problem was, I was not that kind of lawyer, and the sum total of my knowledge of American asylum and immigration law was gleaned during a few sleepless hours in the middle of the night. I thought of my law school criminal procedure professor, a grizzled old defense lawyer of some note. He impressed on us the old chestnut that 'if you don't have the facts, argue the law; if you don't have the law, argue the facts; and if you don't have either, attack the other side.' It looked like the law was on my side, and we had great facts, so we wouldn't have to attack anyone except North Korea. Well, maybe Gordon Planter also, though since he had dealt with Henry, North Korea's man in San Francisco, our government would want to talk with him. That meant keeping him alive, even if the North Koreans had other ideas. One thing was certain: Glenn Murray Cohen, Esq., would not be representing Gordon.

The door opened, and Oliver entered the room. Two men dressed in suits followed. I didn't know the small Asian man who walked behind Oliver, but was well-acquainted with the tall black man.

"Glenn Cohen," he said when he eyed me. "I knew you were CIA material the first time I laid eyes on you, and I was right. First you kidnap a Russian and get him smuggled back to America for trial, now you bring me a rather important North Korean defector, and you've busted open a North Korean drug ring. Glenn, you make me look really good."

"Well, you do look good in that suit," I said, trying to hide my shock. "Office job these days?"

"Just a disguise," he said, extending his hand. "Like the one you're wearing." We shook, and it made me feel safer.

Rodney was the CIA agent assigned to oversee the little gang of NJA friends the CIA hired to kidnap a Russian gangster and turn him over to Rodney and his partner. Rodney's partner, Charlie's old friend Billy Sloane, tried to kill us, but my bodyguard, sent by the General, shot him through the head first. That bodyguard, Wang, the NJA Club cook, stood ten feet away from us, on the other side of the door, a military assault rifle cradled in his arms.

"By the way, this is Mr. Ling," Rodney said. "He's a North Korea specialist with the State Department. He's also a lawyer, and the US Asylum Office has given him the authority to review an asylum application and grant parole into the US when and where he sees fit. Easiest way to do it. Stationed in Seoul but just happened to be in Bangkok for a meeting." Wang nodded at me. I knew parole meant Cho would be allowed in but not officially admitted in any status until the government decided they got all they could from her. A way of keeping control.

"He's also fluent in Korean, both the North and South dialects," Rodney added.

"I don't need an interpreter," Cho said. "I speak perfect English. Better than his Korean, I'm sure. He's not even one of us. He's Chinese." She dragged out the last word the way one would refer to something nasty on the sole of their shoe.

"I'll be happy to speak with you in English if you wish," Ling said. "Or Mandarin Chinese, if you like. You speak it quite well, if my memory serves me well."

"What do you mean 'if your memory serves you well'?" Cho asked. A few muscles pulsed on her otherwise still face.

"You may not know it," Ling replied, as impassive as Cho, "but we were watching you every second you were in China. You don't think we'd miss an opportunity to learn a little about the granddaughter of a general who fought with your founder against the Japanese, the South Koreans, and the Americans?"

"I'll be damned," Oliver muttered. "We've really got a North Korean princess on our hands."

"Actually, she's in our hands now," Rodney said. "But your valuable assistance will be duly noted."

"How much?" the General asked.

Rodney smiled and placed one hand on my shoulder, the other on Ling's.

"I'll let you know after these two gentlemen and Ms. Cho have concluded their meeting. I'll thank the rest of you to leave us in privacy."

"Of course," the General replied.

"And don't even think of eavesdropping," Rodney added. "I'll be sweeping for any active devices, and if I find any, it comes out of your tip," Rodney held what looked like a cell phone from his pocket and looked at the screen.

"I see they have all been deactivated. Oliver, was that you?"

"Yes, it was," the big Australian said. "I think I know the drill."

"You do, and this isn't a drill anymore," Rodney said. Oliver, the General, and Sleepy Joe left the room, and Rodney closed the door. The four of us sat around a table. Ling pulled a legal pad from his briefcase and set it before him.

"Let's start with your life story," he said to Cho.

SHE WAS BORN in Pyongyang and lived there for the first twenty years of her life. As the granddaughter of a hero of the revolution and the daughter of an air force general who became the head military advisor at the foreign ministry, Cho lived a life beyond the wildest dreams of the average North Korean. Her family enjoyed every luxury they craved, even a private automobile. Until she went to China and started to hear what defectors were saying, she had no idea that there was widespread starvation and repression in her nation.

"At first I didn't believe it," she said. "Then I just ignored it. Finally, I accepted that my pleasant life was built on their suffering, and it would do no good if I disowned it and suffered myself."

Some of her friends, also from powerful families, had also been granted the rare privilege of traveling and living abroad, and a few used it as an opportunity to defect. Cho was well aware of the suffering imposed on their families. Her parents made certain to let her know, ostensibly an expression of disdain, but Cho saw it as an appeal to not allow that same fate to befall them. Cho accepted this as an obligation to her parents and grandparents. As time passed, the obligation became less compelling.

"My grandfather was killed by soldiers who were in rebellion against the leadership," she explained. "You probably never heard anything about it. Hundreds of rebels were executed in the most horrible way.

"My other grandparents had already died." Cho then told us her mother had been diagnosed with stage four breast cancer shortly after she arrived in Bangkok. Cho was not supposed to know, as any loosened ties increased defection odds, but her mother sent word through a diplomat at the North Korean Embassy in Bangkok, a friend from childhood. The same friend sent her the news that her mother had died a few months ago. She could not show that she knew, as it would have meant serious problems for her friend and probably her as well. She had to mourn in silence. How difficult it must have been, I thought.

Rodney and Ling looked at each other.

"Good work, Glenn," Rodney said. "We never knew any of this. Remember what I told you about a job that's always been available."

"I'm happily unemployed," I said. Cho continued.

"I am an only child. When my father passes, which will not be long from now, I will have no family left. All of my uncles, aunts, and cousins died from war, starvation, or old age. Some were sent away, and those people almost never return." She then returned to her professional history.

The stint in Beijing was a test. She knew she was watched around the clock by Chinese and North Korean intelligence, but she never considered that Americans were keeping an eye on her. Her handlers assured her Americans were stupid and clumsy.

After passing the test in China, she was sent to Bangkok. On the surface, she was managing one of their cash-cow restaurants, a lawful means of obtaining hard currency.

"But really, I was sent there to compromise a high-profile target," she explained. "American."

Rodney asked how she was expected to do this.

"Any way I could," Cho said. "I'm an educated, attractive woman who speaks perfect English. I've been trained to think like an American. You would be amazed at who comes into the restaurant. Not just businessmen and tourists, also people from the Embassy. Even CIA agents. But they are not coming for the kimchi, and I don't try to work them."

"What was your game plan?" Rodney asked.

"Whatever it took," Cho replied. "Seduction, set them up with hookers, give them drugs, whatever they would not want their bosses to know. Then they belong to us."

"And what success did you have?" Rodney asked.

"Nothing major," Cho said. "Managed to get a few expatriates in embarrassing situations. But they were, at best, people we could use for small things."

"Like coming around the NJA Club, asking about me?" I said. She did not answer.

"Glenn, I think it's best if you allow Mr. Ling and I to ask the questions." He was right.

Rodney asked more questions about Cho's work in Bangkok, and then Ling took over. He spoke in a flat, slow manner, taking copious notes as Cho answered his questions. Most of what he asked was out of my league: questions about people in the North Korean government and military, questions about how they sent and received hard currency, things that are important but boring to any listener who's not an intelligence officer. My boredom faded when Ling asked what she knew about North Korean drug trafficking in America.

"I don't know anything about that," she said. "That's not something I'd be told."

There was the slightest quiver in her voice, so slight I almost missed it. It told me she was lying. That criminal lawyer's sixth sense or radar, or whatever it's called, is infallible once developed. Mine was developed over the course of countless cross-examinations, and it never fails me. No point in interrupting the experts' questions, but I filed it away for later. Ling and Rodney showed no indication of how much they believed. Ling kept writing with a Montblanc 146 fountain pen. When I was a lawyer in America, I toyed with the idea of getting one, so that in the presence of clients, I could sign retainer agreements and other documents with the appropriate flourish. They were going for over seven hundred dollars back then, and Office Depot was selling bags of pens for a few bucks. Looking back, I wish I'd bought the Montblanc. Ling looked supremely confident and officious gliding that beautiful fountain pen across his pad. I made another mental note, this time to buy the Montblanc if we survived.

21

THE QUESTIONING WENT on for an hour. I again lost interest in the minute details Ling was slowly dragging out of Cho: who was in and who was out in Pyongyang's inner circles; which Americans did business with North Korea, knowingly or otherwise. Not being very invested in questions or answers that didn't have to do with Henry being killed, or me being next on the list, my mind wandered. Then, as minds often do, especially male minds, my attention focused on Cho. She was an attractive woman, and her self-confidence sheltered a smoldering sexuality which my well-trained eyes detected. Sitting there in a tight dress, legs showing to the middle of her thighs, I found myself wondering what she must be like in bed. My eyes constantly take in women, and my mind asks the same question. This conflicts with my feminist views, which I'm trying to work out. So far, the best solution has been to keep these thoughts to myself. Based on past performance, I would never get beyond the wondering stage with Cho. Meanwhile, every little move she made, each wave of her hand, watching her body twist as she moved in her chair, raised my concerns about an embarrassing erection. I almost forgot she was a North Korean agent who would have been happy to see Sleepy Joe and me killed a few hours ago.

Ling plied Cho with more questions about foreigners she knew from Pyongyang, or North Koreans working undercover in Bangkok and the US. As Ling dragged on, instead of monitoring the proceedings, I was monitoring Cho's skirt as it moved up her thigh when she responded to a question. My mind was pulled back into the present moment by one of Ling's questions.

"Do you have any fear of returning to North Korea?" he asked.

"Of course, I do," she said.

"And what exactly is it that you fear will happen to you if returned?" Ling asked Cho.

"I'd be immediately convicted of treason and blasted to tiny pieces by an anti-aircraft gun," she replied. Cho noted this on his pad.

"Do you have any documents or other evidence in support of your claim?" he asked.

"Ling, don't be an ass," Rodney said, patting him on the back. "It's not like Kim Jong Un is going to provide a letter. And that little creep would indeed do something as barbaric as our friend predicts."

"Understood," Ling replied. "I'm just following the protocol given me by the US Asylum Office."

"I think we'd be better off taking our legal advice from Mr. Cohen," Rodney said. "Why don't we take a little break so that the two lawyers can iron out some details? I'll stay here and keep an eye on Ms. Cho."

Ling and I rose from our chairs, getting ready to leave the room. I felt Cho's hand lightly grip my wrist. I looked at her, but her face revealed nothing. But that good old criminal lawyer's sixth sense detected fear.

"SHE'S THE REAL deal, no doubt about it," Ling told me in a small bedroom where we ensconced ourselves. He sat on the edge of the bed, with me on a fragile-looking chair meant for a woman to sit on while putting on makeup. "She's spot-on about every place and every person in her capitol, and there's just no way your ordinary North Korean knows any of those things. Cho's no ordinary North Korean. If she were, she would never have been sent to China, where I monitored her, and no way she would be trusted to run the operation here."

"And you think she's lying about some things," I said, more as a fact than a question.

Ling paused for a moment.

"I would say that there are two forces at work here. One is her genuine desire to avoid returning to North Korea, no matter what that requires. Her fear of how she would be treated is precisely what I'd predict."

"Would they kill such a member of their inner circle?" I asked.

"Kim, like his father and grandfather, cares only about hanging on to power and being personally revered or feared by every North Korean. That means making people deathly afraid to be one foolish enough to act against the regime in any way. He does this by regularly demonstrating what happens to those he suspects of disloyalty. That's all it takes, a suspicion. There's no concept of justice or fairness," Ling explained. "You must understand that in North Korea, failure is the same as treason. A North Korean who fails at something is disposable, and it's a good way of sending the message not to fail."

"That's insane!" I yelled. The room's door opened, and Sleepy Joe's head protruded through the open space.

"Everything okay here?" he asked.

"Fine," I replied. "I'm just having such fun I had to scream for joy."

"If you say so, mate," Joe said as he closed the door.

Ling waited silently a moment before resuming. He tilted his head so his ear faced the door. He must have been listening for Joe's footsteps, making sure he wasn't listening in from the other side. We had nothing to fear from Sleepy Joe, but I respected Ling's professionalism.

"Cho might be shown some leniency, based on her family lineage and her past record of service to the state. But in North Korea, leniency means years in a labor camp, living on less than a thousand calories a day, shivering in the winter, frying in the summer, always hungry, and if you get sick, they work you until you die. If you survive, you can be slowly rehabilitated, but never back to where you were. And that only happens to the lucky few. Our friend made a quick but wise choice to jump into your car."

I ran through the basics of asylum I had learned on the internet, hoping to show off my legal acumen.

"We can assume that my client has demonstrated a well-founded fear of persecution, based upon membership in a clearly defined social group, namely North Korean defectors. She has a subjective fear of being incarcerated or executed if returned to Korea, and her fear happens to be objectively reasonable. We can provide expert opinion on conditions in North Korea, but I believe the Asylum Office will take administrative notice and incorporate, by reference, the State Department Country Report on Human Rights." I looked into Ling's impassive face when done.

Ling cracked his first smile of the day. It was more like a slight upturn of his lips, but I'd call it a smile.

"I see you've done some legal research, which is to be expected from an attorney of your caliber," he said. "But actually, there's no need to make a case. This is a done deal. There is no way on earth the US government turns away a North Korean defector on this level."

"So she just walks out of here with an asylum grant, and then a year later she applies for her green card?" I wanted to make sure Ling knew how smart I was even though he said it didn't matter.

"Not quite," Ling replied. "We'll give her a grant of parole later today, which we can revoke at any time we wish. In the meantime, we will bring her to one of our debriefing locations back home, where a team of experts will question her for weeks, maybe months. We have just started, haven't even cracked the surface of what we will learn from her. Once we determine she is absolutely a legitimate defector, which seems to be the case, she'll get her asylum and then green card. Plus, some money and, of course, protection until we can be certain that Pyongyang won't bother her."

"Why would they give up?" I asked.

"Maybe they'd figure at that point it's not worth the consequences. Maybe they'd decide this is one deal they better stick with."

"We make it part of the deal that she stays safe, of course," I said.

Ling shook his head.

"We'll of course have that as part of the deal to turn over Gordon and no local prosecution of any North Koreans. We could get the Thais to charge someone if we really wanted."

"Wait a minute," I said. "The last time I spoke with my group, the question of what would happen to Gordon was still up in the air."

"With all due respect, Glenn, this is no longer a matter for you to decide. It's a US government decision."

"Are you telling me that the US government has a policy allowing it to turn American citizens over to North Korea?" I asked.

"By and large, no," Ling said. "But the CIA makes its own rules, as you are now aware."

"Is there anything we can do to stop this?" I asked.

Ling leaned back in his chair and looked at me.

"Glenn, there is nothing you can do. And don't be so judgmental. The only reason we have Gordon in our custody is because you guys took him off to Chiang Mai, tied him up, and are keeping him there until we could take him off your hands. You're into this as much as anybody.

"Not that it is necessarily a bad thing," he added.

"And after you turn over a US citizen to be blasted to smithereens, are we guaranteed everything is over?" I asked.

"The question to ask is: does the North ever keep their word?" Ling said. "How many times have they promised no more nuclear action? And didn't they swear they were not dealing drugs?"

"Either way, with us or with them, there are risks and no guarantees," I said.

We sat there in silence for maybe half a minute.

"We should finish up our legal matter," Ling said to break the quiet. "Here's how it's going to go: Cho's getting parole into America right now. Then a green card, and later, citizenship. No application, no interview, but if anyone ever checks, it will come up okay."

"But if anyone is checking, it means real trouble," I said.

"It would. That's why she has you. To protect her."

I didn't like the word "protect." The last time it was used on me was when Charlie badgered me into helping Gordon. That got me under fire from North Korea and forced to deal with the CIA again.

"Against whom?" I asked. "And how?"

Ling laughed. He wasn't doing it just to lighten the moment. He looked like he found my question funny.

"Glenn, don't worry. We don't expect you to be in any shootouts, at least not if you follow our advice. The North Koreans won't know if Cho is here, or in South Korea, America, or anywhere we want to stash her. Rodney and I want you to protect Cho like you did for every client you ever had. When we bring in a defector like her, it's our duty to make sure nothing bad ever happens to them. We'd never get another defector if that happened. That's why we work with lawyers like you in these delicate situations."

"Why would I have to stand up for her in America?" I asked. "The government is supposed to give her legal status and guard her as needed."

Ling stared at me for a moment before answering.

"I wish I held the government in the same esteem as you do, but as a long-time civil servant, I cannot. Rodney and I are CIA and State. Homeland Security, which has jurisdiction over non-citizens within the United States, may not always feel as grateful and honor-bound as we do. They are nowhere nearly as well trained as we are, and to be blunt, they are about as bad a federal agency as you can get. They renege all the time, and they care only about enforcing their irrational and unenforceable immigration laws and nothing else, not even national security. She needs a really tough lawyer in her corner if and when she needs one. Rodney tells me you're a stand-up guy. So does Charlie. If DHS tries to screw her, even from Bangkok, you'll shove a writ up their ass like it was an enema." I was surprised to hear a State Department guy like Ling talk like a criminal lawyer at a bar after work.

My insides flooded with a mixture of unclear emotion and physical cramp that is most often associated with the onset of certain kinds of food poisoning. Mention of Charlie causes the same symptoms.

Not to mention it was worrisome to hear a State Department lawyer confide that the Department of Homeland Security was duplicitous, inept, and not really protecting us. On top of that, Ling was implying that I played a role in unwittingly delivering Gordon to the CIA and then to Mr. Kim.

"You know Charlie?" I asked when the flooding stopped. "How?"

"Rodney knows him. Don't you recall that Charlie was a college roommate of Rodney's late partner?"

Of course, I knew. I was present on a dock in Pattaya when Wang caused Billy Sloane to become Rodney's late partner. Shot him right in the head, and Billy fell into the drink, as they say in gangster movies. I was told the CIA would clean things up, but for all I know, he's still there. Ling continued, and I listened.

"As soon as we got the call from Oliver, Rodney got Charlie on the phone. He pretty much corroborated what you told us about his dealing with Gordon."

One question after another poured from my brain through my lips.

"How did you guys get Charlie on the phone so easily? I've had a hell of a time. And didn't Charlie bring up attorney-client privilege and confidentiality? And how could you guys trust Charlie in the first place?"

"There's no reason not to trust Charlie," Ling said. "According to Rodney, Charlie has never lied to them. Nor has he ever lied to you. He told you what you were getting into last time, with the Russian, and you were well paid."

"Well, he sure didn't tell me what I was getting into when he sent me Gordon," I replied.

"Charlie didn't know the real story, or he would have never sent him," Ling said.

Once again, I felt that food-poison sensation.

"The full story being?" I asked.

"Gordon Planter has been working for the North Koreans for years. They distributed their drugs through him. Henry was one of his dealers. The phone wasn't Henry's. It was Gordon's. He's the one who was calling Pyongyang."

LING LAID IT out. He and Rodney had assembled the pieces of the puzzle after Oliver told them what we knew, supplemented by their talk with Charlie, and what information they could squeeze out the DEA.

North Korea had been distributing cocaine, methamphetamine, and opioids in America since the late eighties. They were a relatively small segment of the market, almost negligible in terms of American drug consumption, but a significant source of hard currency for the Hermit Kingdom, which had few other such avenues. Members of their U.N. mission used their diplomatic immunity to bring in most of the drugs, and Ling made clear the CIA believed some other nations not friendly to America helped them with the rest. For a fee, of course. North Koreans could not play any visible role in the United States, and they needed Americans to do the dirty work.

"Somehow, they connected with Gordon's late wife, the one you call the Prune. We aren't sure exactly how or when they met, but it was when the Prune was living in Japan for two years with her first husband, who oversaw local operations for an American company. There's no question but that she had an extramarital affair with a man she believed to be an executive for a South Korean corporation. Apparently, she was a sucker for con men and criminals of all sorts. By the time she learned that he was a North Korean agent assigned to compromise her, there was no turning back. She gave the agent copies of highly protected bank records stolen from her husband's files. Divorce was the least of her worries should her lover talk. As it turned out, there was no need for a threat. The Prune was probably in love with her handler but more in love with the thought of making millions of dollars without working hard. Her handler was sent back to Pyongyang, her husband died shortly thereafter, and she came back to California, eventually finding her way into the arms of Gordon

Planter, at the time, once again down and out. She also found herself involved with North Koreans again, this time as a drug dealer. We think they set her up for it while she was in Japan, but she's in no position to confirm this."

"I don't get it," I said. "If North Korea wanted to distribute drugs in America, why would they enlist her?"

"Because she was smart, tough, didn't look the part, and was easily manipulated by men like Gordon. Hooking up with him made it a sure thing the North Koreans could keep her under their control. Once Gordon got a taste of the easy life, he would not want it to end, and he'd keep her in line. Don't be surprised. The North Koreans are all over Northern California. They want as much info as they can get from Silicon Valley, and they can easily pose as South Koreans or Chinese. We've caught on to that, so these days, they are more likely to use people that look like the Prune and Gordon." Ling didn't look the least bit self-conscious talking about the physical differences between Asians and white people. Why would I assume he would? This guy was a State Department professional to the bone. That was his race, religion, ethnicity.

"Why would the North Koreans want to deal with a fool like that?" I asked. "Couldn't they have arranged for her to meet someone else?"

"Because he's not the fool you think," Ling replied. "He sure showed you that to be the case, didn't he? Charlie too. Even Oliver couldn't figure him out completely. But give Oliver a big hand for figuring out that the cell phone had a tracker inside. Gordon never knew, never figured his bosses were keeping tabs on him. Gordon was concerned the phone might get him in trouble, but knew it could also prove he was part of a North Korean drug ring. He spent enough time around you and Charlie to know that the government prosecutors would be far more interested in that than in busting one lowlife grifter. He never realized just how much information could be gotten out of that phone. It gives us a picture of how North Korean intelligence units operate in America. Gordon didn't fully appreciate this when he split. So he knew he had something of value, but just not how valuable. He made up the story about stealing it from Henry to hide the truth from you. Maybe we don't like the way he operates, but it worked for him, because he's still alive, and you fellows are sitting on a small fortune, which our government will pay."

"You're saying he also fooled the Prune and the communists?"

"I'm sure he charmed the Prune and made her think he would always be there for her. She bought it enough to confide in him and bring him into the drug dealing. Almost all cocaine, sometimes heroin. Eventually, the Prune let Gordon take over her responsibilities, which were mainly picking the stuff up from an unwitting North Korean asset, who had no idea what was in the boxes the pain-in-the-ass lady was picking up. He'd break it down, bag it, and deliver it to her network of dealers, all of whom were handpicked by the North Koreans. Gordon was enjoying a good and easy life, supervising a few local dealers, collecting money, delivering drugs, accounting all to his wife and she to the Koreans. Oh, yeah, Gordon was able to get high on coke any time he wanted, which was a lot. The Koreans took it out of the Planters' cut. I'm sure the Prune wasn't too pleased, but she was bamboozled by Gordon and let it go."

"Here's what I don't understand," I said. "If Gordon was on easy street, living high on the hog and snorting coke at will, why on earth would he run the risks he did by committing mortgage fraud and trying to deal cocaine on the side?"

"Because all the money went through the Prune. She more or less doled out an allowance. She may have been in love, but that did not dull her sharp financial and business acumen. You can love someone, and still acknowledge who they are. But she didn't realize right away just how greedy and selfish a man she had married. She squirreled away where Gordon couldn't get at it once she figured it out."

"I take it the mortgage scam was really just to get the money and leave the Prune?"

"Yes," Ling said. "And he knew he was also going to have to get himself out of the clutches of the North Koreans if he wanted to enjoy his money. And there's more."

"What more can there be?" I asked.

"Nothing he told you about him and the Prune was true, except that he didn't love her. Nothing he said about Henry was true, except that he was a dealer."

"What is the truth?" I asked.

Ling placed his elbows on the table, interlacing his fingers. Then he dropped his hands to the tabletop and spoke.

"Henry was killed on orders of Gordon's higher-ups. Gordon had to execute the plan, if not the victim. The only reason Henry was getting drugs from the Koreans was because Gordon recommended him when one of their long-time dealers died in a car crash with ten kilos of cocaine in a bag in the trunk. Somehow Gordon got to the scene before the cops, and grabbed the bag. He brought it to Henry, who sold it the next day, and Gordon handed the cash over to his handler. Everyone was impressed, and soon after, Henry was part of the family.

"Then someone Henry sold to was arrested, and Gordon's North Korean handlers feared the customer would want to snitch his way out of a jam, setting off a trail leading to them. They had the potential snitch killed and decided Henry had to go as well, in case the cops figured out he sold the coke to the dead snitch. Since Henry was Gordon's man, the assignment went to him. That's how the North Koreans play it, really test your loyalty. Henry called on some Colombians for this. That's where the Antonio from the gym came from. Gordon really did meet him at the gym and figured out he was an enforcer for a Colombian drug ring. Gordon used Antonio to kill, not to score."

I nearly fell off my chair as it dawned on me that the "old friend" Charlie had sent me was, in fact, a cold-blooded murderer. Suddenly, Charlie's suggestion to trade Gordon for an end to this nightmare made perfect sense. Still, I didn't want Gordon dead. I'm just not that kind of person. Sometimes I wish I were, but I am not and never will be.

Ling continued.

"After Antonio—if that's his real name—dispatched Henry with a machete, Gordon had him kill the Prune. There never was a car accident. She died of a broken neck, snapped by Antonio, who was a martial arts expert. Charlie didn't know this, any more than he knew of Gordon's involvement in Henry's murder. With no other evidence, it could just as easily have been a fall out there on the driveway. Gordon, of course, cleared the Prune's death with his North Korean bosses. I'm sure a team of North Koreans cleaned the house of anything that might remotely point to them."

"Why kill the Prune?" I asked. "She was no threat to anyone."

"That did not originate with the Koreans," Ling said. "That was Gordon's idea. He told his bosses that the Prune would crack under pressure if the law found her. Made sense to those paranoids. They weren't worried about Gordon. They'd just seen him have his friend killed to keep things quiet. That's the sort of thing that impresses them. The Koreans thought he was someone they'd want to keep around for future work. They must have known Gordon didn't care about the Prune, and they surely didn't. They did him a favor and got rid of a potential problem. What they did not know was that Gordon wanted the Prune out of the way because he was planning to disappear without a trace and didn't want anyone around who might help in finding him. Not to mention that if the Prune were busted, she'd likely give Gordon up in a nanosecond after realizing he had played her for years."

"Are you saying it was at Gordon's order to kill the Prune?" I asked once I was able to speak. Having Henry killed was reprehensible, but having his wife murdered out of greed was, to me, unmeasurable depravity.

"Technically speaking, all orders come from Pyongyang, so let's say it was Gordon's suggestion, and when the North approved it, he was assigned to carry it out. The North Koreans are paranoid to begin with, so it takes little to persuade them they were getting rid of someone who might lead law enforcement to them, just as they'd done with poor Henry. Then Gordon realized he could well be next on the list, and ran to Charlie for help. He knew if anyone could figure out a way to hide him, it was Charlie. With lies, of course. Charlie would never help a murderous traitor." *That's good to know*, I thought.

It took me a few minutes to absorb all of this. My vocal cords needed time to unfreeze. No intelligible sound could come forth. Up until now, we were working on the belief that Gordon was inadvertently dragged into a North Korean criminal operation, and was trying to make lemonade out of lemons by selling the phone. Now it was clear that Gordon was helping our sworn enemy try to destroy our country from within, because it afforded him an easy life, and was willing to murder his friend Henry and his wife so he could steal from her and run away. Gordon was far worse than a conniving deadbeat. He was a traitor, a murderer, and one of the most thoroughly evil people I'd ever met. For a San Francisco criminal defense lawyer, that's quite a statement, but it is true. It will never be known who despised him more, the North Koreans, or me. Still, I couldn't bear the thought of him being killed. One more death does nothing to improve our world.

"Are you telling me that we should fear Gordon as much as the North Koreans?" I asked when I could speak instead of croak.

"The North Koreans are going to keep hunting Gordon," Ling said. If he happens to be with any of you when they find him, you'll be what they call collateral damage."

"Why are they after him? I thought you said they like him because he was such a cold-hearted bastard. They had no idea that he was ripping off the Prune and planning to split."

"When he stopped answering their calls and they couldn't find him, they figured he had taken off with the phone. He didn't know they could track him."

Of course. Those Koreans who showed up at Charlie's office looking for Gordon, and the flunkies poking around the NJA Club.

"Couldn't Gordon have avoided all of this by simply taking over from the Prune and keeping all the money for himself? Did he really have to run away?"

"Well, Glenn," Ling replied. "As an experienced criminal lawyer, you know that upon discovering the Prune's body, some cop is going to look at Gordon. While they may never have been able to pin the mortgage fraud or murder on him, there is certainly a good chance they'd look at everything about him, and sooner or later, the drug dealing would be revealed. Once that happened, it would be too close for comfort for the North, and like I said, Gordon was well aware that these folks were paranoids and he could wind up like Henry and the Prune. He thought he was smart enough to fool everyone."

"Good luck to him," he added. "He's going to need it."

"Assuming the North Koreans get their hands on Gordon, are the rest of us safe?"

Ling released a long exhale.

"Whew," he said, "that's a tough one. I'd say that the Koreans realize that aside from a general idea that they were dealing drugs in our country, you have no detailed information that isn't already known. They know about the General and Oliver, and now Sleepy Joe. They recognize professionals when they see them. And there's nothing personal involved here. It's not like you guys pose a threat to the Kim dynasty. They expect that just as they must keep up their end of the deal, so must you. No attacks in Thailand, no revenge against you people, but you all keep quiet. In other words, no books or interviews. I sincerely doubt any of you are that foolish. Then they will leave you alone. Killing you guys is not worth jeopardizing their many more productive operations."

"How do we make all this happen right away?" I asked.

"Easy," Ling replied. "Just give them Gordon."

This time, I said nothing.

LING TOLD ME he and Rodney had business to attend to and would be back that evening.

"We'll be bringing Cho's request for asylum, her parole into the US, and some agreements for the two of you to review and sign," he said. Rodney and Ling had made clear that "parole" meant Cho would not be officially admitted in any legal status, but would be allowed to physically enter and would later receive the actual status if her handlers believed she was straight with them. That was what I learned from my all-nighter with the law books. My job was to make sure all went through without a hitch, which seemed to be the case.

My strategy was to hand them an asylum application and demand prompt adjudication, or at least prompter than they had in mind. Ling had tipped me off that we could not be totally assured of Cho being helped a few years down the road because the Department of Homeland Security was not trustworthy. I had to close the deal soon, before she departed Thailand. Reminded me of fighting to get a deal or a promise before I allowed a client to become a cooperating witness. The government had a nasty habit of forgetting their promises once they got what they wanted. Cho should get asylum, and a year later, permanent residence, the so-called green card, which of course, is not green. Five years after that, she would be a US citizen.

When Ling and Rodney were gone, I summoned the General, Oliver, Sleepy Joe, and Nahmwan. Cho was sleeping in a bedroom, the door slightly ajar, two of the General's armed men standing guard outside, occasionally peering in. I felt the urge myself.

I told the four of them about my conversations with Ling, revealing only my talk with him, and nothing of those with Cho. Attorney-client confidentiality was burned into my soul.

"We've known from the beginning that turning Gordon over would end our problems," the General said. "Now that you know he is a traitor to your great country, and a cold-blooded murderer, you can have no further objections to giving him to North Korea," he added, staring at me. I sensed everyone else in that room agreed with him.

"Murder does not stop being murder just because the dead man was a traitor, or even a murderer themself," I added.

Sleepy Joe frowned and shook his head with such force that his long, stringy hair fell in front of his face. Nahmwan gently pushed it away.

"Glenn, everyone at this table would die for you. But not for Gordon. A man who sells out his country for money has no right to live." The other three showed their agreement by nodding their heads. Sleepy Joe had turned, and there went my only ally on this question.

"Why not just turn him over to American authorities?" I asked. Oliver answered.

"Because right now, the only thing the Koreans want is Gordon, because he could cause them serious problems with you Yanks. They know they can't have Cho. Even if they get the phone, the damage is already done. The CIA plumbed it for all it is worth, which is a lot. The communists really don't care about the rest of us. The only reason we killed their people is because they tried to kill us. Like Ling says, to the North Koreans, failure is treason. In their eyes, we killed a bunch of traitors. Not worth making a fuss over. They are as happy to deal and put an end to this as we are.

"The only thing we have to give, the only thing left for them, is Gordon." Oliver scanned the table by moving his neck to face each of us briefly. Approval was shown by all but me.

"We're supposed to despise Gordon as a traitor because he put himself above his country, and now you're telling me we should deprive America of all this knowledge about North Korean drug dealing in our country because it benefits us?" I asked.

"Big difference," Oliver said. "Gordon did not have to throw in his lot with the North Koreans. He chose to betray his country for money. He had his wife killed out of greed. We are simply trying to stay alive. We have shared with your government everything we learned, for which they are most appreciative and will express this in a most generous manner when this is over. Your own government says to give Gordon to the North Koreans; he's really theirs. We walk away safely, the US government hands us money, and Ms. Cho gets asylum. What's there not to like? Let Rodney and Ling continue to save America, and we save ourselves."

"The man's right," Sleepy Joe said. Nahmwan nodded in agreement. I couldn't help but wonder if the change of heart was really his.

"People die all the time in war," the General said to all, but I knew it was meant for me. "We are at war. A good general wants to minimize casualties and not fight needless battles. Oliver knows how to reach anyone, even North Korea. The CIA and the State Department are happy to work with him, and the North Koreans will know that even though he is a private party, not even American, he's speaking for the US My people up in Chiang Mai will deliver Gordon to Rodney as soon as Oliver and his contacts set it up. The life of one man who is the cause of many deaths is a very small price to pay for a truce. I think we and the North Koreans will be sure to stay out of each other's way from now on."

"Four to one, mate," Sleepy Joe said.

Oliver rose from his chair.

"I've got a call to make," he said.

SLEEPY JOE TRIED his best to lift my spirits. We were sitting on the edge of his bed.

"Listen here, mate. There's a lot of good coming out of this mess. For starters, I finally met a woman who can hold my attention. She's my equal in every way. No, even better than me. In every way. We're all alive, and now we hear your government wants to give us more money. What's to be sad about?" I was happy for Joe, being in love and all, but I could not countenance the murder of anyone, not even Gordon Planter.

"We're participating in the murder of an American citizen by North Koreans," I said.

Sleepy Joe let out a laugh that seemed to come from his nostrils, not his mouth.

"Some American he is, mate. Sold out your country to the commies for some dirty money. Had his friend and his wife killed. Told us one lie after another, nearly got us killed. He wouldn't mind all of us dead so he could be the only one to profit from the phone. Sounds like he's getting what he deserves."

"He deserves a trial," I said.

"I'm sure he'll get one in North Korea," Joe replied.

22

THE GENERAL ENTERED the room without knocking.

"I am going to be on the street with my men, to make sure the North Koreans don't double-cross us. They're known for that, as you learned at their nightclub. It should go well, assuming they learned their lessons. Rodney and Ling will be here in a very safe diplomatic vehicle, to bring you and Cho to your Embassy to prepare her papers. Right after that, she is off to the US. She'll spend months, maybe years, being debriefed. Your CIA knows that every word she says must be checked and doubled-checked for verification." He turned and left without another word.

"Back in command mode again, and he loves it," Joe said.

Joe was right. He and the General were warriors, and no surprise they rose to the occasion in war. They thrive on it. That just wasn't the way it worked for me. My wars had been fought in courtrooms, using my mind, my training, and sometimes the law as my weapons.

Not this time.

I THOUGHT NAHMWAN was joking when she offered to teach me how to shoot. I was in the small bedroom given to me to work, planning to review my notes on asylum law yet one more time, hoping to sound just the like the lawyer I was supposed to be. Even though I had spent most of my adult life being one, I didn't feel like a lawyer.

Being away for eight years may have had something to do with it. Passing myself off as an expert in asylum law, of which I knew nothing before that day, may have also been in the mix. Dealing with the CIA and North Korea were not generally part of the legal milieu in which I had worked.

"Don't you think the sound of gunfire might concern the neighbors? Or maybe tip off the North Koreans that we're here?" I asked.

"There's a shooting range in the basement," she said. "Soundproofed."

"A shooting range in the basement?" I repeated.

"Isn't that what I just said?" she replied.

"You're starting to sound just like Oliver," I said. She laughed as she took my hand and pulled me to a closet inside the pantry, with a set of stairs against the wall. This time, I knew the grasp was that of a teacher and a student, not two people attracted to one another. I was fine with that. I had someone else creeping into my mind, even though lawyers are not supposed to think about their clients in that way. Nahmwan pulled me down a flight, and we were in a basement. There were two shooting lanes, and all the accoutrements for practice set out on a table: headphones, bullets, magazines. I saw enough of those items as a criminal lawyer to recognize them. I told Nahmwan I had never fired a handgun.

"Don't worry, I'm a certified instructor," she said. "A few years ago, the General sent me to Taiwan to learn."

We spent well over an hour down there. At first, the recoil of the nine-millimeter Smith & Wesson pistol caused me to jerk the barrel upwards too high, and once or twice, my bullet sailed over the target. It didn't take long to factor in a correction, and I was soon hitting the silhouette target between chest and head almost every time. The magazine held seventeen rounds, and I must have filled it five times. It surprised me that I could do so, and it surprised me even more that I enjoyed myself.

"Not bad for a beginner," Nahmwan said as we wiggled our way back up the narrow staircase and sat at a small table in the pantry.

"But Joe is a lot better. A natural. Not that he needs it, or would want one, but he can handle a firearm."

"You've been down here with Sleepy Joe?" I asked.

"Only once," she said. "I'd like to get him down here again, just in case he ever needs the skills. But he tells me that if he has to rely on a gun, he's already lost, and the idea is to make sure it never gets that far."

"That's Joe," I said. I'd seen Joe kill three men on the Russian operation, and he added three more in the North Korean restaurant that very day, two with his bare hands. The dead men were all armed. My morbid recollections were interrupted by Nahmwan's voice.

"May I ask you something about Joe? I know you two are very close. Joe told me that you are more than just best friends. He says that you are like brothers."

"It's true," I said. "We may look very different, and we have had very different lives, but we are identical in so many ways. We love the same music, the same films, we're both pretty tolerant people, and we both enjoy a good laugh."

"And you also enjoy smoking *ganga* with Joe," she said.

"He told you that?" I asked. Joe and I were always extremely cautious about who we told about our mutual love of weed. In Thailand, one does not want such information to fall into the hands of the wrong people, though somehow, it often does.

"Sleepy Joe told you that?" I asked again when she didn't answer. I couldn't believe Joe had opened up to a total stranger.

"While you have been working, we've been getting very close," she said. "Very close." She turned her eyes down, as if she had said something embarrassing.

It took me a few seconds to fully grasp the importance of her words. Aside from some scattered references to a favorite masseuse, Sleepy Joe had never discussed relationships with women. He mostly listened to me complain about mine. His romantic history was a mystery to me, and I always thought that if he had anything to say, he would, but he never did. My brain scrambled to figure out how and when the two of them found time to consummate their relationship. Must have been while I was in a closed room trying to make heads or tails of what was going on. Or maybe when I was sleeping. Joe was always the best at covering his tracks. Not that my best friend had any reason to hide this from me.

"Now I know what they mean when they say 'could knock me over with a feather,'" I sputtered.

"It's not feathers I'm worried about," Nahmwan said. "We're hopefully going to practice again, but I think if you had to, you could defend yourself now. So take these, keep them in an easy-to-reach place, and use when necessary. She handed me the Smith & Wesson and a small box of bullets. I hesitated, then grabbed the gun with one hand and the bullets with the other.

"I'd call on you or the others first," I said.

"Assuming you have the chance," Nahmwan replied. She walked away, and I went back to the little room.

I put the gun and bullets inside the briefcase the General had given me. Then I rolled a joint and smoked it to the very end, crushing the stub repeatedly in an ashtray.

"I HEARD YOU are now quite the marksman," Sleepy Joe said after he shook me awake. That last joint put me to sleep.

"Are there no secrets anymore?" I asked.

"Not from me," Joe said, flashing what would have been called an ear-to-ear grin, had his ears not been hidden behind the stringy, dirty blond hair hanging over them.

"I guess I have to figure that from now on, when I'm talking to Nahmwan, I'm talking to you as well. Hope it doesn't work that way in reverse."

Joe sat down next to me, reached his arm across my back, and patted my shoulder.

"Mate, no one is ever coming between us. Man, woman, or a combination, no one comes between Sleepy Joe and Glenn."

I stared at him and slowly shook my head.

"Joe, I don't recall you being with any woman that didn't present a bill after the massage and extras," I said. "No offense, but a normal relationship does different things to a man's head and heart."

"Well, you ought to know," he said. "I can recall at least three of your relationships ending rather badly. But going well or not so well, none ever had any effect on us being brothers. So why do you think it's going to be different with me?"

Whenever thoughts of my failed relationships flooded my mind, they depressed me. And that was only the three absolute failures in the eight years in Thailand. There was a failed marriage and a string of un-successful relationships buried back in America. Not to mention the many women here in Bangkok that wouldn't even give me a chance.

"Joe," I said, "I'm pretty experienced in these things, and look at the problems I have had. No offense, but you haven't been there yet. That's why I might seem a little concerned."

Joe let out the loudest laugh I'd ever heard come out of that skinny body.

"Mate, you thought I was a burnt-out hippie who couldn't fight his way out of a paper bag. Turned out you were quite wrong on that point. Maybe that's not the only place where you're wrong."

I was about to apologize if I hurt his feelings, when he held up his hand to silence me.

"You take care of your end, mate, and just remember always, no one and nothing ever comes between us. Got that?"

Before I could say "yes," he was out the door.

I GAINED A new respect for my colleagues in the immigration law field. Back in San Francisco, I viewed them as lazy, unlettered lawyers seeking to exploit a vulnerable population. Funny thing was, many people saw criminal defense lawyers the same way. It became clear to me, through my cramming, that a good immigration lawyer must be intimately familiar with a wide range of statutes, regulations, and federal case law, starting with the Constitution. They also require a good working knowledge of family law, criminal law, and constitutional law. Most of it is way over my head, and thankfully, asylum law was the only part needed for my client.

Ling confirmed what my lifetime of legal experience taught me: The government could not be trusted. According to the law books, Cho needed to prove "a well-founded fear of persecution" based on her political opinion or membership in an identifiable social group. As a defector who jumped to the Americans, Pyongyang would see her as a traitor, taking care of the political persecution part, and her being a high-ranking defector placed her within a clearly identifiable social group, at least as far as North Korea was concerned. If she could do this, the government would have to grant her asylum, and eventually a green card and then citizenship. There were no obvious bars to this because there was nothing to show she had ever persecuted anyone on account of their beliefs or committed any crimes under American law. My job was to make sure we established a political asylum claim that could stand up to any scrutiny and could never be taken away.

I was filling out the asylum application online, to present it to the government when we met, whether they wanted one or not. Oliver had left me a piece of paper with Cho's biographical details, at least as much as he could get from her and his sources, and I had my notes of our discussions and her interviews with Ling as the basis of the persecution claim. Oliver said he would get me documentation of what happens to defectors if the Kims get their hands on them.

I finished the application and printed a copy. It was time for another cup of coffee. If luck was with me, there was a pot ready for me. Otherwise, I'd have to grind and drip on my own. I could review the application and my notes while sipping a cup. I stuffed the file into the briefcase and went to the kitchen.

While grinding, I heard a noise coming from the general area of the front door. I stopped the grinder. This time, I heard what, from my experiences in Chiang Mai and the basement shooting range, I recognized as gunfire. I ran from the kitchen, through the living room, and stopped at the vestibule before the front door.

More gunfire sounded from our street. I looked through the windows and saw no one. Oliver was still gone, Rodney and Ling had not yet arrived, and I had no idea where Joe and Nahmwan might be. Perhaps on the street with the General, perhaps snuggling in an upstairs bedroom. I heard shouting from the other side of the door in what sounded like an Asian language, but with all the noise, I couldn't be sure which one. An explosion followed, then the sound of concrete banging against glass, but the windows did not break apart. The General got his money's worth from his shatterproof glass windows.

My briefcase dropped to the floor. I almost followed, then remembered the Smith & Wesson was in the briefcase. I reached for the gun and the box of nine-millimeter rounds.

I dumped the bullets on the vestibule's table, and loaded seventeen rounds into the magazine as fast as I could, just as Nahmwan had shown me: flat end of bullet toward flat end of magazine, push in and up. My hands shook slightly, but I concentrated on loading the bullets as the gunfire increased and the shouting grew louder. I stood still, feet apart, wrapped my fingers and thumbs against the grip, as Nahmwan demonstrated, and walked toward the door and the sound of the shouting.

The door was suddenly blown open and fell to the floor. If there was an explosive, it was drowned out by gunfire and shouting. Two men in uniforms and balaclava moved through the entry and toward me, assault rifles at chest level. I conjured Nahmwan standing with feet hip-width apart, erect, pistol held between her chest and chin, eye on the sight. I placed my finger on the trigger, aimed at the soldier nearest the door, and squeezed. The noise and the recoil were just as when practicing with Nahmwan. The soldier fell. My hand moved an inch to the left. I pulled the trigger, and a second soldier fell. Another came through the damaged door. Gunfire sounded from all directions as I lined up my sight on the third soldier and fired. He fell forward, his head not more than a foot from my feet. I swept my gun as I looked for other invaders, but stopped when I heard the General calling out in English. "Stop firing, they're all dead." Another voice yelled out in Thai, *hyut ying*, or "stop shooting." Armageddon was replaced by a beautiful silence.

It was the sight of the three dead soldiers, crumpled on the ground like discarded cigarette packs, that accomplished what the bullets could not. I fell to the ground and all went dark.

23

THE COLD COMPRESS awakened me. My eyes focused and adjusted to the light. Cho's face looked down at me, a bulky washcloth in her hand.

"Don't worry," she said, "you weren't shot. You fainted at the sight of blood." She gently ran the cold compress across my forehead. I felt the ice cubes wrapped inside. The cold rush jarred me enough to understand what had just happened.

"I didn't I kill anyone, did I? It must have been the General's men. Or Nahmwan. Maybe Oliver."

Cho was still, her face betraying no thoughts.

"No," she said in a near whisper. "It was you."

"They were yours, weren't they?" I asked.

"Were mine once, but now they are not. They came to kill us both. I told you that in North Korea the penalty for failure is death. So is success, if it comes at their expense. But we're safe now. After you killed those three, the General's men finished off the ones out in the street. Four more, if I count correctly."

We sat next to each other, perched on the edge of the bed.

"I've never killed before," I said. I struggled to hold back tears as fear yielded to sorrow, but I couldn't allow my client to see me cry. "I never even hurt anyone. I fight in court, not with guns. I always say I could never kill anyone."

"Well, time to stop saying that," she said. Her hand rested on my knee, and she leaned against my shoulder. "If not for you, we would both be dead." She pressed her body harder against mine.

"For a lawyer, you're a pretty good shot," she said as she pushed me down on the bed and straddled across me. She placed one hand palm down on my chest, and the other grabbed my crotch.

"Is this what they taught you in those great universities?" I asked as I pushed her off me. We sat on the edge of the bed. Anger and disappointment flooded her face.

"Lawyers cannot have such relations with a client," I said. "It could complicate the relationship."

"What difference could it make?" she asked. "I thought we had a deal with the US government."

"A deal Ling hinted might be over once you're not needed anymore. That's where you'll need me."

"Sorry, but I just thought that was what you American guys wanted all the time. That's one of the things they taught us. Guess it's not true."

"It's not true that we want it all the time," I explained. "Or better said, we can control our desires when necessary. At least if you want to survive."

"So you're saying that if we had sex, you couldn't be my lawyer? I don't understand why. What does having sex have to do with being a lawyer?"

Cho was worldly and sophisticated for a North Korean, but apparently that was a very low bar.

"Cho, sex usually involves emotions. Emotions can make people do things they should not do. When a lawyer becomes involved with a client, their objectivity will probably fall away and be replaced by emotions. Those emotions could include anger, sorrow, feeling of betrayal. That's why most states don't allow sex between lawyers and clients."

"Who said anything about emotion?" Cho asked. "I'm a normal young woman who is never going to see my country again, and no North Korean would risk having anything to do with me now. South Koreans really don't like us very much. I may not like the idea of having sex with a non-Korean, but I've had to do it before, and at least this time, it's my choice. You know, Glenn, for a non-Korean, you are a pretty good guy and handsomer than most. More fit. Plus, you just saved my life. We could have a great time."

"If my representation is ever over, we can pick up this discussion," I said.

Cho looked down and then at me. There were hints of water in her eyes.

"I really need you, Glenn. I made my decision, but it's going to be hard to get by. At least for a while. I would like to have you with me all the way."

"I will be," I said. "But only as your lawyer." I felt strong enough to stand.

"We'll see," she said, gently tapping my cheek. I left the room.

THE GENERAL'S MEN arrived and removed the three bodies. First, they ripped off the balaclavas, and had Cho positively identify them as North Koreans. She had seen one of them several months ago at the North Korean Embassy. Their uniforms bore no insignia. The bodyguards collected the rifles and pistols from the dead men. I walked out the door to the yard, sidestepping small puddles of blood. The front gate slid open and a black SUV drove through. As the gate closed, the General emerged from the car. He did not look happy. As soon as he was in the house, he stopped and spoke to one of his men before turning to me.

"I lost one of my best men, guarding the street," he said. "It would have been worse if you hadn't stopped those three bastards. You should be proud of yourself."

"Somehow pride is not what I feel right now," I said.

"Sooner or later, you will," the General said. "But right now, we've got to get Cho out of here and to America. It's her they want, not us. They know she hasn't told us much. They're trained that way, you realize. She's testing us as much as we're testing her. But Oliver tells me it is going fine. Your government has experts in getting information from people like her. It's all about gaining trust with someone like Cho. But that's for Rodney and Ling to worry about. Let's just focus on our group staying alive. Except Gordon, of course."

"You can't let them have him," I said.

"I'm sorry, Glenn, but I must disregard your advice this time. You can now see why a deal is the only choice if we want this to end with all of us alive. If the communists decide we are never going to deal, they will keep coming after us until they at least have the satisfaction of knowing we don't get to enjoy any victory, because the dead don't get to celebrate. With a deal, everyone will walk away feeling they came out the best they could. Except Gordon, who deserves whatever he gets. Oliver has channels who can reach the North Koreans, channels both sides can trust. We'll give them Gordon and the phone, which your people have already mined for its information. Oliver made sure we also share it with Australia, and needless to say, I'll make sure the right people in Thai intelligence get it as well. In exchange, they leave us and Cho alone, and no more violence in this Kingdom. Not hard for them to agree. They really couldn't touch her in your country anyway, and the damage to their drug dealing has already been done.

"And what will it be like for Gordon?" I asked.

"Your client will know better than me," the General replied.

"THEY'LL WANT TO know everything Gordon told anyone, including you," Cho explained.

"And anyone who dealt with Henry. Once they get it all from him, and they will, he'll be shot and will disappear forever. But they will leave you alone. You're nothing to them once this is over. I don't know that's the case with me, Glenn. But as of now, the only one who is facing death is Gordon."

Cho must have seen the look of despair on my face.

"Don't feel bad," she said. "He deserved it."

"Because he betrayed his country?" I asked. "Or because he's a murderer?"

"Neither," she replied. "I betrayed my country as well. No doubt people have died on some of the operations I've been involved in. We just saw Joe kill three, and this attack here was an extension of the war. I know my people. You hit us; we hit you. We're even, so this is the time to deal. Ask Oliver or the General.

"Gordon's problem was that he went over to the wrong side, and I went over to the right side," she added.

There was nothing more to be said. Gordon's fate was decided. My client was Cho. Hope Gordon got a good defense lawyer in Pyongyang, though I doubt there were any.

"On that note," I said, "my government will be questioning you. I know that you have a lifetime of being taught to hate and distrust us, and your training is to be an excellent liar, but you really need to tell them the whole truth."

"Because North Koreans aren't the only ones who can play rough?" she asked.

"You know the answer to that one," I said. She touched my hand briefly with her fingers. It tingled.

"Don't worry, if the Kims taught me anything, it is how to survive. My ticket is to America, and I am going to ride it all the way. And like I said, you have nothing to worry about. There's a deal, and killing you isn't worth the response from the US if they reneged like that."

"Thanks for the ego boost," I said. "I guess you mean at least I'll be alive."

"What I mean is, you're free to visit me any time," she replied.

PEERING THROUGH THE broken door, I saw the hole blasted into the wall where it met the sidewalk. It was barely wide enough for a person to squeeze through.

"They had some sort of shoulder-fired explosive," the General said from behind me. I turned to face him.

"Probably fired from a moving vehicle," he continued. "Then they used a small concussion bomb to blow the door off its hinges."

"Like a miniature grenade?" I asked, hoping to sound smart.

"Exactly," the General said. "Do I detect you are developing a taste for combat?"

Why are you asking me? I thought. *Maybe because I just killed three men in about a second and a half?* But that was not what I said.

"Please don't joke about that" was my response. "As a favor for a friend."

"You already owe me one favor," the General said.

"General, I've given this some thought." That was not true, as I was making it up as I went along, just like when caught by surprise in court years ago. "You got Sleepy Joe arrested, helped me bail him out, and took a nice cut of the bribe money I put up. And I'm supposed to owe you a favor?"

The General is a bit shorter than me. He arched his eyebrows ever so slightly and tipped his head to look me in the eyes. I thought he was going to tell me I indeed owed him, and maybe even raise the ante. A lump formed in my throat.

"Glenn, you're the best *farang* friend I've ever had. You just killed three men and saved Ms. Cho, a most valuable asset. She is going to make us a fair amount of money, courtesy of your government. Not to mention that for Oliver and me, it opens even more doors than we had before. The favor is waived. You owe me nothing."

The lump in my throat melted away. The fear I had lived with for over a year melted with it.

I thanked the General for waiving the favor. The tightening in my chest loosened, and the queasy feeling in my stomach faded.

"I have a different favor to ask," he said. The tightness and queasiness began creeping back.

24

"I LOVED THE time that we traded stories from our past, and would like to do it again." When the General says he would "like" to do something, he means you better do it. Not a problem for me. Telling stories was what lawyers do. The tightness and queasiness bid farewell again. At least the tightness that came from owing a favor. The part that came from an assault by North Korean commandos stayed longer. Sometimes I think it's still with me.

Before Charlie's greed and my own unrequited love for Noi dragged us into the CIA kidnap plot, the General decided that if we told each other a story from our past, one that revealed how we became the men we did, our bond would grow stronger. I was flattered. So much for these *farangs* who say it's impossible to make Thai friends.

The General told a story from when he was commanding officer of troops fighting communist guerrillas in Isan, and Wang the cook was one of his men. Wang is a native of Isan, like my friend Lek. Rich Bangkok elite like the General usually look down on these hardworking folks, which rankles me enough that I have been known to argue with them. Noi, the woman I loved and risked my life to save, is also from Isan. She is now in America with her US husband, and I'm here, wondering how I became the only rich and handsome *farang* who is alone. Well, not quite alone. I've got the NJA Club.

The General told me how he spotted Wang as exceptional, despite his generally low opinion of Isan people. He appointed Wang as his adjutant, over the complaints of his fellow officers, who had their favorite—and well-connected—soldiers panting for that job. The General's perception proved astute. Wang saved the General's life more than once, and helped him beat back the Reds with few casualties. When the General became rich, he bought the NJA Club for Wang. The cook was so humble, that for years, I thought he was merely an employee, and the General was the owner. Wang is always available for special assignments, if needed by the General, but the Club never misses a beat, always open for business. I was going to say "unless the law says otherwise," but there have been occasions where we've quietly gathered, even when the law compelled a "closed" sign on the door. Thailand can be very mysterious.

The story I told the General at that time was about one of my first criminal trials, where the defendant was a transvestite. She wore a dress to court, though when the indictment was read to the jury, the defendant had a man's name. I told the jury about my client's sexual orientation before they were selected. It must have worked, as we got a jury that paid attention, was fair, and acquitted my client. The lesson learned was that honesty is always the best policy.

"I enjoyed that as much as you did," I said. "But I believe that before all of this happened, Rodney and his colleagues were on their way to get Cho and me."

The General looked at me and shook his head.

"Glenn, I called them and explained that we had just been hit by the North Korean Green Berets, and we needed a little time to clean up and gather our dead. Rodney understood. We've got the time."

"Wouldn't they want to get over here and grab whatever intelligence they could?" I asked.

"Rodney's right; you think like them. Yes, they would, but this is a Thai matter. This is our country that was attacked, and we can deal with it. We'll be happy to share whatever we learn with our friends."

"Or we'll figure out a way to get it anyway," I said. He threw me a look that said not to say that again.

"Will I be treated to another war story with a new hero?" I asked.

"No," the General said softly, looking into his martini glass. "This time, I will tell the story of my first *mia noi*."

"It's not like you haven't had any since then," I replied. Every few months, the General pulls out a picture of the latest occupant of the office, and tries to persuade me to join them, along with one of her friends. The General has revealed almost nothing about his family, other than that his son was following in his footsteps when it came to *mia noi*. I have never met the son, or any other family members. I find it strange that the General would introduce me to his lovers but not his family.

"This was different," he said, still meditating on his drink.

"How so?" I asked.

The General put down the drink, lifted his eyes and aimed them at me.

"It's complicated."

"Why is that?" I asked.

"Because this one, I really loved," he said. "And that's for starters." "

SHE WORKED FOR the Thai military here in Bangkok around 1980. The year Ronald Reagan was elected your President."

The General was a great admirer of our fortieth President. Nothing to do with politics or economics. The General was simply in awe of Reagan's popularity.

"They loved Reagan," he explained. "Your people just loved him. Never needed to send out the troops." That couldn't be said about half of Thailand's Prime Ministers.

"After the communist insurrection up North ended, I was rewarded with a plum post at what was then called the Supreme Command Headquarters," the General said. "Today they call it the Royal Thai Armed Forces Headquarters. The name change was not too long after I retired.

"It was a great opportunity. I was assigned to Intelligence because of what I learned fighting the Reds up in Isan. I worked with many

Americans, military intelligence, and CIA. No doubt it was these connections that caused my government to later send me to America as a military attaché in Washington. That's where I learned to speak your language so wel, and learned so much about America and its people. And got to see Ronald Reagan close up." I didn't have the heart to tell him I did too and didn't find it quite so exciting.

"You Americans are quite difficult to understand, but if one takes the effort and gets to know Americans, you'll find it well worth the trouble."

"That's sort of how I feel about you Thais," I said. What might have been a very slight upturn momentarily grasped the General's lips, the closest he ever comes to actually smiling. "But what does any of this have to do with the love of your life?"

"You're such an American, Glenn. Asking a question when all you have to do is sit back and listen, and the answer will come."

He was right. I listened.

AS I SAID, she worked at Headquarters. A beautiful woman, not quite two years older than me, and I must have been around thirty when we met. Have you ever had that feeling when you look a woman for the first time, and know that you won't be satisfied until you have her?"

"Just about every other day," I replied. "But I never seem to have any success."

"That's because you're an idiot who won't listen to me," the General said. "Anyway, for a young officer looking to rise up, getting involved with a married woman working for the military was not a smart idea."

"You forgot to mention that she was married," I said.

"I'm getting there. She was married to one of your people."

"A Jew?" I asked.

"No, an American. Whatever religion your countrymen follow, they are all Americans to me."

"You should be our new President," I said. "You have a much better attitude than that jackass we're soon going to have."

The General ignored me and picked up his narrative.

"The husband worked at your embassy. Supposed to be an economic adviser, but everyone at headquarters knew he was CIA. My superiors suspected she was passing sensitive information on to her husband. Of course, the Americans are our friends and allies, and we share almost everything. But not one hundred percent. We thought she was giving him the stuff we Thais like to keep to ourselves."

"Like what?" I was genuinely curious.

"Things that don't concern non-Thais. And anything sensitive about our dealing with countries with whom yours has problems, like China and Malaysia."

"And I guess North Korea as well," I said. "You guys did allow them to come here and set up shop. Make hard currency and spy. Don't you think we'd want to know things like that?" I was surprised at my own patriotism.

"Of course, I do," the General snapped. "Do you think for one minute I would have allowed any of those commie bastards to come into my country and run wild as they wish? The only good communist is a dead communist."

"Let's get back to the woman," I said.

"I HAD JUST been promoted to major when I was summoned by my direct superior, an old colonel who began his career right before the Second World War. He never got over the way the Japs occupied our country and killed Allied POWs."

It wasn't exactly an occupation. The Thai government decided that Japan passing through Thailand en route to ransack Burma beat having them ransack Thailand. Thailand went too far as to declare war on the United States. However, the Thai ambassador in Washington, D.C. refused to deliver the declaration and spent the entire war in

America as if nothing had happened. This is a very sensitive topic for Thais, among the world's most nationalistic people. It surprised me to hear the General speak so critically of that long-ago decision. I passed on a comment about the war, but I did let the General know I didn't appreciate his ethnic slur.

"We call them Japanese today," I said.

"When the Japs hold your country hostage, you can call them whatever you like," the General replied.

"Back to the woman," I said.

"Yes, back to her," the General replied. "My colonel showed me the evidence that she was passing military intelligence to her husband. It was all what you American lawyers call circumstantial. Our sources inside your Embassy were telling us that the CIA guy seemed to know an awful lot of things that were never officially transmitted, some embarrassing to important people. Businessmen. Politicians. Even military. We suspected someone was making copies, jotting down notes, once in a while even sneaking a file out and then back the next day. But we couldn't prove it, and we had to find out and stop it. She was the only person we could identify who had both access and motive."

"Weren't we going to learn all this information on our own anyway? We've been dropping the ball lately, but our defense intelligence services are still pretty good."

The General nodded.

"Yes, they are. For the time being anyway. And they could have learned it all without violating our sovereignty. That was no excuse for betraying her loyalty and acting against the best interests of the Thai nation. People could use the information to twist things around and make us look bad."

"Do you really think America would do something like that to our allies?" I asked.

The General took a moment to answer.

"Highly unlikely," he said. But, Glenn, we had to worry about more than just you people getting the information. Just as she could deliver it to your government, she could do the same to nations not so friendly to us."

"Why would she do that?"

"Many potential reasons, Glenn. Anyone who has worked in intelligence knows them all. Money. Love. Blackmail. Deception. Manipulation. If a hostile nation got wind of what she was doing, they could pressure her to do the same for them, or else reveal what she and her husband were up to. It would not end well for either, especially the woman.

"My colonel told me that I would be going undercover, and then he laughed and said he meant I would be going under the covers."

"That translates the same way in Thai?" I asked.

"You're getting good, Glenn. The colonel used the English word for 'undercover' and the rest was all Thai. Good thinking.

"The colonel figured it out. We discovered that the American husband had a young Thai girl on the side. He wasn't like you, Glenn, and he knew a good thing when he saw it. Being a *farang* man here does have its advantages. We would make sure the wife found out about it. Then they would send a dashing young officer and war hero to console her, Thai to Thai, a pretty woman betrayed."

"Where were they going to find that guy?" I asked.

"IT WAS NOT easy seducing a woman married to an embassy *farang*. My colonel set it up perfectly for me. He used his influence with the Americans to get them to hire a Thai woman as a clerk in the embassy. Needless to say, she was one of ours. No way she was going to get the truth from the wife, but she was able to gain her trust and then pass on the information that her husband was cheating on her. Her cover story was that she was having lunch at a local hotel, when out walks hubby and the younger lady, his *mia noi*. Not long after that, our plant convinced the lady to join her for a few drinks with her after work. Of course, it just happened to be where I was enjoying a martini. Claiming that we were cousins, our agent introduced me to the aggrieved wife."

"How did that go?" I asked.

"Very well," the General replied. "I told her that the Thai military was lucky to have someone with her experience, and much as we know she loved her husband and his country, America, it's always better when a Thai works with their own, and I was glad she made that choice. If what I said reached her, she showed no sign. No doubt, her CIA husband taught her a few deception tactics. It had to have some impact, though. We Thais are rather nationalistic, you might say."

"I've noticed that."

"I had the impression her only reason for betraying us was love for her husband. Or maybe she was just controlled by him. I'd find out. When the husband was back in the States for a few weeks, I made my move. Went out to dinner a few times, talked on the phone. She began to confide in me. About how bad her marriage was. Husband sounded like a real jerk. She told me a lot. Your friend would be proud of me, except it was his CIA I was spying on."

"We haven't heard hubby's side," I said. "And Rodney Snapp wasn't born yet."

The General ignored me.

"*Vesak* fell during her husband's absence. You are familiar with that holiday, as I recall."

I felt my face heat up, and it must have been tomato red because of how the General grinned at me.

"I'll never forget it," I replied. That was true. *Vesak* is the most important holiday on the Thai calendar. Sometimes I hear it described as the day The Buddha was born, but others claim it celebrates the day of his Enlightenment. I was fine with either. My uncomfortableness with *Vesak* had to do with the fact that it was the day I was dumped by my first Thai girlfriend. I thought we were in love. We spent a beautiful day at the temple, washing a statue of the Buddha, listening to monks chanting in Pali, the language of the Buddha, not spoken as a vernacular for two thousand years. We left the temple with string bracelets on our wrists and love in our hearts. Or in my heart at least.

When we returned to my condo, she told me she was going back to Isan to marry her old boyfriend. The General was the first person I met at the NJA Club the next day, and I unburdened myself to him. He was not very sympathetic.

"They're a dime a dozen," he advised me. I had learned not to try and argue with the General over his disdain for Isan people aside from Wang the cook. It rankled him that his dear *farang* friend chose an Isan woman.

But this was the General's story, not mine, so I focused on the General's story about his woman and pushed the memories of my own back into the deep caverns of my mind.

"We spent the day at a temple, and we began to open up to each other. One thing led to another, and we spent that night in an apartment my colonel had arranged for me.

"We spent many an afternoon in that apartment," the General continued. "I was doing my job, but falling in love as well. This woman was smart, sweet, and quite pretty. And amazing in bed. Many a time when we were done making love, I'd lie there and think what an assignment this was for a military officer."

"Where do I sign up, my General?"

He shook his head.

"You have to be Thai, Glenn. Sorry."

"No apology necessary, General. I understand."

"Not really," he replied. "Now allow me to continue uninterrupted."

I nodded, and he kept talking.

"ONE DAY MY colonel suggested it was time to lay our trap and see if she really was guilty as we suspected. We knew my good times had to come to an end. The lady was hinting she was ready to leave her husband for me. When we were alone in the apartment, I told her that I was tasked with a most important assignment, one that was of the highest degree of secrecy. I told her I trusted her because I loved her. Then I explained that there was a leak in our headquarters and I was expected to find it and plug it up. If successful, I was on the path to being a General. Failure meant my career was going to fail as well. I said majors were expendable in the Thai army, because there were so many of us.

"Darkness covered her face, and she began to cry. She confessed to exactly what my colonel suspected. Her husband, the cheating bastard, used her to steal from us. He never cared about her. He used her same as we did. Except I really cared about her.

"Everything she said was recorded in the little device the colonel hid in the lamp on the night table."

"Well, 'Mission Accomplished' might be appropriate," I said.

"Once again, not quite," the General said. There was a softness and hesitancy in his voice I'd never heard before.

"You see, I'd fallen in love with her. If I brought back the proof of her treachery, her life was over. The best she could hope for was decades in a Thai military prison. If I did not turn it over, it meant the mission was a failure, and this major was never making it to colonel, forget general. Maybe they would stick me in some boring clerical job, hoping I would quit the army and disappear."

This was the first time the General had ever used the word "love" in reference to a woman, at least in my presence. He wore the usual poker face, but the change in his voice and the ever-so-slight slump of his shoulders told me all I needed to know.

"So my dear General was in love at least once in his lifetime—not counting his wife," I said.

"Just make it once," he replied.

"Is that all?" I asked.

"Not quite," the General said. "That same night, she told me she was pregnant. First missed period. She stopped having relations with her husband at least two months before, when she learned of his infidelity. The father had to be me."

We sat there in silence, lips closed and eyes open, for what couldn't have been more than thirty-seconds but seemed like an hour.

"So what did you do?" I finally asked. "The woman you loved? Mother of your child?"

"I'm not telling you," he replied.

"What do you mean, you're not telling me?" I called out loudly. "You have to tell me!" For emphasis, I slapped a hand on our table, just hard enough to hear the ice in our glass clink.

A rare smile momentarily flashed across the General's face.

"You're good at figuring things out. That's what you lawyers do. Figure this one out."

"That's not fair," I said. "What kind of story is this? A story with no ending?"

The General leaned toward me and gently placed a hand on my arm.

"Glenn, everything has an end. A beginning and a middle as well. I've told you all you need to know. Figure it out. We'll talk shortly. I have to talk to my men outside." He rose from his chair and walked out of the house, bodyguard trudging faithfully behind him.

TEN MINUTES AFTER the General left, I got it. I dialed him at once.

"You figured it out a little sooner than I thought," the General said. He held a bag in his hand. "I had one of my men run out and get you some street food. I always enjoyed eating a little something after a battle."

He laid the dishes out on the table. Street food, especially where Thais buy, is excellent. Genuine Thai, not the toned-down slop one finds all too often along lower Sukhumvit. An order of *som tum thai* the spicy papaya salad—to me, national dish—sat before me. The General knew how much I loved real *som tum thai*, the spicier the better. A plate of diced chicken with basil lay a few inches to its side. A handful of sticky rice was wrapped in paper. I didn't realize how hungry I was until I began scarfing it down.

"You always remember," the General said as I sat and just before shoveling down a mouthful of the salad.

"You may never have learned how to speak like a Thai, but you surely have learned how to eat like one," the General said.

I wiped my mouth clean before speaking.

"Your wife is not the mother of your son."

"It's only you, Wang, and my colonel who know," the General said.

"I figured it out, but there are still some things missing. How did it end?" I asked. He explained.

"My colonel was not a vindictive man and had no interest in punishing a Thai woman used and betrayed by a *farang*. Then again, in a sense, by her own country. Through the young major's efforts, my colonel confirmed to his superiors that an American intelligence officer, operating out of the US Embassy, was using his Thai wife's trusted position to steal information that was none of their business. Of course, he and his aide put an end to it. The colonel became a general, and the young major, who actually broke the case, replaced him as colonel. The newly minted colonel asked only that the woman —whom he now described as his agent—be spared any punishment, to which the newly minted general was happy to comply. As we know, Thais are not a vengeful people."

"Tell that to some of my ex-girlfriends," I said. The General continued.

"Our reports stated that she had been turned by me and had provided us with valuable information, not just about her husband's actions but a lot more. She probably didn't even realize how much she gave us just by providing names, dates places, physical descriptions of people. Things we would have never known otherwise."

"What about the husband?" I asked.

"He was transferred to be an intelligence liaison assisting Thai forces in the South," the General said. "Sadly, he was killed in action when Muslim guerrillas ambushed the Thai patrol he was with. We posthumously awarded him a medal."

The sixth sense possessed by all criminal trial lawyers flashed a message that something was not kosher.

"May I inquire as to how many Thai soldiers died in that incident?"

"None, fortunately," the General replied.

"Any casualties on the other side?" I asked.

"None that I know of," he said. "But of course, we may have wounded a few, perhaps some even fatally."

"Perhaps," I said.

"General, that wasn't right," I continued. "You didn't have to have a man killed to steal his wife. Have you never heard of divorce?"

The General laughed.

"Did your King David ever hear of divorce when he sent Bathsheba's husband off to the front lines, knowing he'd be killed? All because he wanted Bathsheba?"

The General keeps surprising me with his knowledge of the West.

"You've read our scriptures? The whole Judeo-Christian thing?"

"Just the Old Testament," he said. "I have no interest in what the Christians have to say. They're always trying to convert us. We can't stand it."

"My people are with you on that one, General."

We sat in silence for a few seconds more.

"Tell me what tipped you off," he asked.

"You always mention your son. You've told me a few little nuggets. He takes after his old man when it comes to *mia noi*. He helps out in whatever business you do, and I don't even want to know. He drives a Mercedes and has a Hummer, just like you.

"You never talk about your wife. You only mention your son. You never mention any other children. I don't know if you have any, and I don't think your wife wants anything to do with the seed of the only woman you ever loved. Since the woman you loved is the mystery lady from the past, and not your wife, my guess is you married for money. You're just a tough nut to crack."

The General sighed.

"My colonel, actually then my general, could save the woman, but the two of us being together was impossible. A young officer with a good career ahead of him could not marry the widow of an American spy, for whom she stole sensitive documents from her own government. If I wanted her that badly, I'd have to resign my commission."

"Which you were not about to do," I said. "Not even for love."

"Of course not," the General replied. "I was a soldier, a commissioned officer in the Royal Thai Army. My sworn duty was to defend our King and Kingdom. There is no walking away from that oath, not even for a good reason. Not even for love, as you say."

His drink arrived, and the General looked into it before taking a long sip.

"As far as the world knew, the child, a boy, would be the seed of her late husband. He could have obtained American citizenship, but he didn't. I think that was part of the deal to let the woman off with no punishment. And I was not to see him until he was twenty-one years old. By that time, all wounds had healed, and I could acknowledge my own offspring. The Army understandably wanted to bury this one, where no one came out looking good."

"I don't get why they didn't want you to see the kid," I said. "Why would they want to punish you?"

"There was no intent to punish me, Glenn. On the contrary, they were trying to protect me. I was in love, which could have clouded my judgment. My superiors understood that she was a woman who had betrayed her country, and her marriage vows, and she could do it again. They were willing to spare her for my sake, but they didn't want her anywhere near a rising star who was going to have access to a lot of top-secret material. They were right, you know.

"The Royal Thai Army is honorable, Glenn. You *farangs* might hear different, but I tell you almost everyone in it is a person of honor. Our oath is to protect our King and Kingdom, and that is our reason for being. Yes, we have some bad people in our army, but so do you. I am reading about your President's National Security Advisor, a retired four-star general. He seems to be a traitor, working for the Russians against America. We all have our disgraces, Glenn."

"No argument," I said.

"My colonel, who was soon a general, made sure my son had whatever he needed. They got the woman a job somewhere, and put whatever she needed in her bank account. I assume she was smart enough to just take the money and shut up. In the meantime, I had to find a wife. Marrying into a good family would give me the stature to hasten my rise in the military and fulfill my dream of being a general. It would also allow me the financial freedom and resources I needed to make sure that happened. It wasn't a marriage for love, Glenn. I feel somewhat bad about this, but I gave up love for my country, so maybe if it gave me money and a generalship, it's a fair exchange."

"How has your wife handled your having a son by someone else?" I asked.

"My wife has barely acknowledged that I have a son. She never wanted anything around that might remind me of his mother. She's barely mentioned him over all these years, and we never talk about my relationship with him today. For the first twenty-one years of his life, I couldn't see him, but there was never any doubt in my mind that we would someday become father and son. My wife and I do have a daughter, so it's not as if she got nothing out of the marriage. And she enjoyed the perks of being a general's wife. I'm the one who suffered, not seeing my son all those years." That was the first I ever heard about a daughter.

"Obviously, you and your son were reunited," I said.

"Yes," the General said softly. "About a dozen years ago, when my son reached the age of twenty-one, my colonel—I mean general—set up a meeting between us. Up until then, my son had believed his father was a soldier killed fighting Muslim guerrillas down South. Now we are very close, like father and son should be. He works with me, and someday, he'll inherit most of what I own. I'm going to leave my wife the house off Soi 16, and plenty of money, not that she needs it. Same for my daughter, to whom I will leave money and a few luxury cars. She is married to a very rich man and needs nothing more from me. She'll get everything that my wife can leave her. Neither of my children will ever have to worry about money. So maybe now you won't judge me so harshly for my *mia noi*. Life is never as simple and clear as you Americans make it out to be."

Of course, that wouldn't explain why his son needed *mia noi*, or why so many rich Thai men who don't have a rift between a wife and a son, and married women they love, also enjoy younger women on the side. They just don't have as compelling a story as the General.

"Did you ever see the woman again?" I asked.

"Now that's a story for a different day," the General said.

THE GENERAL KEPT his word. He showed me a new side, one that helped me understand him better. Not the tough, secretive but honorable man I knew. He revealed a man who was consumed for decades by an obsession to be a father to the son he abandoned. Today, the obsession had been transformed into a burning desire to make up for the lost time, if that can be done. Throughout this, the General has wallowed in a loveless marriage, albeit of his own making for his own benefit. Meeting and bonding with his son brought him a joy he had not experienced since his time with the son's mother. The General was happy. In the end, isn't that what every one of us wants? All of us are just beings with feelings and yearnings. The General probably spent all these years at the NJA Club for the same reason as mine. I was honored that a Thai man, and such a prominent one, would share his deepest and most heartfelt secrets to a *farang* like me. Or maybe there were no *farangs* like me.

The General did not allow me much time to reflect on any of this. "Now let's hear your story."

25

THIS TIME, MY story was not from my life as a lawyer. I drew on that part the first time we traded stories. This time, I dug deeper into my past.

"When I was growing up in New York City, there was a kid in the neighborhood named Max Flugel, but we called him Weasel. He was the most unlikable person I ever met, prior to Gordon Planter."

"Must be quite a bastard to be called Weasel," the General said.

"And that was what his friends called him," I replied.

I told him how Weasel assembled a knot of bullies by inviting them to parties at his home on the frequent occasions his parents were out of town. I was never invited, but he did sic his bullies on me a few times. On other occasions, he would try to goad me into a fight, knowing that the second I got the upper hand, the bullies would jump in and beat me to a pulp. I'd witnessed it happen to others. So, when this occurred, I had no choice but to back away. I wouldn't mind a beating if I could get in a few shots at Weasel's ugly puss, but the bullies would never allow that to happen.

Weasel's modus operandi went like this: he would wait until he was holding court in public, surrounded by his willing bullies. He would challenge some unfortunate to a fight, very often me. The chosen ones were well aware that if they dared land a blow on Weasel, the mob of bullies would be on them in a moment, pounding away like human jackhammers. Weasel would be standing on the side laughing. Everyone learned that to avoid pain, let Weasel win the fight. He was a weakling whose punches were not much stronger than a young girl's, so that wasn't going to hurt very much. It was the humiliation of being forced to let him get away with this that hurt, not his pitiful punches.

"Weasel sounds like some Thai guys I've run into," the General said. "Let them try that with a real soldier," he added. "We could take out five of them at a time. Maybe more."

"Well, I couldn't," I said. "But one day, circumstances went my way."

The General seemed excited.

"Really? Tell me about it," he said.

"That's what I'm trying to do. Just sit back and listen."

I explained that one day, in my senior year of high school, I wound up hanging out at the apartment of my friend Tony Bernelli; this time, it was his parents who were out of town. We were watching the Mets play the Giants.

Besides Tony and me, my good friends Shaul and Horse were there, along with Tony's older brother Frank, and their next-door neighbor Eddie. Frank Bernelli was six years older than Tony and me, and had just been honorably discharged from the Marines. Before enlisting right out of high school, he was the finest athlete our neighborhood ever produced. He was also a really nice guy, the way accomplished people often are. It's more often punks and cowards like Weasel who are unlikeable in every way. Football, baseball, basketball, Frank Bernelli was the best. Back in America, whenever you bumped into someone from the old neighborhood, we'd share a Frank Bernelli memory. ("I'll never forget that touchdown against that Catholic school . . . ten seconds left and he throws thirty yards.") I never understood why he couldn't play some sport in some college somewhere. Maybe he just wanted to be a Marine.

Weasel came by with one of his goons sometime in the middle of the first inning. The goon was named Kenny Pelko, a beady-eyed psychopath known for jumping people from behind or punching them in the stomach without any warning. I once overheard my mother tell a neighbor that Kenny Pelko was seeing a psychiatrist. It didn't surprise me. With Pelko around, Weasel needed no other assistance. The neighbor said she'd heard that they wanted to give Pelko some sort of drug to restrain him before he hurt someone really badly. To my relief, Pelko left right after the third inning.

Weasel was a die-hard Giants fan, even though the team left New York before he was born. I lived and died for the Mets. When we pulled ahead by a run, thanks to an error by the Giant's right fielder, I couldn't contain myself and let out a whoop loud enough to be heard blocks away.

Weasel turned to me and told me to shut up. I let out another whoop.

"I see it's gonna take a beating to get you to shut up," he said. "Is that what it's going to take to make you stop?" he asked.

"I guess, so, Weasel," I replied and stood up to approach him. He rose as well, looked to his left and right, and realized that his bodyguard, crazy Kenny Pelko, was gone. He took a step back.

"I'll let you off this one time only," he said.

"Fuck you" was my reply, as I delivered a right hook stronger than I thought possible. I haven't thrown a punch like that until I cold-cocked that poor plumber. It connected with the left side of Weasel's face, and he fell to the floor. As he struggled to stand erect again, I hit him with a jab under the chin and back down he went. I sat on top of Weasel and punched him once more in the face, ready to make hamburger out of that ugly puss. I felt two strong hands grab my shoulders and pull me off Weasel, who was bleeding from the mouth and nose, trying to act like it didn't hurt. Tony's hands pulled me away.

"What the hell are you doing, Tony?" I screamed. "This little prick is getting his due!"

Tony and Frank led me into the bedroom they shared and gently pushed me to sit on a bed.

"That was a hell of a right hook, and the jab wasn't half bad, either," Frank Bernelli said. Tony agreed.

"From now on, I'm calling you 'Poke,'" Tony said. "Way you poked that son of a bitch. He had it coming, that's for sure."

"Then why did you yank me off him just when I was getting started?"

Tony put his arm on my shoulder.

"Because this guy is a punk, and if you hurt him bad enough, left some marks, word got around, hey, sooner or later you're gonna have to pass Weasel and his gang. You know what that can be like."

"It will happen anyway," I said.

Frank held up a hand.

"No, it won't. Last thing a punk like Weasel wants going around is that you kicked his ass. Three punches on the floor. Hey, his nosebleed and split lip will be gone tomorrow, and none of us are going to say a word. I'll make sure Weasel is on board. After he cleans up." I would have loved to have been the fly on the wall when Frank Bernelli told this to Weasel. Whatever it was, it worked.

I explained to the General how I was angry for a few weeks, but then, after passing Weasel and his cronies without incident several times, I understood the Bernelli brothers.

"Interesting," the General said when he realized I was finished. "Never would think you were a boxer. Well, maybe that's why you study our Muay Thai. Just don't go knocking out any more plumbers," he said.

We sat in silence for about ten seconds.

"I did get the point, Glenn."

"Tell me then, my dear General. What was the point?"

"You showed Weasel you could hurt him any time his gang wasn't around. Like your great boxing champion, Mr. Joe Louis said, 'You can run, but you can't hide.' It was important to you that Weasel accept this, which he did. You had no further trouble with him or his gang. That too was something important to you. You got everything you wanted, and he got nothing but a little embarrassment and banged-up face. That's quite a win, I'd say."

The General's insights impressed me.

"But next time, tell me another one of those courtroom stories," the General said. "Love that Perry Mason stuff. Always watched *L.A. Law*, too."

There was nothing more to say. There wouldn't have been time anyway, because Rodney and Ling walked through the door.

26

"DON'T YOU EVER get hot wearing a suit and tie in Bangkok's heat?" I asked Ling when we were seated at the big table in the dining room. He ignored the comment. Rodney spoke.

"We're taking you and Cho to the embassy. Actually, a subbasement of the embassy. We want to make sure we are safe and our discussions secure. You and Ling will go over the paperwork, and one of our North Korea experts will interview your client."

"I thought he was the North Korea expert," I said, tossing a thumb in Ling's direction.

"He is, but for the State Department," Rodney replied. "We CIA folks like to use our own. Different perspective. I'm sure you understand."

"Is this sub-basement one of those where they torture people?" I asked. I liked Rodney but not the CIA.

"Oh, no," he said. "That one's in a different part of town. Couldn't have it on US soil. As a lawyer, I'm sure you understand."

"Not really," I said. "I'll leave that legal niche to our friend Ling." Ling's face grew dark.

"I'm with State, not CIA!" he exclaimed. I looked at Rodney.

"You see? Nobody likes you guys."

"Except for North Korean defectors," Rodney said as he stood up. "Now let's get over to the good old USA."

Cho and I walked out the broken door, toward a dark van parked by the front gate. Wang stood off to the side, a cigarette in one hand, the other steadying the automatic rifle cradled in his elbow.

"Won't the police respond to all that shooting? Maybe even the army?" I asked Rodney as we climbed into the van.

"I think the General has that under control," he replied.

The van did not turn left toward Sukhumvit. Instead, it turned right, and then right again, making its way through narrow side *sois* lined with older apartments and storefronts selling food, clothing, auto parts, cosmetics, and pirated DVDs. Massage parlors and salons alternated among the storefronts.

Ten minutes into our meandering, the driver turned left and we cruised along Wireless Road, an upscale boulevard filled with foreign embassies, including the largest, the US. We passed our embassy, and a few blocks later the van turned into a side *soi*, then another, going in the direction we had come from. A few hundred meters later, the van turned into a driveway and wound its way deep into a basement. We parked next to a steel door. Rodney looked into a camera by the side, and the door opened. We walked down a flight of stairs.

"Securest sub-basement in Bangkok," Rodney said as we walked down. "They haven't invented the eavesdropping device that can pierce this baby."

"What about your CIA sub-basement?" I asked.

"What CIA sub-basement? There's none here in Bangkok." He smiled.

Another door greeted us at the bottom. Rodney pressed his palm against a black rectangle above the knob, and the door opened into a room with a table and a half dozen chairs around it. A rolling table with thermoses, bottled water, and several kinds of sandwiches sat against a wall.

"Everything brought in from home," Ling said. "We've even got some real pizza if you want it."

I motioned for Cho to sit. She eyed a sandwich. Rodney reached over, put one on a plate, and handed it to her.

"Roast beef," he said. "Hope you like it. Can I offer you some coffee?" She nodded.

"I was able to get all the American food I wanted back in Pyong-yang," Cho said. "There are restaurants for the connected."

"Well, you won't be welcome there anymore," Ling said. "Right now, we just want to get some more basic information, and then our North Korea intelligence expert will talk to you. Your lawyer will be here with you the entire time."

I smiled at Cho. She did not smile back.

"That won't be necessary," she said. "I'm quite confident I can handle this on my own."

Rodney shook his head.

"No, you can't. Some of our people can be just as duplicitous as yours. The difference is we have laws and lawyers to protect you. That's Glenn's job to make sure no one in our government pulls a Kim and reneges on a deal." Cho's jaw moved a centimeter at the mention of the name of the leader she was deserting.

We ate our sandwiches and drank coffee. When we were done, I opened my briefcase and handed Rodney the asylum application. He looked at it for a few seconds before taking it.

"This really isn't necessary," he said. "You've already been assured that we're paroling her into the US, where we expect asylum to be granted."

"I believe it was your advice to not trust the Department of Justice or Homeland Security," I replied.

Rodney glanced at the application before shoving it into his own briefcase. "We're not planning to do this in the ordinary course of business," he said.

"I understand, and I don't doubt your good intentions, or of the Department of State. But other departments of government may not want to honor your promises, and that's why she needs me. I'm just trying to make sure no one can later say that my client is fabricating a recent claim of fear if any of your fellow agencies go sideways on us."

Rodney looked at Cho and smiled.

"Now you see why I wanted him on your side," he said, nodding in my direction.

"So your government really is not all that different from mine," Cho said. "Except for the lawyers."

LING'S QUESTIONS TO Cho were pretty much along the lines of what he had asked her earlier that day at the General's safe house. He went into greater depth about matters that still seemed trivial to me, like which diplomats frequented certain restaurants, what kind of cars certain government officials drove, and whatever gossip he could pry from her about Pyongyang's elite. I'm sure Ling had good reasons for asking.

Rodney asked fewer questions, but all were precise and aimed at specifics. Cho said she knew nothing about the American drug-dealing operation, but Rodney asked how the top people paid for their fancy imported luxuries, and how overseas intelligence officers received necessary funds. Rodney's job was to track the bad guys and their money. It was clear to me he didn't believe her denials.

It was close to midnight when Rodney told us they were finished with Cho, and we would meet the CIA North Korea expert.

"It's midnight," I said. "I think my client needs a good night's sleep. So do I, come to think of it."

"It'll just take an hour or so," Ling said. "Introductory stuff. We can get you some fresh coffee if you'd like." He and Rodney left the room.

THE NORTH KOREA expert gave his name as Dawson. He didn't look CIA at all. Long black hair tumbled over his ears and collar, and an unkempt beard the texture of steel wool sprouted from his face. He spoke in a slow and deep voice, first used to address Cho in Korean.

"He has the accent down perfectly, and if he called Pyongyang, they'd think he was a native," she said.

"Why don't you tell him what I told you?" Dawson asked.

"You said you knew all about my father. That he was a good man who tried his best to help his country in the face of all the insanity. You said he would want me to help America and live there."

"Is he right?" I asked.

"There is a reason they call him the North Korea expert," she said. Cho and I signed papers swearing not to tell a soul anything discussed in that room. I had no plans to do so and eagerly scrawled my name, as did Cho. Dawson spent the next hour going over the same things Cho had been asked first by Oliver and then Ling. I was growing more bored than I thought possible, listening to them once again discuss streets and meeting places in Pyongyang, the details of operating overseas restaurants, and more of Cho's days in Beijing. At least, she said the same thing every time. Then the questions shifted back to Cho's father.

"Your father had a lot of issues with his government, didn't he?"

Cho's body stiffened ever so slightly.

"I see no reason to speak of my father," she said.

"But I do," Dawson replied. "Your father spent his entire life fighting for his people. He was a decorated officer in the Korean War, barely twenty years old. He went on at least three overseas missions to Africa to train troops your leaders hoped might become allies. He was utterly loyal to the state. But he didn't like those slave labor camps very much. Especially when they grabbed people he'd fought with. He intervened many times to save those he thought were unfairly swept up. He was one of a handful of people in the country who could broach such subjects with the leader or their top aides, and usually get what he wanted."

Cho sat in silence and stillness.

"As long as good old Kim Il Sung and Kim Jong Il were running the show, your father was safe, because they understood that he might be unhappy, might grumble, but he remained totally dedicated to your communist system."

There was not a sign that Cho even heard this. She sat there like a street performer impersonating a statue.

"Then that crazy kid took power. And Kim Jong Un doesn't give a rat's ass about what his father and grandfather thought. The first two heads of the dynasty might have allowed the most minimal expression of a different opinion by a famous war hero, but not this little fat boy. One wrong word and it's the anti-aircraft guns trained on you."

Still not a sign of life from Ms. Cho. Dawson continued.

"This little prick would love to wipe your father off the face of the earth, because if there were any traces of humanity or loyalty left over from the first two Kims, Number Three didn't inherit any. The brat feared that a senior and respected officer like your father might be listened to if he complained loud enough. Others might agree, especially when the kid's brutality made the first two Kims look like humanitarians.

"But the little jerk knew he couldn't treat your father the same way he treated his uncle or others he killed out of fear. Your father helped the careers of just about every person in the inner circle, and over the years, many had implored him to use his influence to help friends and family swallowed up in your gulags. He did, and this made him a lot of powerful friends. Even in North Korea, there are political factions, and one hand washes the other. And all of the hands on either side have firepower. So Little Fat Boy had a real problem on his hands. If he left your father alone, he might slowly undermine the Kim Jong Un regime. If he killed your father, that might spark the coup Rocket Man fears twenty-four seven."

Aside from an occasional blink, Cho did not move a muscle.

"But our little man is nothing if not clever, and even less of nothing if not diabolical. Leave it to him to come up with a solution."

I wondered if Cho was even breathing.

"Send the daughter overseas on some most delicate missions. Keep the father under unofficial house arrest, nothing at all like the gulags, of course. He is, after all, a member of the ruling elite, and this was business for Little Kim, nothing personal. So long as the daughter served Kim well, the father was safe, probably be released to live out a graceful retirement. But if the daughter were to fail, or even think of defecting."

Cho got up from her chair, straightened herself out to stand at her full height of five foot five. I spotted her as pretty the first time I saw her, but close up and stretching, she was beautiful. There was a smoldering sexuality that even a lifetime as a North Korean communist could not extinguish. As Sleepy Joe noted, who knew commies could be so hot? Hot and cool manner at the same time.

"How do you know all of this?" she asked.

"You called me the expert," Dawson replied.

Dawson noted Cho's father was barely twenty during the Korean War. He would be well into his eighties by now.

"We have people in Pyongyang," Dawson said. "You know we do, because every few years, you catch a few and murder them. Maybe I shouldn't include you in that crowd anymore. Certainly not your father. He wanted his country to become a normal nation that was part of the world community. He was never a fan of isolation."

"My father had nothing to do with any of this. It is my decision to defect," Cho said. She was struggling to remain calm, but even the thickest ice will crack when the heat gets high enough.

"We know that, but does it make any difference to the regime?" Dawson asked. "It's not he they would be punishing. It would be you."

"Are you telling me they would hurt my father? He's eighty-four years old. He is a hero in my country."

"They can't hurt him now," Dawson replied. "We had one of our people get word to him that you were Public Enemy Number Two in North Korea. Gordon Planter is number one right now."

"Why did you have to bring my father into this?" Cho cried out, speaking louder and faster than before. "Isn't it bad enough you dragged me in?"

Dawson smiled.

"Dragged you in? Ms. Cho, if my facts are correct, your people tried to kill Glenn and his friends. Glenn made a peace offer, came to your place to speak candidly and avoid bloodshed, and how did you folks respond? You tried to kill Sleepy Joe and kidnap Glenn. When you realized you screwed up big time, you made the wise decision that if you can't beat them, join them. We're happy to have you aboard, and from now on, life will be very good to you."

"And my father?"

Dawson took his cell phone from his briefcase.

"Let him explain it himself," Dawson said, and a voice speaking in Korean poured out from the phone.

THE VOICE SPOKE for less than one minute. As the recording played, the look on Cho's face grew darker, and halfway through, she slumped forward on the table, folded her arms, and buried her head in the crooks of her elbows. Her sobs filled the small, windowless room.

"What did he say?" I asked Dawson when Cho stopped crying and raised herself back to seated position.

"Her father explained that he chose to take his life so that there would be nothing left for Kim to hold over her. It was painless, a fast-acting poison. She is now free to act as she pleases. Kim no longer has a hold on her. Her father's last message to her says that all his life he tried to do what was right for his country, but it went wrong in a bad way. He asked her to stay alive so that she might tell the truth. He told her that she can trust the Americans, just as he had. There are many Korean people in America and the rest of her life will be good."

"He was a spy the whole time," she said. "How else would an American agent be visiting him? I suppose your people gave him the poison."

"Actually, no," Dawson said softly. "Many high-level Koreans carry a secret stash of such poison in case the regime turns on them. Better than torture or being blown to bits by an anti-aircraft gun."

Cho leaned across the table, bringing her face less than a foot from

Dawson's.

"I've heard that South Koreans don't like people from the North. Is that how it is in America?"

Rodney smiled and patted her hand. She quickly pulled it away.

"Some do, some don't. But it doesn't matter, because the identity we are creating for you makes you a South Korean. You'll have all the documents needed, if anyone ever asks for them. And we'll give you enough details to fool anyone."

Cho nodded.

"As I expected," she said. "But right now, I'd like to be alone. I have much to process, as you Americans say."

"We'll take you to your temporary quarters," Dawson replied. "You'll be staying there for a few days, until we finish these interviews. Then you fly off to the US for a new life." He turned to the wall behind him, reached over and pressed a button. Not more than twenty-seconds later, a woman wearing a military field uniform without any insignias entered the room. She wore a stone face that rivaled the General's. Dawson spoke to her.

"Ms. Kennedy, would you please escort Ms. Cho to her quarters, and make sure she gets whatever she wants? We'll see you later," he said, turning to Cho.

Cho stood without saying a word and followed Ms. Kennedy out of the interview room. The door closed automatically.

"Who is she with?" I asked Rodney when we were alone.

"You don't want to know," he said. And no, her real name is not Kennedy."

"How did you know that's what I was thinking?" I asked.

"Because I'm an expert," he said.

DAWSON TOLD ME he had to leave, but not to worry; I'd be taken to a safe place until the North Koreans were dealt with. I didn't ask what "dealt with" meant, nor did I really care. I was worried about

Cho, my friends, even Gordon. Oh, yes, myself as well.

My concerns were interrupted when Rodney Snapp entered the room. He wore a new well-tailored suit and a red-and-blue tie.

"Meeting the ambassador?" I asked.

"Not quite, he replied. "But like I've been saying, you're on the right track. You're a natural, and the job offer still stands. Actually, I'm off to meet a bunch of Iranians, who think they can bribe a deputy consul into giving them visas. All they are going to get is a ticket to the nice little interrogation center we run near here, courtesy of our Thai friends."

"Terrorists?" I asked.

"One way or the other, they are up to no good. As for the exact details, we'll get them after a few days at the center." He shook his head slightly as if he were somewhat sorry, but I didn't think he was.

"Being as we're old friends," I said, "can you maybe fill me in on where I'm going to be stashed until this all blows over? And while you're at it, explain how it gets blown over and what that means. Oh, yeah, and what's happening to my other old friend, Gordon Planter?"

Rodney slipped into the seat Dawson had vacated and, elbows on the table, clasped his hands to form a triangle. A perfect isosceles triangle. It seemed that everything Rodney Snapp did was perfect.

"You'll be staying for a few days at our little guest center," he said. He must have caught the look on my face.

"Don't worry," he said. "You won't see, hear, or smell any of our intelligence gathering, or be near it. We have some very nice guest apartments, and I've made it clear that you are to get the best one. Anything you want, you just ask for it. Even women, though I know from meeting you and reading your profile, that it's unlikely we'll be bringing in one of our hookers."

I didn't know what bothered me more: the government having its own hookers or having a profile on me.

"Oh, and lest I forget," Rodney continued, "needless to say, we can provide you with all the weed you want. Top quality. Just ask."

"Don't you guys work hand-in-hand with the DEA?" I asked. "How would they look at you getting weed for a friend?"

"Who do you think I'm getting it from?" he replied. "That's how I know it's the best in the world. Might even stop by your little hide-away for a few tokes." Then he rose from his chair and motioned for me to follow.

27

RODNEY DID NOT exaggerate in his description of my quarters. A one-bedroom suite with a bar, kitchenette, flat screen on the wall, slippers and robe in the closet.

"There's a phone on the desk," Rodney said. "A menu right next to it. Anytime you want anything, pick up the phone. We tried to get you some clothes that matched your style. If you don't like anything, call and we'll get it."

"How much clothing will I need? How long do you expect to keep me here?"

Rodney handed me the key card.

"You'll need this to get back in and to get into the gym down the hall." Then he left.

I looked in the closet. It was filled with clothing. Shirts, pants, shoes, socks, underwear, suits, ties, sweats. They did look like the stuff in my closet. Too much clothing for just an overnight stay.

I turned on the television. A few clicks on the channel button, and I was watching CNN. The news was the same as always, so I flipped through the channels until I found the music choices. I settled on a classic rock station. Led Zeppelin's "Dazed and Confused" blared throughout the speakers. A most appropriate song.

A few numbers later, I felt the first pangs of hunger. I didn't feel like studying the menu. Instead, I picked up the phone and ordered a burger, fries, and a Coke. This was America, after all.

I was grooving on the Stones' version of "Love in Vain" when someone knocked on the door. Rodney Snapp was holding a tray with my food.

"They really get their money's worth out of you," I said as he set my meal down on the little table in the kitchen and sat down. I joined him.

"I brought you a little housewarming gift," he said as I squirted ketchup on my burger and fries. He dropped a little baggie onto my lap. It must have held an ounce of buds and a pack of rolling papers with a lighter.

"Always keep my promise," he said.

The burger was good. I swallowed a large bite before asking my question.

"How long am I supposed to be here?"

Rodney smiled.

"No more than a week," he said. "Probably not more than a few days. By then, the coast will be clear. Everyone will be happy, North Koreans included. Oh, maybe your friend Gordon excepted."

"What am I supposed to do here all that time?" I asked. "I can get stoned and listen to music at home. Have food delivered too."

Rodney pinched a French fry.

"You can always consult with your client. She's in the next apartment."

I ASSUMED THE knocking on my door was Cho. Were it the government, since I didn't answer, they'd barge into the room. In the high-stakes game they were playing, an unresponsive Glenn would mean trouble.

I dialed the room phone and asked for Rodney. Two minutes later, he called. To my surprise, he readily agreed to get Charlie on my line.

"Ten minutes and he'll be with you. Sit right," he advised. He was a man of his word.

"You're becoming a regular caller," Charlie began.

"Well, who can blame me? When a lawyer has a question about professional ethics, who better to ask than you?"

"Are you implying that I am ethically deficient?" he asked, in mock outrage.

"Ethically lacking would be a better description," I said. Then I asked him about the California State Bar rules on lawyers sleeping with clients.

"We don't prohibit it outright," Charlie explained. "The test is whether the attorney-client relationship is adversely impacted." I told him this involved an application for political asylum that had been submitted and was pending.

"I would stay away from sleeping with her," Charlie said. "We're talking about a refugee, fleeing persecution, seeking asylum in the US. Needs you to get it for her. Sounds like this could never be seen as a truly voluntary and consensual relationship. But once she's granted asylum, no problem. That's what you were hired to do, and once it's done, she's no longer your client. Just make sure that's made clear."

I thanked him for his advice and told him to send me a bill. He laughed.

"How come none of my clients ever want to sleep with me? Am I not likable?" he asked.

"Charlie, you're likable enough," I said. We said goodbye.

It dawned on me that Charlie had not asked or said a thing about Gordon.

I STAYED IN the guest apartment for two more days. Both days, I was taken out to a pleasant yard with high brick walls, where I passed a few hours reading, listening to music or radio, and eating lunch. I called twice to ask Rodney when I could leave, and both times he assured me it would be soon. I took that to mean there was a count-down on Gordon's life. It troubled me, but then again, I wanted my own life back.

On the morning of the third day, Rodney came to see me.

"The asylum application you submitted has been reviewed, and I'm pleased to inform you that the application has been granted. He handed me a manila envelope. The paperwork is all in here. Make sure you explain it to your client. Or should I say your former client," he added with a wink.

"You bastard," I said. "Listening in to my conversation with Charlie!"

"Well, I am CIA, aren't I?" he replied. I looked into the envelope, saw a sheaf of papers, and when I looked up again, Rodney was gone. Just disappeared, as he'd done so often in the past. Someday I'll figure out how.

I made myself a cup of coffee and sat down to study the papers so I could advise Cho. When I was done, I brought them with me down the hall and knocked on her door.

WHEN I RETURNED to my own guest apartment the next afternoon, Rodney was waiting for me, seated at the kitchen table, sipping coffee.

"It's done. You're free," he said. "We're taking you home in about ten minutes."

A lead ball sank to the bottom of my stomach. I couldn't force any words out of my mouth.

"Where is Gordon?" I was finally able to ask.

"I wouldn't be much of a secret agent if I revealed my secrets, would I?" Rodney asked.

The lead ball settled, and it became easier to speak.

"In that case, I'm not leaving until you tell me."

"Suit yourself," Rodney said as he carefully picked his suit jacket from the back of the chair and put it on. "It doesn't cost us anything to keep you here. And the promise of weed is still good." This time, I watched him leave. He opened the door, walked through, and closed it, just like anyone else.

Thirty seconds later, he walked back in.

"That was just a test," he said. "You passed. I'm telling you, Glenn, you really ought to reconsider that job offer. It's always outstanding. We could really use you."

"I'd rather be in a North Korean labor camp," I said.

Rodney laughed.

"We could arrange that, if you'd like. But because you passed our little test just now, we are going to let you know what happened to Gordon. You must first promise never to tell anyone, not even your closest friends at the NJA Club."

"I'll be as tightlipped as an Aldebaran shellmouth," I said.

"Captain Kirk, original *Star Trek* series, circa 1966," Rodney countered.

He then explained how Gordon was to be taken to a secure location in America, someplace no one would ever think of looking, and given a new identity. "After we finish debriefing him," he said. "Only the CIA and you know the truth. Your friends will think he died in North Korea, and the rest of the world, if they care, will think he's just some grifter who disappeared under suspicion of fraud and murder of his wife. That's if anyone still cares."

That's when it dawned on me.

"You were never going to allow Gordon to be handed over to the North Koreans," I said. "Certainly not when he had all that knowledge about North Korean drug operations in America, and how their agents communicated. And you couldn't turn him over after you squeezed him like a lemon, because then the North Koreans would learn about your intelligence gathering and interrogation techniques. Once Oliver got in touch with you guys, the General and the others realized they weren't going to be able to cut any deal with the communists on their own that allowed us to get out alive. You guys took over, and the North Koreans knew this was the best they could do."

Rodney smiled and patted me on the back.

"Once again, you prove me right. When are you getting off your high horse and coming to work for us?"

"When Phil Funston stops being an obnoxious pain in the ass," I muttered. Rodney must have picked up every word.

"The bald guy from the Club?" Rodney asked. "Musician? Want him to disappear? Consider it done. Shame though, guy's a hell of a blues guitarist."

I started to speak, when Rodney cut me short.

"Relax, I was only kidding. What kind of people do you think we are?"

"The kind I never want to see again," I said.

"Well, I'm afraid to disappoint you," he said. "I'm driving you home, and I'm coming by tomorrow with the money."

"The money?"

"Have you forgotten?" he asked. "Your government is prepared to pay you for your excellent services in providing us with two important North Korean agents and a cell phone to boot."

"How much?"

"A million dollars," Rodney said. "Same as last time. We like working with round numbers."

I had one more question for Rodney.

"Why would the North Koreans agree to such a deal? No Gordon? No Cho? Just a useless phone?"

Rodney shook his head.

"Because the General promised not to blow up their restaurants and embassy, and not to kill every North Korean in Thailand. And they've seen your friend Sleepy Joe and his girlfriend Nahmwan at work, so no doubt they're happy to cut their losses and maintain a way to rake in some hard currency and intelligence. They're not as crazy as you think. In their own way, they're very strategic."

"And you guys don't mind, because I bet you score intelligence at that restaurant."

"How right I am about you," Rodney said. "You were born to be CIA."

When we were walking to the car, I asked Rodney where Cho

would be living.

"That, my friend, is top secret, and even if you join us, you'll never find out. Rest assured, she will enjoy a good life, be safe and sound, never want for anything. It's just that you will never be able to see her again. And neither you nor your friends are to ever mention a word about Cho or anything else about this little adventure. You will keep especially quiet about Gordon not being turned over. If word got out that he's alive, we'd have to act."

"Can I at least say goodbye to Cho before she leaves for America?"

"You're too late for that, Glenn. She's being driven to an airport for a flight to the USA. right now."

"Story of my life," I said under my breath.

"What was that?" he asked.

"Oh, I just said she was really a great client."

As Rodney escorted me to the garage, a small knot of people coming from the opposite direction turned toward the same door. When they were ten feet in front of us, I saw Gordon Planter walking slowly amidst a phalanx of armed people wearing black facemasks. Gordon didn't look worried, but he didn't look very happy, either.

"Keep walking, don't say a word to him," Rodney said as he pushed me through the door ahead of him and pushed me again toward a black Honda. I heard the door lock click, and he motioned for me to get in.

"Didn't look like Gordon was being set up for witness protection," I said as we drove up a ramp to the street.

"Who said anything about witness protection?" Rodney asked.

"You did," I replied.

Rodney chuckled. "I said Gordon was being taken to a secure location in America, someplace no one would ever think of looking, and he'd be getting a new identity. All of that is true. You can imagine that place and that identity to be whatever you like."

"But what's the truth, Rodney?"

"All of our American locations are secure, and his placement will be determined in accordance with everyone's best interests, America's always first, of course," Rodney said as he turned onto Sukhumvit. A motorcycle taxi with two women passengers, one holding a child, nearly clipped his side. "But I'm not promising anything."

"In other words, he's going to jail?"

"Not quite," Rodney replied. "In jail, the prisoners have rights."

We rode in silence until we reached my condo.

WHEN HE DROPPED me off, Rodney reminded me he'd be over the next morning at ten with the money. I texted Joe, Oliver, and the General. They would all be over to collect their share.

I brewed a cup of Black Ivory Coffee. I was alive, so it was a time for the best. I even set up the French siphon, with the mineral water and alcohol fuel. The brewing coffee flowed from one side to the other, the boiling water infused the ground beans, and my cup was ready. I carried it to my living room and set the music app on my phone to shuffle. It selected "Bad Moon Rising" by Credence Clearwater Survival, most appropriate for the experiences I had just survived.

My life had been sucked up, blown about, and crash-landed, all in the space of nine days. I was unhappily reunited with an unsavory figure from my past, dragged into a series of violent confrontations with North Korean agents, learned to fire a gun, and used one to kill. One good point I always felt good about was that I'm not a killer. Now even that's out the window.

I thought something might develop between me and Nahmwan, but I read it all wrong. It was Sleepy Joe she wanted. But when you get down to it, that made more sense than me. They're both trained to do things I don't even want to think about. And Joe will be happy, which is what is most important to me.

My brief dalliance with Cho must be one of the most unusual in history, but it still comes down to a one-night stand. Doubtful we'll ever meet again. If the CIA lets her write a book, I wonder if I'll be in it. Or who would play me in the movie.

BANGKOK WHISPERS

The Black Ivory Coffee was smooth and went down easy, unlike my life.

28

I ALWAYS WAKE up at six thirty, a habit formed as a lawyer, when I needed an early start to get to court or stop off at the office for some urgent paperwork. I left that life behind, but not the early rising part. I like to go out on my balcony with a cup of coffee and watch the sun rise over Bangkok. It's surprisingly pretty, with soft shades of orange, pink, and yellow. Maybe it is the pollution, but it looks pretty to me.

This morning was no different. My internal alarm woke me, and shortly after, I was on the balcony with a cup of black Ethiopian. The sound of CNN International drifted onto the balcony from my living room. Investigators had found even more connections between the Trump campaign and Russia. The Rolling Stones announced another concert tour, assuming their gerontologists approved. There was another assault rifle massacre in the US, but those were hardly news anymore.

Faced with this barrage of events, there was only one course of action. I rolled a joint, sprinkling in some of that Indian hashish our English friends had bestowed upon Joe. I took a deep drag, lay back on the chaise lounge, and the next thing I knew, Rodney Snapp was shaking me awake. The sun was moving up the horizon, and it was getting hot outside.

"Ten o'clock, Glenn. Lucky this isn't court or you'd be fined."

"Well, Rodney it's not like I have to let you in," I said. "Do you carry lock-picking equipment with you?

"A smile can open any door," he replied.

"I haven't found that to be the case," I said.

"Let's go into the living room," Rodney said. "I can pay you and then I have to run. There are a few folks I have to torture later today."

He must have seen the look on my face.

"Just kidding," he said.

We sat on my couch, and Rodney counted out stacks of bills he drew from an attaché case. They were in bundles of ten thousand dollars each, in crisp hundred-dollar bills.

"Trust me, it's one million," he said.

"Why are you doing this?" I asked. "We weren't working for you."

Rodney smiled and pushed a few bundles off to the side.

"You're always working for us, whether you know it or not," he said. "Besides, you are a really good negotiator."

"Wait a minute," I said. "I never negotiated anything with you. So why the million?"

"That goes to show just how good a negotiator you are," he said. "I advise you to set up the shares for your buddies. I'll take Charlie's and see that he gets it." Rodney scooped up the bundles he'd pushed aside and put them back into the case. "A hundred grand, like last time." He stood and started walking.

I grabbed his arm before he could leave. There was something on my mind.

"I want to make sure nothing bad happens to Gordon. I've killed too many people already."

"You haven't killed anybody," Rodney said. "More like suicide. A few North Koreans broke into your lodging and walked into a hail of your bullets. Had they stayed home in Pyongyang, they'd still be alive."

"As if they had any choice," I replied.

"But Gordon Planter had a choice," Rodney said. "His choice was to betray our country and help our enemies make money poisoning our people with heroin and cocaine."

"That doesn't justify killing him with no due process at all," I said.

Rodney clapped my back as he advanced toward the door.

"Who said anything about a killing with no due process? I thought we were good on this. He lives and you shut up about it. Relax, Glenn, take a break, enjoy your money. Let us deal with Gordon. We do this all the time."

"That's what's worrying me," I said.

"Don't let it," Rodney countered. "Anything else I can do for you before I go?"

"Any chance you can make Charlie disappear? Or at least stop calling me?"

"And cost you and your friends all that dough?" he asked. He was out the door before I could tell him where to shove that next round of money.

SLEEPY JOE CAME prepared with a backpack emblazoned with the Australian flag. He stuffed two hundred thousand dollars into the pack.

"This is getting to be a rather pleasant ritual, mate," he said. "We really must do this more often."

"This is it for me," I said. "If Charlie calls again, I'm not taking it."

"Well, give him my number, mate. In the meantime, let's smoke a symbolic joint."

I still don't know what he meant by a symbolic joint, but who am I to argue with Sleepy Joe on joints? When we were finished, he grabbed his pack and stood up.

"Have to go now," he said. "Meeting Nahmwan for lunch."

"I'm really glad for you," I said.

"We'll see next month if you can still say the same," he replied. "Just kidding. But I'll stop by tomorrow to say goodbye. We'll finish off that Indian stuff and listen to some music."

"What do you mean 'say goodbye'?"

"I'll be doing a little work for the General," Joe said. "Should keep me busy for a month or two."

Then he too was gone.

EVEN SLEEPY JOE has a girlfriend, and I don't. What a world.

And just in case I was amenable to forgetting this, the General did all he could to assure I would not.

"Glenn, you've got to loosen up. Let's just be happy we're all alive. How about this weekend? Come on down to Hua Hin with my son and me and our *mia noi*. We have somebody lined up for you. Perfect, you can't miss it. And you get to meet my son. If you like me, you'll like him too."

"What about if I don't really like you?" I asked.

"Then you are the best actor in the world," the General said.

"I think I'll pass on the weekend but would love to meet your son someday," I said.

I placed two separate piles of bills in front of the General. I told him the large pile was his, the small one for the family of his man killed defending the safe house when the North Koreans attacked. He slowed them down enough to allow me to defend myself inside.

"You are most kind and generous," the General said. "I am also going to help them. I will deliver this to them after the funeral." He put the money in a black briefcase and snapped it shut.

"Glenn, listen to me. Your life is not complete without a woman. I can help. It's not like you have been doing such a good job on your own."

"What do you mean?" I asked.

"Glenn, look at your last three relationships, if they can be called such. A money launderer. A prostitute. A North Korean communist spy. You need me."

"Those aren't the only ones," I said, feeling indignant at this representation of my social skills.

"That's right," the General said. "I forgot about the woman who tried to stab you, and the young condo manager who went out once with you and said you reminded her of her father."

When it came to manipulating my past, the General was as adept as Charlie, who used that talent to lure me into the whole mess. Not this time, I told myself. Don't be manipulated again, a voice told me.

"Tell you what," I said. "If I haven't found someone six months from today, we're on."

"Make it three months," the General countered.

"Who's the lawyer here?" I asked. We settled on four months. I watched the General make an entry on his iPhone.

"Counting down the days," he said.

OLIVER ACTED AS if the money didn't matter to him at all. He swept his pile into a pack without a word.

"Joe told me about that hashish you guys came up with. Wouldn't mind a hit, that is, if there's any left."

"Just a few crumbs," I said. "But that's all it takes." I rolled a thin joint and sprinkled in half of the remaining hash. I was already struggling to stay awake, so I handed it to Oliver. "It's yours."

"In that case, I'll just hang on to it until I visit my favorite masseuse later today," he said. After we're all done, we'll smoke this." By "after we're done," Oliver meant he was getting more than just a good massage.

"Suit yourself," I said. "And how about next time, someone else does the heavy lifting, and I just show up and collect a few hundred thousand?"

"You mean there's going to be a next time?" Oliver asked.

"Actually, not if I have anything to say about it."

Oliver threw back his big, shaved head and let out a roar of a laugh.

"As if you ever do," he said.

We sat in silence for a few minutes as we experienced the Indian magic, each in our own way. Art Blakey's Jazz Messengers filled the room, and the sound of Wayne Shorter's tenor sax grabbed me as always. He didn't switch to soprano sax until the late sixties, and I was playing one of his early albums from the early sixties. Oliver broke the silence.

"Glenn, maybe you should think about spending some time on Koh Phangan," he said. "If Charlie or Rodney ever call again, I can guarantee you won't want to leave paradise to fight Russian gangsters or North Korean assassination squads."

"Don't be so sure," I replied. "You're not necessarily any more fun than they are, and you don't pay as well." Truth was, I'm a city boy who can enjoy a break on a beautiful island but must live in civilization.

"I thought none of this was about money, Glenn. Don't you already have enough?"

He had a point. I reflected upon it for a few seconds.

"But if it isn't the money, then what is it? If you think I don't need money, I have news for you. I don't need to be shot at. I don't need to deal with the CIA, or Charlie. There's no good reason for me to get mixed up in this craziness ever again. I've learned at least that much."

"And while you're on this learning curve, maybe learn a little about women. Jeez, a money launderer, a hooker, a North Korean agent? And you look down on Funston?" That hurt.

"That's almost word-for-word what the General just said before you got here," I exclaimed. "Are you guys passing around a script?"

"No, Glenn," Oliver said softly. "We're just observing."

Some small talk and the album was over. Oliver took his pack and bid me good day.

"See you at the Club. Tonight," he said.

Of course. Where else would I be?

I ARRIVED AT the Club a little early. The last of the corporate crowd were leaving. None of my friends were there yet. Phil Funston sat in his usual corner, looking like a hound dog who had a bad night. He glanced in my direction, forcing me to recall the threat he'd made after his disastrous gig at the Blues Club. Here I was, in the line of fire, with no backup. He motioned for me to sit with him. *What choice is there?* I thought. It would be worse if I ignored him and he chased me around the Club. The easiest thing to do was get it over with.

Mai the waitress provided temporary respite. She seated me at a table a foot from where I stood and sat across from me. From the corner of my eye, I caught Funston fuming. When his shaved head reddened, you knew he was angry. I ignored him, but couldn't ignore Mai.

"I hear you dump girlfriend, *ka?*"

"First of all, Mai, she was not my girlfriend. Second, it's better if we don't talk about this."

I thought the only people who knew about Pim were the General and Wang, the NJA Club's cook and owner. Wang hired Mai as soon as he took ownership of the Club ten years age and worked with her daily ever since. No surprise the two Thais gossiped about the rich *farang* so unskilled he paid a hooker for companionship. Most Thais would not expect such behavior from an affluent American lawyer. I'd agree with them.

Mai moved her face inches away from mine.

"You hurting, you want to talk, anytime."

I was hurting but not over Pim. The relationship was short, ended many months ago. I needed some sensual release after surviving the CIA kidnap scheme and having my heart broken by Noi. But I'm not Phil Funston, and in my world, relationships with hookers don't count. My wounded heart had not fully recovered from the cold-water-in-the-face realization that my love for Noi, for whom I'd risked my life, was never going to be returned. She was off in America with her husband, free from legal problems, thanks to me. More than a year later, it still hurt. I thought she really cared about me, when all she wanted was to use me. Perhaps Noi was right, and we were only meant to be good friends.

Mai knew Noi as an NJA regular and, like everyone else at the Club, knew my feelings for her. Mai thinks my heart can jump from one woman to another with no recovery period. Many *farang* men do this, but not me.

Mai would never believe I hired Pim, a Pattaya hooker, to pass for a sexpat, as my cover in a CIA plot to kidnap a Russian gangster, and I could never tell her. Sexpat was not a look I wanted to cultivate, but the CIA insisted. After we succeeded, I broke my rule against sleeping with hookers. A seasoned *farang* should have known better. I've issued that warning to others countless times, before it was my turn to be stupid. It definitely reinforced the no-hooker rule for the future.

No doubt Mai would be there for me if asked. She has lobbied for a relationship the entire eight years we've known each other. By the time this was clear to me, other women had been pulling my strings. A *farang* would be lucky to have a woman like Mai. She was born in Chiang Mai, Thailand's "Lanna Kingdom" of the North, with the full body and light skin often associated with that region. Northerners are said to be reserved, but Mai is a regular chatterbox, as well as headstrong and proud. When Phil Funston hurls a lewd and demeaning remark at her, she cuts him down with a reciprocal insult. Phil has left her alone the past few weeks, since she questioned his manhood and claimed he was growing breasts.

That day, Phil Funston served a useful purpose. He provided an avenue to end my discourse with Mai while not hurting her feelings. The path of my relationships in the Kingdom is equally hazardous to my health. My second Thai girlfriend tried to knife me when I told her we were through, and unrequited love for another woman got me entangled with the CIA and near-death. Rejection by a younger woman deflated what was left of my ego. Then there were the two Thai women who dumped me. With three strikes plus, perhaps I was permanently out. One wouldn't know this from Mai, who didn't count strikes. I can't get involved with Mai. Failing with her would mean avoiding the NJA Club, or feeling uncomfortable there, either of which is unthinkable. The folks at the Club are my family.

"I need to tell Phil how much I enjoyed hearing him play the other night," I said.

"Okay, *Khun* Glenn, I can call you later," she said as I slipped away to Funston's table. Never knew she had my number.

This was as good a time as any to try and put out any fire started by the night at the Blues Club. I sat down across from Funston. He was working on a cup of espresso, a folded *Bangkok Post* on his lap. The year before, the General had bought an espresso machine for Wang, mainly because he liked to enjoy a cup once a day, and I often indulged with him.

I sat down and instinctively flinched, expecting another Funston fusillade. Instead, I got a sob story.

"Someone stole my guitar," he said. I understood then that his look was not sullen; it was sad. "Near Patpong. Bent down to tie my shoelace, and some kid comes out of nowhere, grabs it, and I have no idea where he went." Patpong was famous for rip-off go-go bars, and I couldn't figure out why Phil Funston was walking around there with his beloved guitar.

"That Les Paul, I've had it forever," Funston continued. "Got it not too long after I arrived here. Worth maybe six, seven grand in the States right now. Here, the yaba head who took it will probably sell it for just enough to buy the next fix, and that lucky buyer will find a musician to pay maybe four grand." It probably was a methamphetamine addict who stole it, especially around Patpong.

I suggested that if four grand was the going price, Phil might just have to spring for another one. He threw me a look as if I'd suggested he step into the nearest Muay Thai ring and fight the local champ.

"Four grand? Might as well ask me for four million," he said.

I had always assumed that Phil had some money tucked away. He didn't work—unless you count the occasional student and rare paying gig—but he never seemed to have trouble paying for his drinks or breakfast at the Club. You learn something new every day. I told Phil I'd put his espresso on my tab.

"I'm sure it will work out," I said.

"I'm not counting on it," Phil replied. "I've been here a long time, well over a dozen years. Hasn't gotten me very far. I'm heading home,

Glenn, back to the States. I know I can drum up some students, and America's a big place with lots of music. I'm sure I'll find work. It pays a lot better over there." If he wanted to convince me he felt good about this, he would first have to convince himself.

Not a bad idea, so go for it, I thought. *You've pissed off every musician and club in town.* Needless to say, my life would be more pleasant once Phil Funston was out of it. I hoped he followed through.

The General walked in, bodyguard a few paces behind, and I told Phil we had something to discuss. Ray the bartender saw me get up and started preparing martinis for the General and me.

I told the General what Phil had said, and how excited I was that he'd soon be gone. I expected the General to share my feelings. He did not.

"Glenn, the last two times we met, all you could talk about was how terrible you feel about killing those communists. Never mind the only reason it happened was that they tried to kill you. I know you *farangs*, especially you *Khun Yew*," using the Thai word for the Jewish people. "Feel guilty when there's no reason. Only you would feel bad about killing people who were poisoning your country and threatening to blow up the world. But when you get down to it, can't question you guys on anything. Look at all the Nobel Prize winners you produced. And what an army you guys have."

"Actually, General, I'm an American, not an Israeli."

"Well, your army is pretty good, too," he said. He continued dispensing his advice.

"You are going to carry this guilt within you for a long time, maybe forever. It may actually affect your karma, even though you didn't do anything wrong. These constant bad thoughts can do it to you," he explained. "Best thing for you is to accumulate some good karma, or merit as we call it. That will make you feel better, and balance out any bad karma you might have built up. Who knows, maybe you could have avoided killing those commies. Maybe you should never have gotten mixed up in that Russian gangster kidnap. Maybe there were other paths to take. I'm not saying you could have, or should have, but look at this good karma as an insurance policy. The world never suffers when someone does good."

"You seem to know an awful lot about this for a man who spent his life as a soldier," I said. Actually, he didn't seem to know any more than I did, but it would be the height of arrogance for a *farang* to say that to a Thai.

"I learned a lot of dharma when I was living in the temple," he said. I had my martini in hand, and it nearly fell when he said this.

"You were in the temple? You were a monk? When? How?"

"That's a story for a different time, maybe when we swap again," he said. "Meanwhile, take my advice. Help out Funston. You know, he is a musician, and he is good. People like listening to him. Right karma for you, all around."

"How do you know if he's any good?" I asked. I couldn't see the General grabbing a beer and listening to music at the Blues Club or Saxophone Club, or anywhere else Funston might have played.

"How long till you figure out that I know everything that happens in Krung Thep?" he asked, using the Thai name for Bangkok. "At least the parts that interest me."

"I still think we ought to let him go back to America," I said.

"And I think you should go back and tell him you're loaning him the money for the guitar."

PHIL FUNSTON'S BALD head glowed red as if it were radioactive when I told him. That's also how it looks when he's angry, which is often. Happy, angry, it's all the same for Phil Funston.

"I never thought you were that kind of a guy," he said. "Sorry about all those bad things I said about you."

"I love music, and that's what you make," I said. At least, that wasn't a lie.

"Okay, Glenn, any time I'm playing, the cover charge is waived for you."

"That's awfully nice of you, Phil. Just make sure your manager gives my name to the gatekeeper. Don't need to get into arguments with tough Thais." Only tough Russians or North Koreans, of course.

Phil pressed his lips together and pulled his eyes deeper into his face. That's how he lets us know he's thinking, usually about the next bar fine he plans to pay. Maybe that's why he was broke.

"Manager, yeah, that's what I need. Someone who can set up gigs, handle payment, run the business side. Deal with the clubs and the promoters. You were a lawyer. You have to be better at dealing with people than me."

"Phil, anyone is better than you."

"You get ten percent of whatever I make," Phil said.

"That's a few thousand baht a year right there," I replied. I had no idea how much a musician was paid in Bangkok, but suspected that even for a maestro like Funston, it wouldn't be enough to support either a musician or a manager, certainly not at ten percent.

"Wouldn't do it for twenty percent," I added.

Funston thought for a moment. "Okay, lawyer, you drive a hard bargain. You'll drive them for me too. Twenty percent it is."

Before I could object, Phil stood and draped an arm around my shoulder.

"Got to run now, Glenn. You draw up the papers and we'll go over them tomorrow. But I trust you, and you can start lining up gigs." I was still sputtering obscenities under my breath as he made his way to the door and into the street.

WHEN I WORKED my way back to the General, Oliver and Sleepy Joe were also there. I told them about Phil's idea that I manage him.

"A great idea," the General said. "I can get him booked in a dozen places right now. Get a little present from the owners and another from *Khun* Glenn."

Oliver approved as well.

"Think of the intelligence you can pick up in a club. People getting drunk, at their lowest. A tidbit here, a nugget there, and pretty soon you have some real intelligence," he said. "Plus, I'm sure I can wrangle some club on the island to book Phil, and we can hang out for a while."

"You guys can't be serious!" I shouted. "What's the incentive to bring more Phil Funston into my life? It can't be the money. Good music? Bangkok's full of it. Plus, I've got my stereo system."

I felt a tug on my sleeve. It was Sleepy Joe.

"Any time you can work in the music industry, you do it, mate."

We all agreed twenty percent was high for an agent or manager, but under the circumstances, it was fair.

"Remember, you and Phil split my honorarium," the General said. "Five to ten percent, depends on the fee. So you need the extra points Phil's giving you. Now let's vote officially. All in favor of Glenn managing Funston raise their hand."

Outvoted three to one. NJA Club rules control.

"I'm going to need new business cards," I said.

"My son owns one of those mailbox and business service places. They print cards as well," the General said. "He'll give you a nice discount. Like maybe free when I tell him you're coming. Of course, when Phil plays at a nice place, you'll get the best seats in the house for him and his *mia noi*."

"I'll give it a try," I said. "Maybe a few months. If it's unbearable or unproductive, then I'm done, and we can let Phil go back to the States. On the next plane out." *Just as I went to the San Francisco Airport all those years ago and asked for the next flight out. It was to Bangkok. I'm still here and never regretted it. I wonder if it works that way in reverse.*

"Love to be the fly on the wall when you tell Phil," Sleepy Joe said, as he struggled to keep his smile from stretching into a grin.

29

SLEEPY JOE LOOKED around for an ashtray while I cleared the coffee table. He came by the day after picking up his money as promised, to say goodbye before he left on his assignment for the General.

My favorite Elvis Costello album, *Armed Forces*, was playing. It hasn't lost a thing since the 1979 release. Elvis was backed by the Attractions, his best band by far. Joe lit the joint by striking a match with his thumbnail. He dropped the match into the ashtray.

"I do have a lighter lying on the table," I said. Joe took two deep drags and blew out a cloud of smoke that reminded me of a foggy San Francisco morning. Bangkok never had fog, unless you count pollution, but no one comes here for the air. It's not particularly bad for an Asian capital but would never be acceptable where *farangs* come from. Air quality notwithstanding, many a sunrise or sunset has pleased me with soft pastels colors and earth tones. This was such one evening. I motioned Joe to follow me on to the balcony, where we passed the joint as we studied the soft-hued and fading light.

"It will be the same, mate," Sleepy Joe said as he stubbed out the last of the joint and flicked it over the edge. "I'm still your weed contact, not to mention your best friend and guardian angel.

"And I'll be gone two months at the outside," he added.

My eyes were drinking in busy Sukhumvit Road, choked with traffic. Half the buses, cars, and motorcycles already had their lights on. A BTS Skytrain pulled out of the station, each car a different color and advertising a different product in a script I could not read, in a language I did not understand. Yet this is home, and I wouldn't have it any other way. Joe was a huge part of why I felt that way.

"It will be the same between us, but it won't be the same for you," I told him. "There will be more North Koreans out there, more Russians, more enemies of the General, or the CIA, or whoever you're working for. I really don't know and don't care to know."

"That makes two of us," Sleepy Joe said. "It doesn't really matter. To me, it's just a job."

"A very special kind of job," I said. "You only get to screw up once."

Joe put an arm across my shoulder. I smelled the *ganga* on his breath. Mine probably smelled the same. I had some breath mints lying around somewhere.

"I'm ex–Aussie Special Forces, Glenn. We just don't screw up. Never."

"I guess so," I replied. "I'm sure it will all be fine." The look on Joe's face said he didn't believe me.

"There are risks in everything, mate," he said. "You don't really expect me to be a *ganga* dealer forever?"

"Actually, I was sort of hoping you would be," I replied.

"You're covered, Glenn. First of every month. You heard the General. He gives the orders. Happily followed, I might add. While I'm gone, someone will drop off your monthly ounce." It was part of what Joe owed me for getting him out of a Thai jail with no record.

"(What's So Funny 'Bout) Peace, Love, and Understanding" filtered through the open door to the balcony. Written by Nick Lowe, it was my favorite song on the album. It is a cry for introspection by all. Why does there have to be such violence in this world? Where are the people who can change things?

"If you have to be in an army, I guess there's no better commanding officer than the General," I said. "Somehow I don't believe you need a lot of direction. Neither does the General, or he wouldn't have recruited you. Following orders has never been your strong suit."

Joe lifted his head as his skinny chest expanded.

"What do you mean?" he asked. "I was Aussie Special Forces for ten

234

years. You don't know what orders are like," he added in a softer tone.

"You quit to become a weed dealer," I replied.

"And now it's time to get back into action!" he shouted. "And there'll always be you, music, film, and weed."

"And Ms. Nahmwan as well," I said.

Joe's pale white skin turned a noticeable shade of red.

"I was going to tell you sooner, of course," he said. "But I didn't want to disturb you and Ms. Cho."

"I'm just her lawyer," I snapped, immediately sorry for being angry with my best friend.

"And I'm just a *ganga* dealer," he countered. "Allow me to roll another joint while you put on some New Riders." He knew I loved that Northern California group. Full name, New Riders of the Purple Sage, part of the Grateful Dead universe I periodically inhabited. There would be no more concerts, considering Dead Head Jerry Garcia passed away in 1995. The Grateful Dead were no longer a band, and I was in Thailand. But I made it a point to listen to the Dead several times a week. My favorite album will always be *Workingman's Dead*, but my favorite song is "Ripple" from the album *American Beauty*. That day, we absorbed the voice of John Collins Rodney IV, better known as Marmaduke, leader of the New Riders, as he sang their greatest hit, "Panama Red." Despite the band's association with marijuana, that song was not a paean to the potent Central American strain, but about a desperado named Panama Red. Yet whenever I hear it, I taste that earthy flavor, though I'd never actually smoked any. I kept playing Elvis.

"Imagine how different our lives would be if we hadn't met at the NJA Club," I said.

"But it doesn't work that way, Glenn," he replied. "There is no other possibility. The way it was is the way it is." He lit the finished joint. I spilled out my thoughts as he inhaled.

"I guess that means you don't buy string theory. That theory says there are simultaneously an infinite number of variations on any event, each existing in a separate and parallel universe. There could be a universe where we both exist and never meet."

"Can't say I believe it, because I don't know if I understand it," he said. "But it wouldn't be much of a universe if we hadn't met."

Joe sat on a chair across from me on the sofa. He had a palm on each knee, the burning joint pointing straight up between the first two fingers of his left hand.

"Where is the General sending you?" I asked.

"You know I can't tell you," he said, offering me the joint. I waved it off, and he placed it in the ashtray on the arm of his chair.

"What is it with everyone I know?" I said. "You, the General, Oliver, Rodney, not to mention your girlfriend Nahmwan. All of you do things that no one can know about, and always dangerous. All of you seem to like it. Am I the only one who isn't crazy?"

"We've been wondering when you'd figure that out," he said.

THE ALBUM ENDED with a special bonus track of a live version of "Accidents Will Happen," with Elvis accompanying himself on piano. At the last note, Sleepy Joe stood and stretched. "Got to be going," he said.

I walked him to the door, my gaze fixed on this man who looked like he was made of straw and could be carried away by a strong breeze.

"Be safe," I said and put out my hand. Joe ignored it and embraced me instead. His hair reeked of weed. His embrace was strong, much more than would be expected from this wisp of a man.

"Always do," he said as he dropped his arms. "It's you I worry about."

I watched Sleepy Joe walk to the elevator, and when the doors closed behind him, a lump rose in my throat. For a brief moment, my swallowing and breathing constricted, and then all was normal again. The scent of Joe's weed-drenched hair stayed with me as I headed to my kitchen to brew another cup of Black Ivory Coffee, my way of offering prayers for my friend's well-being. I could surely afford the best.

30

SLEEPY JOE HAD only been gone a month, but it seemed like forever. With Oliver spending more and more of his time on Koh Phangan, I passed most of my time at the NJA Club seated at the General's
table, discussing international, American, and Thai politics, spiced
with gossip, rumor, his *mia noi* escapades, and the gloomy notion
that a man I deemed a fascist thug was about to assume the American
Presidency.

"We're used to crooks and strongmen," the General commented
over our daily martinis one late December day. "But nobody as low
class as this man."

"Comes from a rich and powerful family," I said. "Supposedly he's
a billionaire."

"Well, he acts like one of those pimps bugging you *farangs* on Silom or Sukhumvit, with their pictures of naked women," he said.

"That's him to a T," I replied.

With Joe gone, there were many things we did together that I now
did alone: smoking weed, listening to music, watching movies. Twice
I watched *The Big Lebowski* and waited for Joe to shout out his favorite lines. Instead, I was greeted with silence.

It took a while to accept that once outside of my Muay Thai classes
and the NJA Club, I would be alone. It hadn't dawned on me just
how much time Joe and I spent together, all quality time. At least,
that's how we see getting stoned, listening to music, and watching cin-
ema on my television. There was nothing to fill the void. It's not like

I had a girlfriend or even a date. The General could fix that anytime, as he continued to remind me.

I spent more time surfing the internet, checking out subjects of interest. I started following a blog meant for expats in Thailand. The opening page of the site displays a medley of articles the editors deemed most newsworthy that day, and usually they were right. I came to enjoy starting my day with a cup of black coffee and the blog, sometimes at my desk, but if early morning weather permitted, on the balcony. This morning, I sat on the balcony, savoring a cup of Brazilian arabica, soft, low acid with a nutty flavor. The sun had just started to rise. I loved watching Bangkok illuminate and come to life in the soft light and cooler air of early morning, starting my day on a mellow note.

After logging on to the blog site, a piece by a freelance journalist living in Bangkok caught my eye. I'd seen his writing before, and he specialized in the seamy side of Bangkok. The headline read "Foreigner Fished Out of Canal in Thong Lor," referring to a neighborhood not too far from the NJA Club or my condo, an area known for trendy restaurants, bars, and clubs. Joe and I frequented many, especially those with live music. Part of Thong Lor runs along the Khlong Saen Saep, the longest canal in Bangkok. One could travel to Thong Lor by canal boat, and many do, but not me. A few years ago, some canal water splashed into the eye of a movie star passenger, and he died of infection. The canal boat crews are swaddled in the poor person's version of hazmat suit: layers of clothing, gloves, and a bandana around their neck. Not very reassuring.

Divers were searching for something that fell off a boat. Nothing said about what it was; this is Thailand, so there have to be mysteries. They never found what they were looking for but did come up with what was left of a human being after several weeks at the bottom of a polluted canal. The medical examiner quickly identified him as a foreigner, a Westerner, most likely an American. Enough dead *farangs* turn up each year to bestow expertise on these doctors. Just another Bangkok story to me until I reached the middle of the third paragraph.

Dental records obtained from America by the US Embassy identified the deceased as Gordon Planter, age forty-nine, most recently a resident of Marin County, California. Planter is believed to be a widower with no immediate family.

I grabbed my phone and hit a speed dial button.

"Oliver, you get Rodney to call me right now!" I screamed.

"Saw the news, Glenn. Bad break. Let's see what I can do. No promises. You know these CIA guys."

"Obviously, I don't," I replied.

Five minutes later, Rodney called.

"You lied to me!" I yelled into the phone.

"How so?" Rodney asked.

"You told me you were bringing Gordon back to the States, sounded like to some sort of secure home detention setup. Now they fish him out of the bottom of Khlong Saen Saep."

"And we fully intended what I told you," Rodney said, "except he ran away before we could transport him. Happened right after I left to bring you home."

I made him say it all again.

"Gordon escaped from custody of the CIA?" I asked, my hands gripping the sides of my chair.

"It happens. He had help."

"What do you mean, he had help? Who the hell would help him?"

"The North Koreans. At some point, when he was working for them, they gave him a tiny ball that explodes into a thick cloud of smoke, enough smoke to choke a horse. Must have had it in a tooth, like that Nazi at Nuremberg. As soon as the car carrying him made it to the streets, he must have spit it out and stepped on it. Our people had to open the doors, and Gordon just melted into the crowds along Wireless Road. Element of surprise is always an initial advantage. Didn't get very far. We still are the CIA, after all. Found him hiding out in a massage parlor off *Soi* Nana."

"He wasn't handcuffed?"

Rodney nodded his head and frowned.

"Gordon was a lot more enterprising and capable than we thought," he said. "He convinced a masseuse to help him get them off. She told us he claimed to have been playing some S and M games and the lady he spent the night with forgot to unlock him before she left. The masseuse believed him and got some tools to cut off the cuffs. Gordon then managed to persuade some *farang* customers to spot him the money for a massage with a happy ending, which we interrupted." Gordon Planter would never change.

"Then how did he wind up from there to the bottom of a canal?" I asked.

"I threw him in," Rodney said. "After I snapped his neck, of course. No one deserves to die in that cesspool, not even Gordon Planter."

It took a few seconds to compose myself and ask him why. It must have been a lot longer than a few seconds because Rodney asked if I was still on the line.

"Why did you kill him?"

Rodney was ready with his response.

"Glenn, this guy betrayed our country. He sold heroin to our people. He had Henry killed. He had his wife killed. He caused the deaths of people on both sides over here. And bear in mind, he was quite ready to kill you and your friends without any compunction. We offered him the best deal anyone would ever make. We don't have time to be chasing after grifters like Gordon Planter. We have better things to do. And we just can't let him go running around free. He knows far too much for comfort. There's a time when we just have to close out a case one way or the other. That's why he wound up at the bottom of a canal."

"What gives you the right to judge him and make that decision?" I asked. "I thought you represent the law."

I heard Rodney chuckle.

"I'm not your cop on the beat," he said. "Different game, different rules. And what gives you the right to judge me? You killed three Koreans when you thought it was the best thing to do under the circumstances. Like the situation with me and your pal Gordon."

"That's not a fair comparison," I said. "You had a choice. I had none."

"Really?" Rodney asked. "Ever think about running out the back door at the first sound of trouble? Or down to that secret shooting range in the basement? Call the General to get you out? Instead, you reached for your Smith & Wesson and started blasting away. Not saying I blame you, but there are always options. You chose one many would say the best. Great job, I might add. You're definitely CIA material. I'll qualify you for shooting right now."

"No thanks," I said. He was right. When faced with danger, my first reaction was to reach for my gun. Well, I am an American, after all.

"Goodbye, Glenn," Rodney said. "Till we meet again."

"Which will be never!" I shouted into a dead line.

THE SUN WAS a wheel of butter growing brighter in a slow and steady cadence as I watched from my balcony. My little blue wireless speaker rang out the sounds of "Tunji," the first cut on Coltrane's relatively mellow 1964 album, *Crescent*. He worked with his classic lineup: McCoy Tyner, keys; Jimmy Garrison, bass; Elvin Jones, drums. Most people no longer care about things like classic lineups, but I do. Sleepy Joe does also. I sipped my second cup of Brazilian. I smoked a fat joint after Rodney's call and wished there was more of that Indian hash the English kids gave us.

I adjusted my chaise lounge to become almost a bed, hoping to drift back to sleep, blanketed by Coltrane. Instead, cascades of thoughts flooded my mind, as when I went to meditation. Most thoughts evaporated in seconds, but one clung to my mind like Spanish moss on an old tree.

Many years ago, when I was still a criminal defense lawyer in San Francisco, I was asked to join a panel on gun violence at a local youth center. My role was to advise the youths of the legal consequences of being caught with a firearm, especially if used in the course of a crime. I also planned to drop in a few hints about what restrictions the law imposed upon police who felt like doing a search on someone, which I never mentioned to the organizers beforehand. I managed to weave Fourth Amendment rights into the context of telling the youths what could happen to them if there were illegal search and seizure, the most common situation, in fact.

I spoke last. When my presentation ended, a young man stood up and shouted, "Thanks, Mr. Lawyer. I want to have a gun and make sure I don't get locked up for it. I want to have a gun!" Suddenly I wasn't all that happy with myself.

A man rose from the audience. He was a big man, over six feet, heavy, not in the rolls-of-fat way but in the way of a big-boned man with a lot of muscle. His hair was long and greasy, and a thick beard hung half a foot below his chin. My first thoughts were white supremacist or biker, maybe survivalist.

"My name is John," he began. "Former Marine, two tours of combat duty in 'Nam. Let me just tell you one thing." He paused.

"You want a gun, you say? Take it from one who knows. If you have a gun, it means you're willing to use it. And if you use it, that's something you're going to have to live with every day of your life." Tears ran down his cheek, seeping through his beard. He sat down, and for the longest time, there wasn't a sound in the room. We were all done, and everyone walked out in silence.

I pray he's not right.

THE END

What Readers Say About *Bangkok Shadows*

"As an expat living in Bangkok for 18 years, I can tell by the way Mr. Shaiken portrays the characters and places in Thailand, he's done good research and knows Thailand, Thai culture and Thai people well."

MKC, AMAZON

"Great read-and I do hope for the sequel."

TRACY, AMAZON

"S. Shaiken gets Bangkok like only someone who has lived there can."

TCK, AMAZON

"Smooth, balanced writing, detailed and rich characters, and plot that moves along, building the story to the very end."

PACIFIC ORGANIC, AMAZON

"The book is fantastic. I couldn't stop reading. One of the better mysteries I've read."

M, AMAZON

"Awesome read . . . Really enjoyed the character details.Can't wait for his next work."

AEB, GOODREADS

STEPHEN SHAIKEN

"This is a great Asian story of intrigue, life in Bangkok andcolor of living there."

DM, GOODREADS

"Wow! What a page turner!"

KATIE, AMAZON

Acknowledgments

I benefitted greatly when the first quarter of the novel was critiqued by the dedicated writers of Key Bangers Bangkok, forever my writing group. No author could ask for better guidance in those early stages of their novel. A portion was also reviewed by the Tampa Writers Alliance, who provided many excellent suggestions. Special thanks is due to my dear old friend Barry Weissman and my brother Elliot, who volunteered as beta readers, and whose feedback was, as always, invaluable. My daughter Liz helped bring the manuscript into shape. Great thanks to my wife Josie, who endured the struggles of living with an independent author publishing a novel. Most of all, I'd like to thank the Kingdom and people of Thailand, who provide authors with an endless string of intriguing tales and kindness.

About the Author

Stephen Shaiken practiced criminal law in for more than thirty years, the first four in Brooklyn, and the rest in San Francisco. His decades as a criminal trial lawyer are often embedded in his writing. He is a graduate of Queens College and Brooklyn Law School, and earned an M.A. in Creative Writing from San Francisco State University. He currently splits his time between Bangkok, Thailand, and Tampa, Florida.

Stephen's short stories have been published in numerous magazines, and several may be read on his blog. Stephen's two novels are best described as exotic noir thrillers, but he also writes humor, literary, and occasional science fiction stories.

Bangkok Whispers is Stephen's second novel, featuring the same characters as his first, *Bangkok Shadows*. Follow Stephen on his blog and on Twitter, and sign up for his newsletter to receive advance notice of Stephen's future novels and short stories.

Click here to visit the *Bangkok Shadows* page on Amazon.

Follow Stephen's blog:
www.stephenshaiken.com

Follow Stephen on Twitter:
@StephenShaiken

Made in the USA
Las Vegas, NV
25 August 2022

54021237R00138